Funk Foundation Doughnut Location

© Julie Deitrich

Funk Foundation Doughnut Location

A copy of this publication can be found in the National Library
of Australia.

ISBN: 9781921681455

Published by Book Pal
www.bookpal.com.au

To My Friends

Without whose imagination, sense of humour and mindless stupidity this book would only be three pages long.

You know who you are, I love you all.

Jules x

Contents

March 2008

'Look at me! I've got liver disease!' exclaimed Peter the Painter, pressing his face against the wall of my newly decorated coffee shop. Peter thought he was blessed with the timing of a comedy genius — nobody was laughing, he wasn't even funny. Anyway, I really liked the organ-replacement yellow I'd chosen for the walls of my coffee shop.

'Why didn't you bring one of those Dulux matchpots home first to see what the colour would look like on the wall?' asked Peter. He laughed as he climbed down from his stepladders.

'I'll go and check what my sign's looking like,' I replied and trudged outside.

Martin Luther King had a dream, something about wanting equal rights for black people, and I had a dream too. Thankfully mine was nowhere near as ambitious as Mr King's: I wanted to run my own business, escape the shitty nine-to-five I had been working for the past twenty years, and be my own boss. I know I really shouldn't be so ungrateful; people in countries like India and China work twelve hour shifts, six and seven days a week, so I should stop bitching but I'm not planning on stopping any time soon.

I am British, after all, and that carries certain obligations. It's my duty to: bitch and moan on a daily basis; continue to make 'queuing' the great

British institution that it is today; complain about the current government, even though I didn't even vote at the last general election; drink at least five cups of tea every day, with two sugars; and, shout recommendations at the current England football team manager, from the safety of my sofa, even though I only learned what the *offside* rule was about six months ago.

This coffee shop was something I was going to stick at—not like the gym, various diets, my Open University degree, or my marriage. I wanted peace and thought this was the place to find it, whilst feeding my face with cake.

I want my life to be different, but have no idea what I want to do. I'm restless. When everyone around me seems happy to whinge and moan about their lives, I want to change mine. Anyway, I'm planning to make an appointment to see a counsellor to find out why I can't stick to anything (A counsellor who sorts out your problems as opposed to a *Councillor* you write to when your wheelie bins haven't been emptied for two weeks.), but I've decided that I don't want anyone to know about it, as my friends think I have mental health issues as it is.

I can't seem to commit to anything long term, except my mates; I love them, but this coffee shop was just probably going to be another spur of the moment, flash in the pan, whatever you want to call it, idea. I think that these optimistic ideas all make up the rich tapestry of my life but my mates say, 'Make up your fucking mind and stick to something.'

The sign at the front of my new coffee shop read: 'Funk Foundation Doghnut Location'.

I'd scoured the *Yellow Pages*, for four hours, trying to get the cheapest quote for my coffee shop sign, and I was pretty sure that this clown had never won a spelling bee. How can you choose sign writing as an occupation if your spelling skills would make a six-year-old weep? The fucking idiot. The 'doghnut' would definitely have to go.

'What's a *doghnut*?' I asked, pronouncing the word as 'dog nut'.

At first I heard nothing but an uncomfortable silence; I think this may have been followed by a muffled, 'Bollocks!' from said clown, who was hanging precariously onto the top of his ladders.

Me: 'I suppose I just took it for granted that you'd be able to spell, you know, you being a signwriter.'

'Tea would be nice, like piss, two sugars,' he said as, without even turning his head, he flicked me the finger. The ladder shook as he released his grip on it and I willed the dyslexic bastard to fall to the ground, but I'll give him his due, he hung on in there.

Like I said, I'm losing interest even before I've opened the shop just because a couple of things have gone tits up, like the colour of the paint on the walls and that stupid signwriter out the front, the fucking idiot.

The name for the coffee shop, Funk Foundation Doughnut Location, was the result of a festive night with my mates—their getting festive involving copious amounts of alcohol and non-prescription drugs. Personally, I can't stand the taste of alcohol and as for drugs, well, call me uptight but I get just a wee bit nervous at the thought of not being in control of my bodily functions. Anyway, I digress.

Other coffee shop name options included: 'The Mocha Locka'(Mmm … not bad.), and 'Chunky's Chow Down' (Cheeky twats!). Music wise, I had Aretha Franklin's greatest hits on a tape somewhere under the driver's seat of my car, but apart from that my music collection was far from funky. I was going to have to spend some serious cash the next time I paid Virgin Megastore a visit.

I wasn't looking to expand the boundaries of culinary excellence in this establishment; I was going to provide simple fare in a relaxed atmosphere: Baked potatoes, toasted sandwiches, cakes, coffee and doughnuts—it doesn't get much simpler than that.

So, I'd decided to open a coffee shop, and in doing so I had certain legal obligations to my customers with regard to food safety. Apparently, 'food hygiene legislation requires all food handlers to receive appropriate supervision, and be instructed and/or trained in food hygiene, to enable them to handle food safely,' so the website said. A monkey could have completed The Food Hygiene Certificate, now that we have that most wonderful of tools, the internet. Especially, when the test's online and you can gather around a group of friends, provide a few beers, cheese, crackers and dips and they'll agree to help you complete it. It only took around three hours and, to be honest, is worth doing as I learned loads.

Did you know that when you store food in a fridge the cooked foods should be above the raw stuff? I didn't. And they go a little bit over the top on this online course if you get any of the questions wrong. For example, if you fuck up any of the questions in the examination, like putting the uncooked chicken on the shelf above the cooked chicken in the online refrigerator, the screen displays a flashing skull and crossbone sign with 'AAARG YOU KILLED 500 PEOPLE'. Yeah, fucking right, are we exaggerating a little there? I reckon with the size of my refrigerator I'd be pushing it to kill more than ten people, fifteen max.

So, I picked the aforementioned venue as my coffee shop because it was near the seaside, in the quaint seaside town of Saltburn by the Sea, in the North East of England. It sat opposite the number 262 bus stop and a housing development that provided accommodation for the over fifty-five's.

The bus stop, like most in the UK, was a complete waste of space, like an upside down L shape, providing fuck all shelter from the elements. As you well know, the rain doesn't fall vertically in the UK like it does in tropical climates; in the UK rain is usually accompanied by a force five gale and sweeps horizontally making bus stops totally redundant and causing abundant umbrella deaths.

You know you're going to get pissed wet through when it rains, even standing under a bus stop, so hopefully seeing a coffee shop nearby would lure extra customers through the door.

The premises had an apartment with a living area, kitchen, bathroom and two bedrooms upstairs. It was dirt-cheap, with emphasis on the word 'dirt', as the place was a right shit-hole when I first took it over; I found a dead rat behind one of the kitchen cupboards, I nearly shit myself, it was the size of a fucking cat.

The Estate Agents claimed it had a sea view; if you climbed up on a chair in the front bedroom, craned your head out of the window and risked garrotting yourself on the TV aerial then you could have your sea view.

Saltburn is only twenty minutes or fifteen miles outside of the crap town that is Middlesbrough, or 'The Boro' as it is more commonly known, and it is a regular entrant into Country Life's 'Prettiest Village in England' competition. Whilst some of Saltburn's residents may describe their picturesque little town as near to Whitby, made famous by Bram Stoker's Dracula, others may even be as adventurous as to suggest it is near York, with its magnificent Minster and cobbled streets—it's near Middlesbrough, end of story.

Fuck all ever happens in Saltburn. Even if you look at the events calendar on Saltburn By The Sea's very own website, you'll see that the only thing happening in March 2008 is Easter, and Easter's happening pretty much everywhere else in the Christian World. In 2008 Easter came pretty damned early if you ask me, earlier than I've ever known it be before, starting around the 21st March. Who works these dates out anyway? I mean, if I was still in paid employment I wouldn't care as it just means a nice long weekend, where we all get four days off in a row; even better than Christmas because sometimes Christmas can fall on a shit day like a Tuesday or a Wednesday and you only get two days off together, but Easter is a guaranteed four days off for an office worker, which I used to be—*result!*

Anyway, I'm digressing again. I've grown up near the place and it's a bit shit. Then 'Why,' I hear you all ask, 'do you still live there?' And my answer is: 'I have no fucking idea'. It must be the people; that's my apathetic British excuse and I'm sticking with it.

The people in the North East of England are fucking mint; they have a great sense of humour and are the most welcoming people I know. I've been to London a few times and I get the feeling that most of the people there wouldn't piss on me if I was on fire. Mind you, most people tell me that London isn't full of Londoners and that it just takes a while to get to know people down there. Well, I don't have time to get to know people; I'm impatient and you either like me up front or you don't, what takes people so long to make their minds up?

So back to the cafe where the boys, well two of them anyway, you can expect introductions a little later, had built three booths on either side of the shop for me, each seating six people, or four fatties, and there was a large rectangular table in the middle of the cafe. I was aiming for a modern but comfortable look, steering well clear of the greasy-spoon mentality that so often frequented the neighbouring establishments; I wanted to bring a bit of class to the place, but who the fuck am I kidding here? I am to class what Radovan Karadzic is to Bosnian Community Relations.

The counter for the coffee shop was at the opposite end of the premises to the front door and there was a large display cabinet next to the counter for the doughnuts and whatever else I was selling.

So the walls are a sort of jaundiced yellow colour at the moment—it does make everyone look a little sickly so I may have to change it in the near future, when I can be arsed. The booths have big, comfortable, black cushions in them—I'd decided against the plastic padding regularly seen in the American style diners, because I hate the farty noises it makes when you move across it, and the fact that it looks cheap as fuck.

I'd bought a few magazines for the customers, obviously the boys wanted 'Big Jugs Monthly' and 'Hustler' but I decided that 'Hello' and 'Marie-Claire' would be more suitable for the clientele.

There were spotlights in the ceiling, not too many though, just enough to read the menu and recognise who was sitting opposite you. I'd also had the good sense to laminate the menus so that they were easy to wipe clean.

The catering equipment had arrived, so I was all set to go. A cheap coffee maker, I couldn't quite stretch to the Gaggia which came to around eight hundred quid, and was aimed at the home market!

Knowing my staying power, this venture was only going to last six months anyway. I'd bought the plain white crockery and simple cutlery from IKEA because I have a tendency to break things; honestly sometimes I think I might have Parkinson's disease, I seem to have a firm hold of something and the next thing I know it's smashed on the floor—clumsy as.

As a side note, I fucking love IKEA, those Swedes have got it cracked. I was once talking to this Swedish bloke on the train down to London and he said that when a new IKEA catalogue is published in Sweden it's a major event, like a royal wedding or, erm … something else big, like a football cup final. When the Swedes produce such cracking porn, I can't believe that they get excited about the IKEA catalogue. Oh, and apparently they have quite a high suicide rate, especially in the winter months and in the North of Sweden where it's dark for twenty-odd hours of the day. So, officially, the Swedes are as mad as a bag of cut snakes. Obviously, that's only my opinion but you must be able to see my point. Anyway, I digress.

So, I was going to open seven days a week to start with, it was a matter of having to really, I needed to get back what I'd put into it and compete with the more established cafes in the area. Even with that fucking awful paint on the walls I still beat the competition, with their plastic tablecloths and white paper doilies, hands down.

I just had to be polite, customer focused and control any urges to use colourful language. I just have to swear, it relieves tension and when directed at the right audience I think it's funny as fuck.

At a friend's place one night, I was given a five quid bet that I couldn't talk for ten minutes without swearing. I failed miserably and lasted about three minutes before I blurted out 'you're a fucking cock' to an unsuspecting friend. I also had the loving expression 'cock, piss, wank' iced onto all my friend's Easter eggs, thanks to our local confectioner Thornton's; Chocolate Heaven since 1911.

I spend an awful lot of time with my friends, probably because I no longer speak to my family, which is another reason for making the appointment with that counsellor I spoke about earlier—I will talk about this later and with professionals—so I decided that I would chose my own family. Let me explain how.

Someone once told me about this book called the *Celestine Prophecy*. This person told me that, when the time was right, the book would find me. Obviously at this point in the conversation I was nodding my head, had a fixed smile on my face and was thinking 'ABORT, ABORT, ABORT' but, bugger me, within a week I was reading the magazines in a local news-agency, because I'm too tight to buy one, and someone had left a copy of the *Celestine Prophecy* on the shelf just next to *OK Magazine*.

So I bought this book, like a complete sucker, and a lot of it was steamy spiritual shite but there are some parts of it that made real sense to me. The part I liked the most said that we should strike up conver-sations with complete strangers. I mean the book didn't say it exactly like that, it was identifying those brief moments when you make eye contact with people you've never met before and said that they have something to tell you. Yes, it usually is complete bollocks but I have met some really lovely people along the way.

So, after reading the *Celestine Prophecy* I never bought a newspaper or magazine when I travelled on a train or plane. I always tried to sit next to someone and talk to them. Yes, it does look strange when there's only one person in a train carriage and you make a beeline for them but, trust me, it builds your confidence if nothing else.

I will admit, I've had a couple of fuck off tablets from a few people I've tried to talk to, and I'd rather pour acid over my genitals than meet some of them again, but on the whole we're quite an interesting bunch of people here on Planet Earth.

I was once asked if I'd like to join the 'mile high club' whilst on a flight to India. Although shocked, I suppose a meal and a movie can technically constitute a date, so I planted my arse on the baby-changing table in economy class on an Air India flight to New Delhi—I don't know whether that comes under the 'complete slut' or 'desperate' category. Bollocks, it's too late now and I'd never shagged anyone who wasn't white before either, so that's another of life's 'must do's' I can now cross off my bucket list.

The people I liked the best became my friends, and Mr In-Flight Entertainment disappeared at New Delhi International Airport.

As I handed my fucking idiot, dyslexic sign-writer his piss weak cup of tea, my friend Bev walked up to the cafe. One of her work colleagues has been sexually harassing her, in a sort of complimentary way; I think it does wonders for her ego. His name's Dave, he's a nurse at the same hospital as Bev works at and, when they both share the night shift, he'll sit with his trousers around his ankles behind his desk at the nurse's station and just look at her. She knows this because he makes no attempt to dress when she returns to her seat after a patient has called for assistance.

Bev: You've got your trousers down haven't you?

Dave: Is it me or is it a little warm in here?

Bev: It's a fucking hospital, of course it's warm. What if one of the staff nurses walks down here?

Dave: It can be our little secret Bev.

Bev: Yes, yours, mine, Amanda's, Nikki's and Julie's.

He also likes to spin around in his leather, swivel chair, with his tail hanging out. Today, she told us, he'd given her a shoulder massage, and that the conversation had gone something like:

Bev: I can feel it digging in my back, will you stop it!

Dave: Please touch it.

Bev: Fuck off!

Dave: Bev, just look at it.

Bev: Dave, it's a tail. I've seen one before, I'm a fucking nurse!

'He's massive you know Jules.' Bev added, with a cheeky little grin on her face.

Me: Like Biggest Loser massive or he's got a bit knob?

Bev: He's got a big knob, Jules, I ain't no chubby chaser.

The painter had packed up for the day; the decorating was finished, so my friends and I sat around the big table to discuss the day's events and eat chocolate muffins.

There was a bang at the front door; one of my friends Jamie had just driven his wheelchair into it, he's such an attention seeker.

'Let me in,' he mouthed.

Everyone important in my life was now sitting around the large table in the middle of the cafe: Bev, Jamie, Amanda, Kam, Tom, Colin, Nikki and me—it was a big table.

So, I'll start the introductions, ladies first.

I met Bev when I was doing a temping job at James Cook Memorial Hospital. I managed to land myself the lofty position of Data Entry Clerk. I'd rather give myself a hysterectomy with a vacuum cleaner before going back there but, looking on the bright side, I met Bev.

Bev is a nurse: her approach to nursing couldn't really be compared to that of Florence Nightingale, by which I mean she would happily stand by (Pissed.) whilst those in her care were eaten by rats.

Bev is a fiery red-head, 'it's not fucking ginger, it's auburn'. You'd want Bev on your side in a fight but, if the truth be known, she's soft as shite underneath. She is currently single and looking for a man, any man, who still possesses his own hair and teeth—this seems to be proving quite a challenge for her as she's been single for ages.

It seems that everywhere I work I manage to pick up at least one good friend, the type you do actually want to keep in touch with after your leaving party, and Bev and Jamie fall into this category.

Jamie I met at a local mobile telephone company. He'd been hired because this company thought that it would be politically correct, and I do believe it may now be a legal requirement for large organisations in the UK to hire a token number of disabled people. *We've got the disabled access, a brand new lift to the canteen area, and no disabled people to use them, what a waste, best get in touch with Remploy and get a couple of wheelchair users over here on the double.*

We got Jamie fresh from Northampton University, with some business degree that enabled him to undertake the lofty position of Chief Fax and Post Distributor. Jamie is capable of so much more.

'But they call it Corporate Co-Ordinator, Jamie, how good does that sound?'

Jamie's reply was simply, 'Fuck off.'

An avid Darlington Football Club supporter, brittle bone sufferer and potential fire hazard, Jamie is a pleasure to be around. If your idea of fun is emptying piss from a urine receptacle in some dirty, disabled public toilet and you like running the continued risk of having your toes broken as your wheelchair bound, disabled friend thinks he owns the fucking pavement then Jamie is indeed a pleasure to be around.

Amanda is one of my public transport friends. I started talking to her on a train one day and we both ended up sleeping with two best friends. She's a bit of a posh bird, works as an auditor for the local council, and she's the only one of the group that doesn't come from a dysfunctional family.

Amanda likes the finer things in life but is also prepared to slum it with us occasionally. She's a bit of a diplomat as well, which balances out the fact that the rest of us are about as subtle as a kick in the bollocks with a wide fitting boot.

She's a bit of a stunner who doesn't go out of the house without brushing her hair, cleaning her teeth and putting a bit of lippy on, which is more than can be said for the rest of us. Her hair is currently a rich chocolate colour, so the box says, and she's taller than the rest of us girls at around five feet seven inches.

Nikki's a fantastic shopping partner, with a slight tendency to 'spend it like Beckham'. She's currently dating a married ice-cream man (Ever wondered why you get so many broken wafers? Chances are they've been under Nikki's arse.), I fucking hate him, he's a complete wanker and he makes my skin crawl. I don't like him.

On the *shagometer* Nikki is towards the easy end, not quite a slut, but her morals are, shall we say, loose. I got to know Nikki at a friend's Christmas party four years ago. She was absolutely hammered, bollock naked, puking down the toilet whilst trying to take her contact lenses out—class with a capital C.

Nikki has two daughters and numerous grandchildren; I think there might be up to around seven of the little rug rats now. When Nikki's kids were younger she would carry a wooden spoon in the car with her, in order to dish out the appropriate punishment to either daughter who thought it would be a good idea to piss their mum off while she was driving. Nikki's proudest parenting achievement was the day she managed to hit both daughters with one swipe of the aforementioned wooden spoon. And the telephone number for Social Services is?

Kam works at Orange with Jamie. He's a Sikh, but doesn't wear a turban, and is shitting his pants that his family might be arranging a marriage for him in India. He has grown up in the North East of England and would like to maintain his family's culture and beliefs, but not if it means he has to marry and shag an ugly bird.

Kam speaks English and Punjabi and has taught me, about fifty times, how to say 'I'll have a mild, vegetable curry and poppadums with all the trimmings but go easy on the lime pickle', but I still can't remember how to say it. It's too hard this multilingual thing—thank fuck I speak English.

Tom is the local barber and the only member of the group who's seen my vagina. At this point I would like to point out that we were both five years old at the time and he used the same trick to look in all the girl's pants: 'I'll give you ten pence.' To 'feed his habit' he'd been stealing money from the spare change jar his family used to save spending money for their holidays in—this went on until his mum found out and she went off her fucking nut.

Apparently, he'd taken over five pounds from it, the dirty little bastard—I don't even know if Tom knew fifty girls or if he was just a regular client to some of them, I think I showed him my vagina twice because Mars Bars were twenty pence at the time. Anyway, I digress.

Tom also dabbles in a bit of yoga, martial arts, and takes copious amounts of drugs—what a lethal combination when you cut people's hair for a living. When I asked him what drugs he'd used his response was, 'I haven't taken heroin or crack.' Short and sweet. Tom is around six feet tall, dark hair and green eyes, quite a looker really, but to me he's just Tom.

Colin is one of Tom's customers. After a car battery exploded in Colin's face, blinding him, and after he nearly drank himself into a stupor, he enrolled onto a massage course at a local college. This year Colin won 'Remedial Masseur of the Year' and came top of his class—I must admit he gives a mean massage. He's also the only blind raver that I know of in Middlesbrough, he loves dancing.

That leaves me. I'd say I was impulsive, with a low bullshit tolerance level, and a tendency to blurt out offensive language. I do have a reputation for telling the truth, sometimes a little too quickly and without thinking of other people's feelings. Jamie says that I'm too 'black and white' so I am trying to put a little bit of grey into my life.

I'm quite short, around five feet two and a half inches tall, and have mid length brown hair, and hazel eyes. I know, I know; I can hear you all say how the fuck do you get laid looking that plain, on a positive note I have been graced with a fantastic pair of tits.

Whilst my breasts are actually deaf I have had many a bloke talk for hours to them; if they're bum men then I'm fucked, or perhaps not as the case may be, as I have quite a flat arse and am no competition for Jennifer Lopez, which of all the celebrity bums is the one I'd like to have.

My Taurean coffee mug says that I'm good with money, am a bit of a homemaker and hence a bit boring, and have a tendency to be stubborn and overweight as I like the finer things in life—I love cake.

We're all in our thirties, except Nikki who's around forty-something, sorry I can't be more specific but I think age is irrelevant in this group as we all act like a pack of twelve-year-olds anyway.

So this is my family, just as dysfunctional as every other family, but I decided to chose the bunch of weirdos I wanted to hang out with.

The girls were flicking through some magazines and the boys were playing cards. I love it when Colin deals, the cards go everywhere. As he put the remaining cards back on the table he knocked my cup of tea off the edge of the table, it smashed on the floor.

'I'll get that shall I?' I said, bending down to pick up the broken pieces of my mug.

Colin: I'm blind.

Jamie: I've got a disability.

Me: Not those old chestnuts again? What did we all do to end up with sixty-five thousand hours of fucking community service with the disabled? Rape and murder hundreds of old people? We must be giving Harold Shipman a good old run for his money.'

Amanda: Has he just broken your Taurean coffee mug? I bought you that.

Me. I know, he's clumsy as.

Colin: It's a mug you pair of sad twats, now get a life.

Tom: I've taped 'Countdown', where's the remote? Hello Carol Vorderman.

Me: I'm no good at anagrams. If I was on Countdown, I think I'd choose nine consonants and hope I could spell 'rhythm'.

Jamie: Or rhythms.

Kam: Or Gypsy.

Tom: What about crypt or, or, erm … pygmy?

Jamie: Or crypts.

Tom: Jamie, are you just adding an 's' to the end of all the words?

Nikki: What about psych or hymn?

Jamie: Or psychs or hymns.

Nikki: You'd be quite good at Countdown Tom, do you fancy joining my Scrabble group?

Tom: Sorry Nikki, you appear to have mistaken me for a sad fucker with no life, a bit like yourself. Do you remember that time on Countdown when both the contestants could only spell 'wankers' with the letters? That still cracks me up.

Amanda: What is it that you like about Carol?

Tom: She's a filthy slut in the sack.

Me: How do you work that out?

Tom: Don't spoil it. The imagination is all powerful.

Bev: I gave Dave a wank at work last night.

Me: Eh?!

Bev: It is Easter.

Me: I normally give chocolate and shit like that but I suppose I could save a small fortune just pulling blokes off instead.

Bev: I've asked him for some perfume for Easter. Oh, I need some more of your old clothes, we running out of them for the patients at the hospital.

Nikki: Don't you have to provide your own clothes when you go into hospital?

Bev: Some people get rushed in and don't have chance to pack or don't have relatives to bring in anything extra. Some people just have fuck all. Mr Teasdale died the other day in your old black and grey cardigan Tom.

Tom: The Christmas cardigan my Gran knit me?

Bev: Yeah. He got buried in it as well.

Tom: Oh right.

Bev: It's a bit spooky when I walk into some of the wards and all the patients are wearing our old clothes. I can just imagine us in forty years, all sat in our own piss in one of those wards.

Me: Changing the subject a little here, what constitutes funky music?

Jamie: What have you got?

Me: *Aretha Franklin's Greatest Hits*, Lenny Kravitz's *Let Love Rule*, a New Woman compilation album and something from Celine Dion.

Jamie: Well fuck all from Celine Dion for a start.

Nikki: You've got a Celine Dion CD?

Me: I can see where this is going, so let's change the subject shall we?

Colin: What about a bit of Coldplay, Oasis, Eminem?

Me: The customers will have an average age of about sixty.

Colin: Fucked if I know then.

Me: Thanks for that, Colin. I think I'll just choose music we'll like then.

Bev: What cakes are you going to have?

Me: I haven't decided yet. Let's get Delia out.

I opened Delia Smith's *Winter Collection* cookery book and laid it on the table.

Bev: Do you know how to make doughnuts?

Me: Er ... no. They're ninety nine pence for five from Tesco's.

Nikki: Are you really going to buy doughnuts from Tesco's?

Me: Yeah.

Nikki: Oh.

Bev: Just buy everything from Tesco's: cakes, cookies, the fucking lot. It sounds like hard work making everything yourself.

Me: I might as well, I mean, Delia talks a good cake but perhaps if she got laid more often then she'd spend less time baking in the kitchen and more time ordering takeaways like the rest of us.

Tom: Jamie, what's your new carer like?

Jamie: She's really good actually.

Tom: Have you nailed her yet?

Jamie: Not a sniff, she's a fucking lesbian.

Bev: Is it compulsory to be a lesbian, or at least look like one, before you can be a carer?

Jamie: Must be. I've got two carers now that are lessas.

Me: I bet more women have seen your cock than have seen all the other blokes at this table.

Jamie: Probably.

Kam: Do you ever get hard when they're soaping you down in the shower?

Jamie: I just think about an ugly bird and it keeps me soft for an extra thirty seconds.'

Tom: Like Gail from Coronation Street, or Anne Widdicom, yeah she's a right dog.

Jamie: I have actually, my personal favourite is Margaret Thatcher, I can never get hard when I think about shagging Maggie. I've slept with one of my carers.

Nikki: Is that when she turned into a lesbian?

Jamie: Fuck off. She did break my toe when we were shagging once.

Me: How?

Jamie: She went to straddle me and caught my toe with one of her knees.

Me: What was the funniest time you ever broke a bone?

Jamie: It hurts you know, but once I was trying to reach some bread that was on the dining room table at home and I over balanced because I leaned over too far, and ended up hanging onto the edge of the table by my nose. My mum had to save me. She was laughing her head off, the soulless witch.

Tom: So this new carer of yours, is she a lipstick lesbian or butch, you know, like a man but without the cock?

Jamie: Angela is definitely a lipstick lesbian. What about your Aunty? Doesn't she drink from the furry cup?

'Aunty Alice? Yeah, she's been Wendy's 'friend' for twenty years now.' Tom replied, emphasising the word friend. 'I never understood why my dad would always giggle when he said that we were going to visit Aunty Alice and Uncle Wendy when I was a kid.'

Nikki: I think we all need a weekend away before the shop opens, any suggestions?

Bev: What about camping in the Lake District?

Amanda: Will I have somewhere to plug my hair straighteners in?

Me: Can't we have a bit of luxury for once? I'm sick of roughing it.

Jamie: Since when have you ever roughed it? You fucking holiday snob.'

Me: Let's get one of these cheap flights from EasyJet and find a hotel on the Internet?

Colin: I fancy somewhere hot. I don't care where, I can't see fuck all, but I like the sun on my face. I might ask Babs to come with me. Actually on second thoughts I might not.

Tom: How's it going with Barbara? Are you getting plenty?

Colin: It's going alright, but she won't go down on me, says it makes her heave.

Nikki: When was the last time you bathed?

Colin: Shut up fool!

Me: Try putting a TicTac in your jap's eye—only two calories and it will keep her breath minty fresh for up to two hours apparently.

Colin: Babs slapped me last week, I didn't see that coming.

Tom: Well you wouldn't would you?

Amanda: What did she slap you for? What did you do?

Colin: Well you know she's deaf, and she was bitching to me about something and I thought she'd finished and turned away from me but she must have been lip reading when I called her a fucking, stupid mare. And then she bitch slapped me, fucking well hard.

Me: You deserved it.

Jamie: Do you know that together both of you make up Helen Keller?

Amanda: What about Amsterdam? I think EasyJet have one of their cheap flights to Amsterdam from Leeds-Bradford airport.

Jamie: I think I'll get my rocks off then.

Kam: Me too.

Jamie: What do you think happens when you hire one of those ladies?

Nikki: Are you using the word 'ladies' in the loosest sense of the word?

Jamie: I do hope so. Will they just lay me down and ride me for twenty minutes?

Me: How would we know? It'll be more like five minutes and she's not going to call you tomorrow and tell you she loves ya.

Jamie: She might if I slide her an extra five Euros.

Kam: She might after I've slid her a full eight inches.

Nikki: Why are you going to put it in twice?

Kam: It would make you squeal if I stuck it up your arse.

Nikki: Hardly.

Me: It'll be cold in Amsterdam in April; you'll need to buy a coat Jamie.

Jamie: Will you shut up about me getting a coat? I don't feel the cold like you, you puff, I'm sure there's something wrong with you.

Me: I just like to be toastie. Anyway, stop changing the subject, you're getting a coat.'

Jamie: Well actually, you'll be pleased to know I've already purchased one. It's hanging off the back of my chair.

Me: Where?

Jamie: In the Wilderness Ways Extreme Sports bag.

I opened the bag and pulled out a padded, black jacket.

Me: I'm impressed, this almost looks warm. Here let's try it on.

Jamie: The arms are a bit long. I'm going to ask my mum if she'll take them up.

That was an understatement to say the least. After I'd zipped him up all that remained of Jamie was two feet poking out of the bottom of the jacket and his head, from the nose upwards.

Bev: You look like a bag of someone's rubbish.

Tom: Amsterdam it is then.

Nikki: It sounds like a plan.

I think Jamie said, 'Get me out of this coat', although I couldn't be sure as the sound was rather muffled, so we just left him in it.

Mmm …marijuana, Dutch pancakes and porn.

April

We arrived at Leeds-Bradford airport at five forty-five on a fucking Saturday morning.

It was raining and, as per usual at UK airports, the long stay car park was miles from the main terminal. Add the fact that someone had to push Jamie in his manual wheelchair, and he got to hold the umbrella, which meant that the rest of us were piss wet through before we even checked in.

We were not a pretty sight, especially after being told there was a two hour delay due to the pilot being 'uncontactable'; he'd slept in hadn't he, the bone idle, work shy, lazy twat.

Tom: Jamie, if you look at that itinerary once more I'm going to slap you.

'Sorry,' said Jamie, folding up the printout detailing our flights, and he calls me a control freak.

'Jesus, the woman at the check-in desk looks like a hooker,' I declared as we approached the counter. 'I don't think I've seen eye shadow that colour since my Aunty sold Avon in the seventies.'

Amanda: She does look a bit ropey, I have to admit. I thought the airlines gave their staff lessons in how to apply makeup and stuff like that; you know, how to look your best.

Bev: Ah, bless her, she probably does look her best, not everyone can be as stunning as us.

Me: Point taken. Right everyone, give me your passports.

Jamie: You're a bit of a control freak aren't you? You're always trying to organise everything.

'Ah, here we go. You do it then, knock yourself out,' I said, dropping all the passports into Jamie's lap and taking two steps back away from him.

Jamie: I can't see over the counter.

One of the passports slid off his wheelchair and dropped onto the floor. Jamie looked around pleadingly.

'Can someone pick that passport up for me please?'

Bev: No.

Me: You want to be treated like everyone else, pick it up yourself.

Jamie: I can't reach, ya pack of bastards! Here then, if it makes you happy, you check in. He threw all the passports on the floor.

I walked up to the hooker.

Me: Good morning, we're going to Amsterdam.

Up close the hooker looked even worse, like a bulldog licking piss off a thistle, only uglier; she could've at least trimmed her moustache.

Hooker: Can your friend walk to the plane?

I don't know which pissed me off the most. The fact that the stupid bitch asked the question, or that she aimed it at me rather than Jamie, but I felt a streak of mischievousness unleashed within me.

Now at this point let me describe Jamie to you. Jamie has *osteo genus imperfectus,* better known as brittle bones disease, not to be confused with *osteoporosis.* He was born with thirteen broken bones in his body and spent the first six months of his life at Great Ormond Street Children's Hospital, where, as his parents were told that he was not supposed to last long. Jamie has since broken every bone in his body except his spine. Only a complete fuckwit would ask the above question, I hope this clarifies my answer to it.

'I don't know, I'll just ask him.' I raised my voice to screaming pitch, 'DO YOU THINK THAT YOU COULD WALK TO THE PLANE?'

Jamie joined in the fun, 'NO, BUT I CAN DO A MEAN FOXTROT. WHY ARE YOU SHOUTING AT ME?'

Me: BECAUSE YOU'RE IN A WHEELCHAIR.

Jamie: Oh right.

I turned to the hooker and smiled, the joke was completely lost on her.

Me: Tell me, what qualifications or training do you need to stick those labels on suitcase handles?

The hooker didn't answer the question.

As I collected all the passports and tickets I added, 'I think with a degree in Business Administration, you're overqualified, Jamie.'

We all gathered in the departure lounge and waited for our flight to be called. Nikki hadn't arrived yet and was cutting it fine to catch the flight, thank God it was delayed. Kam and I sprawled out across some empty seats and tried to get our heads down for an hour.

Tom: I'm bored.

Me: Who am I?

Tom: Oh, I like this game, are you a man?

'Yes.'

'Are you alive?'

'Yes.'

'Are you British?'

'No.'

'Are you a Yank?'

'Yes.'

'Are you an actor?'

'No.'

'A sportsman?'

'No.'

'A politician?'

'No.'

'A chat show host?'

'No.'

'A singer?'

'No.'

'A TV chef?'

'No.'

'A writer?'

'Erm … sort of.'

'What sort of writer?'

'Play the game properly.'

'Do you write books?'

'No.'

'Plays?'

'No.'

'Films?'

'No.'

'What else is there? Ah, songs?'

'Yes.'

'Are you in your twenties?'

'No.'

'Thirties?'

'No.'

'Forties?'

'No.'

'Fifties?'

'No.'

'Sixties.'

'Erm … yes, or I could be in my seventies.'

'A sixty or seventy year old song-writer?'

'Yes.'

'Liberace?'

'Last I heard he was mincing around St. Peter's entrance.'

'What?'

'He's dead.'

'Oh right.'

'Elvis?'

'I'm alive fool.'

'What old fucking song-writers do we know?

'Are you giving in?'

'No. Give us a clue.'

'He's written hundreds of songs, you'll kick yourself when I tell you.'

'I can't be arsed with this. Who is it?'

'Burt Bacharach.'

Tom: Burt Bacharach! Who the fucking hell's Burt Bacharach?'

Me: A famous song writer, he's written hundreds of songs apparently.'

Kam: Name one that we'll all know.'

Me: I bet you a tenner that you already know at least one of his songs.

'You're on, I'll take that bet for a tenner.' Kam sat up, took his wallet from his back pocket and flicked a dirty ten pound note at me.

Me: Where the fuck has that been?

Kam: Money's money, and anyway I'll be getting it straight back in about a minute's time anyway. Off you go Jules, sing to me.

'Raindrops keep falling on my head, and just like the guy whose feet are too big for his bed, nothing seems to fit.'

Kam: Shut up.

Me: What about this fucking classic? You know this guy, this guy's in love with you. Yes I'm in love, who looks at you the way I do.

Kam: What?!

Jamie: Shut up Jules.

Me: Or what, dickhead? But really Jamie, what are you going to do? I have no issues giving a disabled person a fucking slap when they need one. If you can do better Kam then knock yourself out.

Kam: I will then. Who am I?

'Are you a man?'

'Yes.'

'Are you alive?'

'Yes.'

'Are you British?'

'No.'

'Are you European?'

'Yes.'

'Are you a sportsman?'

'Yes.'

'Are you Michael Schumacher?'

Pause ...

'Yes.'

'Kam, you're shit.'

'I could have picked anyone, how did you know it would be Michael Schumacher?'

'Because you're so predictable and we know you so well. Think outside the square, Kam, surprise us.'

Amanda: Who am I?

'Are you a man?'

'Yes.'

'Are you alive?'

'Mmm, not really.'

'What do you mean?'

'I'm not alive, but I'm not dead.'

'How can you be a man then?'

'It's all in the name.'

'Is it a cartoon character?'

'Yes.'

'Is it anyone off the Simpsons?'

'No.'

'Bob the Builder?'

'No.'

'Fireman Sam?'

'No.'

'Mr Benn?'

'Ooh, nearly.'

'I can't think of any others.'

'It's all in the name.'

Pause ...

'I'll give you a clue, his name starts with Mr.'

'Ah, it's one of the Mr Men.'

'Yes.'

'OK then, Mr Happy?'

'No.'

'Mr Strong?'

'No.'

'Mr Messy?'

'No.'

'Mr Tall?'

'No.'

'Mr Nosey?'

'No.'

'Mr Tickle.'

'No.'

'Fucking hell, how many Mr Men are there?'

'Fifty six.'

'You're fucking joking?'

'We'll be here all day.'

'Mr Rush?'

'No.'

'Mr Greedy?'

'No.'

'But you could change your answer if we guess the right one.'

'Ask what colour or shape he is then.'

Pause …

'What difference will that make? We grew out of the Mr Men thirty fucking years ago?'

'Mr Small?'

'No.'

'You know them all don't you Amanda?'

'Yep.'

'You sad fucker.'

'Keep guessing.'

'Mr Tidy?'

'No.'

'Mr Tickle?'

'You've already had him.'

'Mr Big Cock.'

'Eh?'

'Mr Baldy.'

'Mr Comb Over.'

'Mrs Kappa Tracksuit.'

'They're not real'

Pause …

'This is shit.'

'Are you giving up?'

'Yes, I've given up the will to fucking live.'

'Mr Bump.'

Pause …

Amanda: Mr Bump's better than Burt fucking Bacharach.

Nikki rushed into the departure lounge, 'Sorry I'm late,' she said, sitting down next to me.

'What's happened to your eye?' Bev said, drawing our attention to the nasty red swelling just below Nikki's left eye.

Nikki: June must have found out about Phil and me. I was walking down Linthorpe Road in town yesterday and I saw her walking towards me and just kept my head down as I passed her.

Amanda: And you walked into a lamp-post?

Nikki: No, she smacked me in the face with her sandal. It was one of those Scholl ones with the wooden sole, it smarted like a bastard. Anyway, I ran out of petrol on the way here and had to hitch a lift the rest of the way.

Me: You are terrible for doing that, keep the fucking car filled up you tight twat. You'll look sick if you break down late at night, in the middle of nowhere, don't be calling me up and asking me to come and get you.

Nikki: Have you quite finished?

Me: Yeah.

Nikki: Good, now shut up.

Jamie: Does anyone want to play chess?

Me: I don't know how to play chess but I can play drafts.

Jamie: I don't have any draft pieces.

Me: We can just play with the chess pieces.

Jamie: No, that won't work: we can't crown a piece if either of us gets to the other side of the board.'

Me: Don't be a twat all your life Jamie, we can just play for fun, don't be so competitive.

Jamie: It won't work.

Me: Come on, I'll look really intelligent if everyone thinks I'm playing chess.

'*Flight LS201 to Amsterdam is now ready for boarding at gate number four. At this time we ask that anyone requiring assistance to board this flight make themselves known to the ground staff.*'

Jamie: Saved by the bell.

Result. Straight to the front of the queue.

'There seems to be a high proportion of wheel-chair users on today's flight Jamie. I do hope it's not contagious,' Tom said, indicating the five or so disabled people preparing to board the flight.

Jamie: You'll miss me when I'm gone; I have a reduced life expectancy you know.

Me: That's just not good enough, Jamie, we need dates.

Nikki: How long do you reckon you'll last, Jamie?

Jamie: I'll be pushing it to see sixty.

Me: Sixty! That's not a reduced life expectancy; It's a life sentence for us.

Amanda: Colin, how did you cope with losing your sight?

Colin: I didn't. I just got pissed out of my skull for three years. I bet I shagged some real ugly birds. Ah well, that's one of the advantages of being blind, as long as they feel like a woman you don't care if they look like Bernard Manning.

Nikki: So which is worse? Being born disabled, or becoming disabled during your life?

Jamie: I've never known any different.

Kam: But don't you wish you could have played football? You love it.

Bev: Not really, he supports Darlington.

Jamie: Now don't be *dissing* Darlo.

Kam: At the beginning of the last footy season we managed to forge a letter from Darlington Football Club and send it to Jamie telling him that the club could no longer afford to offer concessions to their disabled patrons, and that he'd have to pay full price for his ticket. You should have seen him throw his toys out of the pram; he was going to wheel straight down there and play the disabled card.

Although there's normally a stampede for seats on these cheap flights having a disabled member of the group does increase the chance of a larger group being able to sit together. It also ensures that you fly straight to the front of queues at most tourist attractions. I would thoroughly recommend making friends with a disabled person for these reasons alone.

When everyone was seated comfortably, we took off.

Me: You have to pay for the sandwiches on here, £3.95 for a cheese and pickle sandwich. Fucking scandalous!

Nikki: We've paid £6.49 each way for this flight and you're bitching about paying for sandwiches.

Me: There's no movie either.

Nikki: That's because the flight is one hour and ten minutes long, you fool.

Me: They could play half a movie on the way out and the rest on the return journey. Or an episode of Friends or Little Britain, something like that.

Bev: I've never been on a plane before. What if we get hijacked?

We all turned to look at Bev.

Tom: We'd be fucked then. Unless of course it's on the return journey and then at least we'll have seen Amsterdam.

Bev: Do you think we could stab the hijackers with the knives and forks you get from the trolley?

Tom: You'd be lucky to cut through a pork chop with this cutlery, let alone stab someone to death.

Amanda: You could inflict more damage with this in-flight magazine. I've just given myself a paper cut.

Jamie: I feel sick.

Tom: We've just taken off.

Amanda: Who's got a sick bag?

Bev: Here.

At least it wasn't me this time. I used to puke my ring up on most flights until I met a Lifeboat Coxon who suggested I tilt my head to one side every time I felt travel sick, something about confusing the liquid in your cochlea so that it stops moving too much and making you feel like you're going to hurl. It works, I've never puked since I started doing it, but I usually get a pain in my neck, which lasts for a couple of hours after the flight.

I got used to the stares as my face turned bright red, my eyes started to water and the veins in my forehead started to protrude. I used to wretch as loudly as I could in the end, and blow kisses at other staring passengers with chunks still hanging from my mouth—pretty much how Jamie looked right now.

Me: You look beautiful.

Nikki: Do you need another bag?

Jamie: No, I think I'll get it all in here, thanks.

I handed Jamie a serviette to wipe his mouth. He carefully folded the top of the sick bag and then dropped it on the floor.

Me: Words fail me. You clumsy bastard.

Jamie: Sorry.

It stunk, everyone within a two metre radius of the drop site gagged for the rest of the flight. I take back my recommendation for befriending the disabled.

Colin: What's happened?

Me: Nothing Colin. Do you fancy changing seats? That window view is lost on you.

Colin: Yeah no problem.

Kam: Julie, you rotten witch.

Colin: Phew, what's that smell?

Jamie: I've just been sick.

Colin: Jules, you selfish twat.

Me: Ssh, just sit back and relax, you need to reserve your strength. You'll be emptying your bollocks into some filthy whore before you can say 'tulips from Amsterdam'.

Kam: You make it sound so sleazy.

Tom: I was thinking that I might not go for the 'full monty' as such, I might just have a blow job.

Kam: I was thinking the same but it's been so long since I had a shag I might blow the back of her head off.

Jamie's suitcase didn't turn up at Schiphol Airport.

Jamie: Where is it?

Bev: Look we're only here for three days. You can turn your undies inside out tomorrow and then go commando the next day.

Jamie: I don't give a shit about my clothes, it's my spot cream I'm bothered about. I'll have a face like a pizza by tomorrow if I don't use it.

Jamie filled in all the necessary lost luggage paperwork, he writes like a total spastic so that took up forty five minutes of holiday time, and then we headed for the railway station, where we boarded the train for the thirty minute journey into Amsterdam.

Tom: Ah ... Amsterdam.'

'Where are we staying?' Kam asked as we alighted at Amsterdam Central.

Bev: Follow me. It's a ten minute walk from here; I booked it on the Internet. It's just off Dam Square, bang in the centre of town.

We all loaded up Jamie's wheelchair with as much hand baggage as it could take, without it toppling over, and set off after Bev with her newly acquired tourist map of Amsterdam.

Jamie: Why do I have to carry all the bags?

Me: You're not really carrying the bags, the chair's doing all the work.

Jamie: I look like a shopping trolley.

Tom: Come on Sherpa Tensing.'

Bev led us, map in hand, to the chosen hotel for our two night stay.

The sun was shining, the Dutch were smiling. The Dutch are a lovely bunch of people, something to do with them taking drugs and having sex all day long. They also make cracking porn, just like the Swedes but the Swedes are in pole position as far as I'm concerned because they have IKEA.

'I couldn't resist' said Bev, as we came to a halt outside one of the hotels.

Tom: Are we really staying at the Kock City Hotel?

Jamie: *Result!*

We checked in and couldn't help smiling as the Receptionist answered the phone with the chirpy 'Kock City Hotel' every time it rang. We dumped our bags in Jamie's room; another result, disabled room my arse, Jamie couldn't even get his wheelchair into the bathroom.

'I'm fucked if I need to take a dump,' Jamie despaired.

Amanda: Especially as you are currently experiencing a severe lack of replacement under-wear.

Me: I can feel a free breakfast coming on.

Tom: Do you reckon? It's worth a try.

Jamie: I'd rather just have an accessible bath-room; do we have to play the compensation card every time someone screws up?

Me: Hell yes!

And the receptionist was more than willing to oblige us with a free breakfast when she realised that they had screwed up and all the other disabled rooms were booked. We'd deal with Jamie's toilet requirements as the need arose.

Nikki: Coffee anyone?

No-one needed any further persuading; it was only a leisurely five to ten minute stroll through Amsterdam before we came across a cosy looking little drug den come cafe.

After briefly perusing the menu, I decided that I would try a slice of Madeira sponge, heavily laden with some quality 'Class B' substance, and a weak latte, like piss with two sugars. I promptly ordered both. Jamie and I were the only ones in the group not toking. I've never smoked anything so it had to be cake; It's always got to be cake.

'Have you ever taken any drugs, Jules?' Amanda asked after she inhaled deeply on her reefer.

Me: Nah, I've never been bothered really but I can't see taking marijuana once or twice doing me much damage.

How wrong could I have been? Somehow the next hour disappeared; I spent the last thirty minutes in total silence. The Dutch must get really pissed off with tourists from countries with stricter drugs laws flocking to their fair cities and getting boxed off their tits giving drugs a bad name.

Someone belched and we all laughed like fuck. Then I started to feel a little weird, my heart started to beat a little faster and I began to sweat like a horse.

Me: I think I'm going to die.

'We're all going to die, Jules,' said Tom, trying to comfort me.

Me: No but, I think it's impending.

Colin: Eh?

Nikki: You'll be alright.

I didn't know what to do with myself. The waitress did advise that I should eat my cake slowly, but as I was a little peckish I'd bolted it down my neck in under a minute. I just sat there moving my head in all directions, like one of those prairie dogs, as I tried to look for … god only knows. Then I started to cry like a small child.

Me: No really, I think I'm going to die.

Colin: Can I shag you while you're still warm?

The lack of sympathy from Colin upset me even more.

Me: Girls, I want you to sell everything I own and share it amongst yourselves.

Kam: What about us?

Me: Fuck you all, you pack of bastards, I'm dying and all you can think of is what you're going to get. Don't anyone let Colin shag me.

Nikki: How much are you worth?

Me: Probably about a hundred and fifty thousand.

Kam: A hundred and fifty thousand, where did you get all that from?'

Me: I think I'm going to die.

Bev: She made loads of money from the Orange share-save scheme.

Nikki: So we'd get a straight fifty grand each then? What would you spend yours on Amanda?

Amanda: I need to get a new car, mine's just about given up the ghost.

Bev: I would love to go on one of those ninety day cruises around the world. I think they cost about ten thousand each though, I think all the food's included as well. I'll be the size of a small house by the time I get back.

Kam: Come on girls, don't we get a sniff?

Nikki: Nah. You heard what she said, she doesn't want you lot getting anything.

Jamie: You greedy bitches.

Bev: Anyway, Jamie, if you had twenty five grand in the bank it would affect your carer benefits.'

Tom: I'll look after it for you Jamie.

Jamie: Like shite you will. Ooh, I need a shit.

Tom: Can it wait?

Jamie: It'll have to, won't it? Oh, it's OK I've just farted; I can wait a bit longer now.

Me: I don't feel well. I think I'm going die.' I rocked back and forth like a nutter at this point.

Colin: Shut up, you'll be alright.

Tom: I don't think I've ever seen anyone freak out on ganja before.

I could hear the blood rushing around inside my head, my cheeks started to feel really flushed like I was burning up with a fever. I stood up quickly, knocking my chair to the ground behind me.

Me: I want to be cremated.

Tom: What, right now? Shouldn't we wait until you're actually dead?

'I'M GOING TO DIE.'

Kam: Come on soft cock, let's get you out of here.

I leaned over the railings next to one of the canals and tried to steady myself. I took deep breaths and after a few minutes I'd started to feel better.

'Come on then, let's see some of this city,' Tom said, leading the way.

There really should be a highway code for people operating electric wheelchairs, especially in cities with canals, and after consuming copious amounts of space cake. This time it was Colin's turn to have his toes run over, bless him, he couldn't even see Jamie coming.

Colin: Ooh, you fucker! What was that? Was it that clumsy crip bastard again?

Amanda: Come on Colin, we're off to the Red Light District.

Colin forgot about his toes.

En route we decided we needed to pay one of the many sex shops a visit. We managed to find one that scored very highly in the 'top quality filth and sleaze' category.

The videos were arranged in an orderly fashion, at eye level on a shelf as you walked into the shop, so that you could judge the content by the pictures shown on the spine of the video case. The movies got progressively more hardcore as you went from left to right along the shelf.

The first video showed a picture of a man ejaculating over a woman's breasts, halfway across the shelf was a fist shoved up someone's back pipe and then finally, to the far right, was someone shitting in a bloke's mouth—a first class establishment.

Tom bought a deck of filthy playing cards showing various cum shots and I decided, in my currently unstable mental state, to buy a four-foot inflatable cock, which I quickly tired of carrying around the centre of Amsterdam with me. The last time I saw my cock, its bell-end was protruding from the window of one of the canal boats where I'd left it.

Like most of the men that window shop in Amsterdam's notorious sex district the boys were all talk and no action, except Colin.

'Babs has dumped me so I'm going to get jiggy with one of these ladies,' Colin declared.

'Ah, I'm sorry to hear that Colin, did she say why?' Amanda asked.

'Apparently, I didn't show her enough love and affection. I mean I shagged her more or less every night, what more does she want?'

Me: That's not love and affection, Colin. How did you shag her? I mean if you were giving her it doggie style every night then you're hardly building up any intimacy are you?

'But I like taking her from behind,' Colin replied.

Me: But every time? Fucking hell, Colin, widen your repertoire.

Colin: And the witch has only taken the fridge and the wardrobe, I know she bought them but I thought, *'Where the fuck am I?'* when I walked into the kitchen. I went to get the milk to make myself a cup of tea and I was like, *where's my fucking fridge?* So I wandered around the flat trying to find out what else the thieving cow had taken, it took me ages to feel my way around everywhere. She'd thrown my clothes all over the bedroom, I nearly broke my fucking neck when I walked in there and got my feet caught up in a pair of my undies that had been left on the floor.

Amanda: Didn't you see Babs moving all the stuff out Tom?

Tom: No, I didn't see a thing. I was behind Colin at the time.

Amanda: Should I assume that you were cutting his hair or sodomising him?

Tom: Cutting his hair funnily enough. Right Colin, we are now standing in the red light district of Amsterdam.

Colin: Thanks for that, Tom. Boys if you could recommend a hot babe for me that would be fantastic.

It was just too much of a temptation for the boys who, deep, deep down, are complete twats, there was a knowing look between them that spelled mischief.

Fifteen and a half minutes later Colin had shagged a pig. We then proceeded for the rest of the weekend to affectionately call him Bacon. Obviously the boys wanted details, and we were there with them so we had to listen.

Kam: So come on then, spill the beans.

Colin: We had a shag, that's about it.

Kam: Was it good?'

Colin: Not really. I feel a bit violated actually.

Kam: What do you mean? What did she say?

Colin: Not a great deal. It was very business like.

Me: Like going into a bank and making a deposit?

Colin: Something like that, but I've never been handed a wet wipe at the bank.

Kam: So what happened? Did you ask her for a blow job or just skip the appetiser and go for full penetration?

Colin: I took my clothes off and laid on the bed, I think the sheets were plastic I was sticking to them, she gave me a quick hand job to get me started and then hopped on for about five, maybe six minutes. And then hopped back off.

Amanda: So it was well worth it then?

Colin looked at his feet, well, looked in the loosest sense of the word, he just hung his head really.

Up until that point the boys had wanted to take in a live sex show, they were, however, a little wary of the signs advertising for 'audience participation'. We decided to find a pub where Colin could have a drink and drown his sorrows.

'Here,' said Kam. 'This place looks OK.' He pushed the large stainless steel door open and we all piled in.

Every head in the place turned to look at us.

Tom: Why are there no women in here?

Tom seemed to falter at the end of his sentence, at about the same time as we all noticed 'Man-O-Man' in neon lights above the bar.

Kam: Let's back slowly towards the door.

Jamie: Why can't we just smile, turn around and walk towards the door?

Kam: Well they might … you know?

Me: What, they might butt fuck you all before we reach the door? Don't be so ridiculous. They might teach you how to dress and dance, but don't flatter yourself, they won't want to fuck you. I'm going to the bar. Are you coming?

I could hear the boys starting to panic behind me but it was about time that the boys realised that not all gay men go around raping and pillaging every straight man they set eyes on. I bought the first round.

Bev: Time for a piss stop.

Tom: Don't you fucking dare leave us!

Bev: Shut up.

It was night club bliss for girls, a clean ladies toilet with no queues.

Amanda: Has your cubicle got a condom machine in it?

Me: Yeah, flavoured ones I think.

Bev: Have you got two Euros?

Amanda passed a couple of coins under the cubicle to Bev.

Bev: Curry flavour, I mean would you? Really?

Me: Chocolate Ripple flavour my arse.

Amanda: Oh bugger, I must have put my money in the wrong slot, I've got a maxi night-time towel.

When we got back to the bar the boys were still standing in silence with their backs towards the bar, we were tasked with striking up a conversation with some of the locals. After about twenty minutes the boys relaxed their sphincter muscles and joined in.

'These homos are alright, you know,' Kam whispered to Nikki.

Nikki: We know.

The guys in the bar that night were some of the nicest people I've ever met. We danced and talked all night to complete strangers. We had a great time, especially Colin. Colin loves to dance and as I watched him move to the music I hoped that he wouldn't miraculously regain his sight and see that both him and the guy that had sidled up to him were wearing tight white t-shirts. I giggled to myself.

We all left at around one in the morning when I had the munchies, big time.

Me: I'm starving.

Nikki: Me too. We've just passed a tapas restaurant just down the road; I think it's still open.

We all turned around and walked the hundred or so yards back to the restaurant. The lights were still on and three or four couples were finishing their meals.

Tom: Good evening, your façade suggests that you are purveyors of fine food and beverages.

Pause …

Bev: What did you just say?

Tom turned to us and whispered, 'I'm sick of all these Dutch fuckers speaking such brilliant English, when I haven't managed to pick up more than two words of their language. I'll show them 'who's the daddy?''

He turned to the waiter with a smug smile on his face.

'We most certainly are, Sir.' the waiter replied; he was Irish.

If you're able bodied, and you don't have to think about manoeuvring a wheelchair around the Formula 1 track that is most restaurants, I've found that you don't really take too much notice about accessibility issues. Jamie once asked me if Rome was disabled friendly, after I'd just spent the weekend there, and do you know, I couldn't answer him; I didn't have a clue, I just put one foot in front of the other and pretty much got everywhere I wanted to go. I tried to be helpful and point out that the Spanish Steps were probably a no go area for him, but he just gave me some derogatory hand gesture.

I did notice some wheelchair users at The Acropolis in Athens though, and we've since decided among ourselves that improved disabled access in major cities is down to the Olympic Games. If a city, in recent years, has held the Olympic Games, then you're laughing tea-cakes if you're disabled because it must be part of the contract when you tender for the Games to provide disabled access to major sightseeing attractions. I think the Paralympic Games are on straight after the Olympic Games anyway; it wouldn't be much of a spectator event if the athletes couldn't get to the stadiums.

Anyway there was this awful grating noise from behind us all, and we turned to find that Jamie had failed to handle a particularly tricky chicane and was dragging along one of the restaurant's chairs which he had caught on one of his wheelchair handles.

'Have I hit something?' he asked, twisting his head over both shoulders and trying in vain to look behind him.

Amanda and Bev unhooked him, while I asked if we could all sit at the front of the restaurant. The waiter then moved us to a table where we could look out over one of Amsterdam's many canals, which was obviously lost on us because it was now around one o'clock in the morning and pitch black outside.

We all ordered a meal, sat back and waited for our food to arrive, while having a deep and meaningful conversation with the boys who told us that homosexuality was just plain wrong, but that lessas were alright as they liked vaginas. When the dishes did arrive we weren't disappointed. Plates of hummus, pita bread, succulent garlic mushrooms, potatoes covered in a spicy sauce, Greek salad, chicken wings, king prawns and pasta dishes; you always order too much don't you?

About five minutes into the meal, when we were all sat stuffing our faces, Jamie started to make a coughing-choking sound whilst eating a chicken wing.

For the next few seconds everything moved like it was in slow motion, nobody said a word. Then there was the realisation that one of us may have to make a monumental decision; here are the two options that we were faced with at that particular moment in time: option one, perform the Heimlich manoeuvre on brittle boned Jamie, break most of his ribs and possibly puncture a lung; option two, leave him to stop breathing and hope the paramedics can save the day, if they get here on time.

Option two was looking pretty good when Jamie, with purple face and blood shot eyes, managed to clear the blockage.

'I think I've just swallowed a bone.'

Tom slowly moved the chicken wings away from Jamie and we quietly continued eating.

We got to bed at around two thirty.

It was around three o'clock in the morning when the noise started: a rhythmic squeaking that is immediately recognisable as shagging, and it seemed to be coming from the room directly above us.

The other girls were making noises like farm machinery, and coupled with the noise of the shagging I had no chance of any shut-eye. After four minutes I'd had enough.

I considered waking the others up, but thought that they might not take kindly to that course of action so I devised a cunning plan. We were in Room 455, on the fourth floor, surely that meant the shaggers were in Room 555? Mmm ...

I switched on the reading light at the side of my bed and quickly read the instructions on how to use the telephone, which were stuck to the cabinet at the side of my bed. All I had to do was dial the room number to get through to any room in the hotel. Here goes.

I heard the telephone ringing in the room above and after a few moments the rhythmic squeaking stopped. Someone picked up the telephone and I quickly replaced the receiver.

There were a few moments of blissful silence from upstairs before the shagging recommenced. I dialled 555 again and the phone was answered just that little bit quicker than the first time; I put the phone down again.

My mischievous streak had been unleashed and I repeated the whole process about ten times in all and was chuckling away to myself as the shaggers were getting more and more desperate to finish the task at hand.

At the final attempt I heard a muffled scream through the ceiling and everything went quiet; mission accomplished. I'm officially a cunt.

The next day we missed our free breakfast by about one and a half hours so we decided to go out for brunch—very cosmopolitan don't you know. I skipped the drugs though, while I think Nikki may have had some sprinkled on her muesli.

We decided to be cultured and went to the Van Gogh Museum. We could tell that we were in a country that treated us like adults; we could have touched Van Gough's painting of the 'Sunflowers', we were so close to it and it wasn't behind any plate glass or anything. Jamie managed to drive his wheelchair into the foot-rail that ran around the bottom of each room in the art gallery, and nearly knocked the painting off the wall but the security guard just looked and nodded at Jamie as he reversed sheepishly away—we were long gone; he was on his own.

Then, funnily enough, back to a coffee shop; I only had a coffee and everyone called me a homosexual.

It was time to go home and Tom had decided he wanted to smuggle some good skunk back to the UK. I had no idea how Tom got hold of the stuff, but apparently there had been a few dealers out on the streets of Amsterdam and Tom had managed to get his hands on some cannabis resin.

As we'd been walking around the city I had heard people whispering 'Charlie' at me and thought, *do I look like a fucking Charlie to you?* Apparently, it's short for Charlie Brown, or cocaine, don't you know? I'm not really very street savvy.

Tom: The stuff out here's so much better than at home. I've brought some cling film with me.

Amanda: To do what?

Tom: To wrap it in before I conceal it.

Me: How are you going to do that?

Tom: I'm going to stick it up my arse.

Me: No really, how are you going to hide it?

Tom: I'm going to stick it up my arse.

Me: Really? Like in the movies? I thought drug smugglers swallowed drugs in condoms and then shit them out.

Tom: That's only heroin, when you want to bring loads of the stuff in. Your arse can only hold so much but your stomach can hold a lot more.

Me: Right. I take it you'll be smoking it on your own.

Kam: No, he'll share it.

Me: Are you going to smoke skunk that Tom's pulled out of his arse?

Kam: It's wrapped in cling film.

Tom: I'm not fucking sharing it, get your own you tight twat and stick it up your own arse.

Bev: I hope they anally probe you.

Tom: Thanks Bev.

Me: Jamie, I reckon you could bring ten kilos of cocaine back to the UK hidden on this wheelchair, and even if the beagles were barking like fuck they still wouldn't dare search you.

Jamie: Let's not though. I haven't got the bottle. I've got an extra litre of vodka in my bag and I'm starting to sweat.

The flight went smoothly enough, I bitched about the price of the sandwiches again, Jamie managed to not vomit and we all succeeded in getting back through customs without being strip-searched. I don't think it would be politically correct to strip-search the disabled.

As we passed through customs we retrieved Jamie's suitcase, which hadn't even left Leeds-Bradford airport, and Jamie applied a thick cover of spot cream to his face.

We arranged to pick up Nikki's car en route back home. Nikki had left the box from her new DVD player on the back seat. Some vandals had smashed the back window to get to the DVD player. Upon realising that the box was empty they had decided it would be fun to piss all over the seats inside as revenge for them wasting their time smashing the car window to steal the DVD player in the first place.

You could smell piss from well outside the car and no one offered to drive the car back to Nikki's, so we decided to call the AA and have them tow it, giving a flat battery as the excuse for the call out.

May

Back home again and it was time to open the coffee shop. Nearby there was a new housing development being built, complete with hairy arsed, hungry builders. So I decided to open the shop early and hoped to make a killing with my breakfast rolls and take-away teas and coffees.

The early mornings were a killer for me; I am not a morning person. On the second day I somehow managed to fall asleep at the counter. When my next customer walked in the doorbell woke me with a jolt. He asked for a bacon sandwich and tea to go, with a big grin on his face the whole time. I smiled back, wishing all my customers were this friendly.

When he'd gone I turned to check my hair in the mirrored tiles behind me and realised I had the remains of a KitKat stuck to my face. I peeled the KitKat from my cheek and finished it off.

I also got help from the local Business Development Officer and managed to employ someone to help me run the place. I got a young girl called Marie; she was seventeen years old and lived nearby. Marie turned out to be a good worker, never late and always stayed in the shop until the last customer left. She was shy and quiet but always polite, and the customers seemed to like her. Marie took a weight off my shoulders—perhaps I would find peace after all.

I couldn't really have picked a better spot for the shop, right opposite a warden controlled housing development for the over fifty-five's. The occupants became my main source of income. The oldies were always telling stories: 'when I was a boy' or 'girl', and when there was rationing, clip mats when they couldn't afford carpets, going for years without a TV, fridge, car etc. etc. Apparently us young ones have it easy nowadays.

I had asked the boys if they'd lend me some of their Marvel Superheroes Comics, but every response ended in … off! I thought *Reader's Digest* and *Arthritis Today* would be appropriate reading material for my clientele but against my better judgement I decided to buy some of those celebrity scandal women's magazines, like 'Hello' and 'Now', and leave them lying around for the customers, who loved them. They lapped up all the gossip, using the shop as a sort of social club.

Colin walked through my door one afternoon. 'This must be the right place, I can smell piss,' he said, walking up the counter, resting his elbow on said counter and knocking a container full of drinking straws to the floor. He's a clumsy twat.

Me: Don't be a complete cock Colin. They're a lovely bunch of people and fortunately hard of hearing. Hello Mrs Jackson, how are you today?

Eighty-three-year-old, arthritis-sufferer Mrs Jackson shuffled up to the counter.

Mrs Jackson: I'm fine and yourself.

Me: I'm good. How's Mr Jackson?

Mrs Jackson: He's OK. He wears a colostomy bag now you know, his waterworks had been playing up again and he kept wetting the bed, we've had to buy a new mattress, the old one had started to rot.

Me: Oh right.

Mrs Jackson: How are you, Colin?

Colin: I'm doing very well Mrs Jackson; I'm just waiting for a young lady, like yourself, to ask me out.

Me: Take my advice and don't go there Mrs Jackson, you deserve better, just ignore him; however, he did get himself an older woman.

Mrs Jackson: A Doberman, that's nice, what have you called it?

Pause …

Me: Barbara.

Mrs Jackson: That's an unusual name for a dog, but I suppose anything goes these days.

I managed to serve Mrs Jackson a cup of tea and a raspberry jam doughnut before I walked away from the counter and cracked up laughing at the back of the shop. I tried to avoid Colin's death stare—well it was as near a death stare as a blind person can give you.

I popped out to Somerfield supermarket for some milk and left Marie in charge. When I came back ten minutes later Colin was standing behind the counter pretending to operate the till.

Me: What are you doing?

Colin: If anyone guesses I'm blind they'll be in here robbing you, asking me to change a twenty pound note and only giving me five, the bastards.

Me: Where's Marie?

'I'm here,' Marie appeared from the kitchen at the back of the shop, she was shaking.

Me: Are you OK?

Marie: I just felt a little dizzy, I'm OK now.

As I turned to the front of the shop I could see Jamie passing on the opposite side of the road. Mrs Jackson's eighty two year old husband clung tightly onto the handles of Jamie's electric wheelchair, allowing himself to be pulled along in his own manual chair.

Me: Mrs Jackson? Where's Jamie taking your husband?

Mrs Jackson shot up out of her seat, dodgy hip my arse, and opened the door of the shop.

'Oi, where do you think you're going?' she shouted down the street after Jamie and her husband.

Mr Jackson: Leave me alone woman.

I love public domestics.

Jamie: We're just off to the pub for a few jars Mrs J, we won't be long.

Mrs Jackson: Don't be coming in drunk and trying any funny business with me! Do you hear me?

What the fuck is funny business when you're in your eighties? God I hope I'm still getting it then, I'd like to get some now actually rather than wait until I'm in my eighties.

The day passed quickly and soon it was closing time. Colin was the last customer out of the door at six thirty, with the remaining doughnuts in a paper bag.

I carried the rubbish out to the passage way at the back of the shop; that's when I heard the shouting.

'Don't give me any shit, just give me your wallet.' The dark figure holding Colin against the wall hissed into his face.

'I've only got four fucking doughnuts,' Colin replied.

Fuck, what was I going to do? A mugging in Saltburn by the Sea, I don't think so. Bingo!

I don't know what it is about our little town but you can always find old furniture left in back alleys. You could probably furnish an entire house with the amount of shit that's left lying about. I spotted a broken chair leg and it was mine. I had no idea what to do with it really but thought hitting this mugger as hard as possible over the head would be a good idea. I don't think rationally in moments like that, any sort of negotiation skills I may have had just fly out of the window.

As I have the coordination of a cerebral palsy sufferer there was a fifty-fifty chance that I was going to smack Colin over the head instead of his assailant. Anyway, I managed to creep up behind the mugger and land the chair leg smack in the middle of the back of his head, it made an awful cracking sound and he hit the ground; he was out cold.

Me: Are you alright Colin?

Colin: Where is the bastard?

Colin managed to get his bearings and then started to swing his leg wildly in the direction of his assailant. After six or so kicks he stopped and leant against the wall, breathing heavily.

Me: Come inside Colin, I'll make us a cup of tea.

Colin: He'll regret ever fucking with me, the twat.

Me: That he will, Colin.

I took Colin's hand and led him into the kitchen. I didn't have the heart to tell him he'd just kicked fuck out of a bin-bag full of rubbish.

Colin took the attempted mugging badly, he was very nervous on his own over the next couple of weeks, so we decided to have a night out to cheer him up.

The Empire night club, in Middlesbrough, hosts a seventies music night every Thursday, complete with resident DJ, Brutus Gold, riding his bicycle across the stage asking, 'Ladies, who wants to ride my chopper?'

We decided to get right into the scheme of things and dress up in clothes from that era, from our local charity shop 'Help the Aged' and decided to meet in the coffee shop at seven o'clock, and then get the train through to 'Middlesboogie', as we locals affectionately like to call Middlesbrough.

Tom was wearing beige, polyester flares and a pink shirt with huge lapels when he came into the shop. He finished this ensemble off with beige platform boots. He actually looked quite good, which made me feel a little uncomfortable.

Tom: What do you think of the shirt then?

Me: It matches your shaving rash lovely.

Tom: Get fucked.

Amanda and Bev were wearing silver boob tubes, with black satin, skin-tight trousers, and pink glitter wigs. Nikki had gone for a white, blue and green patterned blouse in nylon, which made me feel nauseous if I stared at it for any length of time.

If it wasn't seventies night Kam would have been arrested on the spot for pimping. He was wearing his grandma's full-length fur coat, black polo neck and black flares. He'd managed to sneak his grandad's walking stick out of the house and had wrapped some tin foil over the hooked end to try and make it look *bling*—wanker. He looked good but was going to sweat like a bastard inside The Empire.

I looked a bit shit. Even if I really try to look good I can't quite pull it off, and tonight was no different. Mine was a nice little pleated number, in red, black and white stripes, buttoned to the neck. A bit like those old Playboy duvet covers boys used to have on their beds in the eighties. I looked like I should be sat at home, crocheting in front of the telly, with my hot chocolate. Even my American Tan tights had wrinkled at the ankles, oh fuck it, it was too late to change now.

Colin and Jamie somehow managed to get the wrong end of the stick.

Me: What on earth are you two wearing?

Jamie: What do you mean?

Nikki: What we mean is, take a look at what everyone else is wearing. Polyester flares and nylon tops in vomit inducing colours, typical of the seventies. Where did Doctor Who and a Dalek come into it?

Colin: Ah, is that who I am, Doctor Who?

Jamie: In case you haven't noticed I am somewhat restricted dress wise. I am in a wheelchair and where am I going to find flared trousers when my legs are only twelve inches long? Now shut the fuck up and let's go listen to some Jackson Five.

I just love seventies nights, all cheesy glitter wigs and platform shoes, Disco Dick strutting his stuff on the dance floor. We regularly lose Colin at these events, normally Amanda has hold of his hand all the time but if she loosens her grip for even a moment he's got hold of someone else and fucked off over the other side of whichever venue we happen to be frequenting.

All of us then have to split up and, with military precision, scour the surrounding area looking for the blind guy, edging his way around the walls of the Empire, trying to find his way back to us, and saying 'Sorry' every ten or so seconds when he stands on someone's toes. We only lost him twice this particular evening.

Anyway, when we got there, The Empire was heaving with people as per usual, but we'd totally fucked up the nights and there was a Secret Skins Party on instead. So forget the Jackson Five and Donna Summer, it was BlocParty and DJs Dirty Secretz?!

There were still tickets available so we thought, 'Why not?' Luckily everyone was off their tits anyway, and didn't seem to notice what we were wearing.

Initially we stood at the back of the venue; I don't like taking Jamie into the middle of a crowd of piss-heads, you know it'll all end in beers and a trip to Accident and Emergency.

From where we stood I watched a couple with eyes only for each other, acting like they were the only people in the room, arms down by their sides holding hands, whispering into each other's ears and following each comment with a kiss. They smiled at each other and look into one another's eyes, their faces almost touching.

That's what I miss the most now that I'm single: the intimacy. Those long, soft, deep kisses you share with someone you love, not those fumbling, teeth clashing, if he sticks his tongue any further down my throat I'm going to gag, kisses that you sometimes get when you first get it on with someone.

I miss having the back of my neck stroked, having my fingers entwined when I hold another's hand, enjoying someone's touch and enjoying touching them, kind words.

Sometimes I lay stretched out in my bed, eating milk chocolate HobNobs, watching whatever I damned well like on my portable TV, thinking, 'Isn't this great?' And then sometimes, occasionally, and more often lately, I wish I'd fucked every man I ever met.

I wish it could have worked with my ex, he was, is, beautiful, but we're better people apart—stronger. I'll always be there for him; I can talk to him like no-one else, be intimate with him. Jesus, I've done things with him that are illegal in some countries, you can't get any more intimate.

Tonight I was lucky enough to be chatted up by some smooth talking twat, in a pair of black leather trousers and Cuban heels; he must have made the same mistake we did. He had dark Brylcreemed hair combed back off his face and he smelled of fish and chips. His chat up lines went something like this:

Twat: French, Chinese, Italian or Thai?

Me: What?

Twat: The restaurant that I'm going to take you to. Which would you prefer?

Me: I'd prefer to cut my clitoris off with a razor blade.

Twat: No really.

Me: No *really*, I would.

Twat: Now that I've seen you up close, I'd rather have a wank anyway.

Walking to the train station at the end of the night was fun. Everyone except me was pissed and talking complete bollocks; although, I have been known to be sober and talk complete bollocks, so at least the rest of them had an excuse. Just to top it all off, Jamie had forgotten to charge the battery on his wheelchair the night before so we were all taking turns to push him.

Me: You need some new tyres. Only Michael Schumacher should be driving on these slicks.

Tom: It's a right bastard to push.

Me: It's your turn Kam.

Kam: How do you work that out?

Me: We're just coming up to a hill.

Then, somehow, we managed to take the train going in the wrong direction, one stop later and we had to alight in salubrious Thornaby, hot on the heels of Middlesbrough in the crap town stakes, and cross the platform to wait for a train back in the other direction. May I mention at this point that the platform is only around ten metres wide, so crossing to the other side was no great feat.

Thornaby railway station is in the middle of fucking nowhere. The station itself is set down from the road, right next to the River Tees, and under one of the main roads that runs from Thornaby to Stockton Upon Tees; completing the triangle of crap towns, perhaps not a triangle of crap towns, more of a cluster of crap towns because the nearby suburbs of Grangetown, Southbank and Port Clarence are equally wank.

It might have been May but it was chilly. I was only wearing a thin jacket and folded my arms across my chest to keep warm.

'There's someone stood on the bridge,' Amanda said, as she squinted to focus on the nearby bridge, 'it looks like they're going to jump off.'

Sure enough, there was someone stood at the centre of the bridge, it looked like a man. To be honest it's only a hundred foot drop into the Tees, I doubt that you'd do too much damage to yourself. What's the worst that could happen? You'd catch a nasty dose of *gastroenteritis*, a rash or a kidney infection from the dirty water.

We were none too worried until someone muttered that perhaps this guy couldn't swim and we'd had a great night so far, even though we'd ended up in Thornaby, and didn't really want to end the night watching a complete stranger drown to death.

So we all shuffled up onto the main road and made our way to the middle of the bridge. Fuck knows what for; we were as subtle as a curry enema.

Kam: Watch this, I'm going to try some reverse psychology on him. JUMP YOU DAFT CUNT!

Bev: Shut up Kam, you shithouse.

We edged our way nonchalantly along the bridge to where he was standing. It wasn't really that nonchalant, more the nervous shuffle of a five year old child who's done something wrong and is going to get a major bollocking from their mum or dad.

Me: Hello mate, you alright?

'Does it look like I'm alright?' he snarled sarcastically.

Me: Mmm ... not really. Do you want to go for a coffee and a chat?

Bloke: What?!

Me: Would you like to go for a coffee and have a chat?

Bloke: About what?

Me: About what?! Are you fucking joking?

My patience was starting to run out—how can counsellors chat to these fucking nutters for an hour at a time? Thirty seconds into the conversation and I was already over it.

Bev: It's a bit chilly out here, I'll be in McDonald's if you need me.

Bev walked briskly over the bridge towards Stockton, followed closely by Nikki and Amanda.

Jamie: I need a piss, Kam, wheel me over to Macca's. They've got a crip's toilet in there.

Tom: I'll leave you to it then.

Me: Fucking cheers.

Bloke: I don't want you talking me out of this, it's taken me long enough to get here.

Me: I'm not going to talk you out of it. I tell you what, this is what we're going to do, I'll make you a deal. Obviously today has been a bit shit for you hence you are up on this bridge, a whole twenty or thirty metres above the River Tees, which is probably about twenty or thirty metres wide. Look at it from my point of view, are you fucking joking?

Bloke: I can't swim.

Me: OK then, if in thirty minutes you still want to do this, I'll come back up here with you and push you off myself. Now are you coming for a coffee with us? I'm freezing my fucking tits off.

I didn't really give the bloke time to answer, he looked at me without speaking for a few uncomfortable moments. I think he was trying to size me all up really, bearing in mind I'd just offered to push him off the bridge if he didn't feel any better in the next half an hour. He also looked suspiciously at the polyester number I was wearing.

Bloke: Yeah, I'll do coffee. I haven't got any money mind.

Me: That's the story of my fucking life.

We walked together towards the town centre and the warm refuge of McDonalds.

We talked along the way, starting off with how crap Middlesbrough, Stockton and Thornaby were and then moving onto the grittier stuff that makes you threaten to jump from a bridge in the dead of night into a river when you can't swim.

Some people's life stories are heartbreaking; you wouldn't treat a dog the way some of us behave towards others. The bloke's name was Neal. He'd been abused by an uncle, beaten by his dad, ignored by his mother, he'd left home as soon as he could at sixteen, and bummed around for a few years, staying in different places in the UK, slowly trying to drink himself to death.

Then he met a girl, and they had five wonderful years together, before he lost her to breast cancer eighteen months ago; he returned to the bottle.

Obviously, I have no idea what to say to make anyone feel better about themselves because an hour later we were back on the fucking bridge.

Nikki: You are useless and I think we've just missed the last train.

Me: I didn't see you trying to help him.

Nikki: Have you mistaken me for someone who gives a shit? Let him jump.

Me: He's had a shitty time lately, you callous bitch.

Neal: Thanks for taking the time to listen to me.

Me: It was nothing.

Nikki: Obviously.

Me: Please don't listen to my friend Nikki here, as she's a complete cunt.

He smiled and I sat next to him on the wall at the edge of the bridge, trying my best to summon words of wisdom from within. I must have been thinking too hard because I lost my balance. The next thing I knew I was falling and then I hit the icy cold water of the River Tees, fuck me it was cold, and it tasted like shit. I watched this experiment once on the TV, and it's true, you do stop breathing when you're submerged in really cold water.

'Ooh, you fucker,' I shouted as I gashed my leg on something sharp, which I think might have been a discarded shopping trolley, probably from ALDI just up the road.

I clawed my way back onto the riverbank as the others tried to make their way down from the bridge towards me. My heart was pounding like it was going to burst out of my chest and I could hardly speak for my teeth chattering, except to mutter something about being a clumsy twat and question why this sort of shit always happens to me.

Three hours later we were still sitting in Accident and Emergency at James Cook Hospital. It was probably misuse of National Health Service resources to call an ambulance to bring us all here, but Jamie started bitching about the small proportion of taxis in the area that could actually accommodate wheelchairs and before we knew it he'd called the emergency services. I needed six stitches.

Neal: I'm really sorry about this.

I was tempted to tell him to eat shit and die but I thought I would try my psychic powers out on him instead. I raised my eyebrows, flared my nostrils and silently thought those two, sweet words, the second of which is 'off'. Neal fully understood and looked down at his feet. It was quarter past four in the morning and I was freezing my tits off, waiting for the stitches to my calf and wondering how I was going to manage at work that day. All that karma shite, 'what goes around, comes around', was obviously a pile of big, hairy dog's cocks—next time I won't bother.

The doctor took great pleasure injecting the anaesthetic into my two inch long gash, oh er, more tea vicar, and then prodding away at my leg like some apprentice seamstress. I thought of offering to do it myself, but I've never even darned a sock before so I'd probably do an even shittier job of it than he did. It didn't look too bad at the end actually; good old NHS, where would we be without them?

Then I remembered that Bev was a nurse and perhaps she could've done it for me, then I remembered that she was still hammered.

We were ready to leave Accident and Emergency just over an hour later.

Neal: Thanks for talking to me, it was just what I needed.

Me: I wish I hadn't bothered.

Nikki: What are you going to do now?

Neal: I'll try and make a fresh start. Get a place of my own, get off the streets and make some new friends. I can't say that I definitely won't end up back on that bridge though.

Bev: Have you got a place to stay?

Neal: I'll look for somewhere today. I'll be OK.

Bev: What? You haven't got anywhere to stay? Jules you've got a spare room, he can stay with you. Till you get back on your feet Neal, you can help Jules out in the shop.

Neal: That would be really nice, thanks for offering.

Me: I didn't.

Bev: Shut up.

We managed to catch a train going in the right direction on this occasion. The sunrise was fantastic, I can't remember ever being up this early in the morning, I must do it again sometime.

Amanda: You hardly know this bloke Jules, I think it's a bit risky asking him to stay at your place when you've only just met him.

Me: Thank you for those kind words of comfort, Amanda. I've just had six stitches in my leg, can hardly walk, and now you're highlighting the fact that Bev may have invited a potential murdering, rapist into my home. I didn't even invite him, fucking ginger over there fucking asked if he wanted to fucking stay.

Tom: Are you quite finished?

Me: No, not really. Oi, Neal, are you going to help me out today, bearing in mind this is all your fault?

Neal: I'd love to. I used to work in a sandwich shop.

Me: Right, fuck it, you're on the early shift with Marie.'

I slept until midday; I was knackered. The painkillers that the hospital gave me were marvellous, they knocked me right out; I had a dream that I was a prostitute and ended up shagging this complete stranger, I was filthy, it was great.

I hobbled down to the shop at around 1 pm. Blow me, Neal and Marie had done a marvellous job, the shop was ticking over nicely.

Neal: It's been busy but we've managed. How's your leg?

Me: Smarting like a bastard, thanks for asking.

Neal: I'm sorry.

Me: Don't worry, it was an accident, I'm a right clumsy twat. Anyway, thanks for helping me out here.

Neal: No worries. I'll stay as long as you need me.

He smiled. I was seeing him for the first time in daylight and I noticed his big, green eyes, shiny, dark brown hair and easy smile. I leaned back too far on my chair to look at him and fell over backward, cracking my head on the floor. Why do I always make a fool of myself when I'm trying to play it cool? Let's be honest, I'm far from cool.

June

Tom and Colin's barber's salon come massage parlour is located about half a mile away from my coffee shop. Tom cuts hair downstairs and Colin massages clients upstairs.

The building sits on its own about twenty metres from the Saltburn to Marske railway line. The front rooms on both floors are where the boys work and the living areas are at the back of both floors.

Tom charges five pounds for a haircut; short back and sides, or 'I'll just have a trim', which accounts for around ninety five percent of all requests. Anyone asking for a cut that's a little out of the ordinary, or possibly in fashion, ends up with a short back and sides anyway.

Tom gets a bit of a kick when young kids bring in a magazine shot of one of their favourite celebrities, they ask Tom to try and emulate their celebrity's hair style and he then goes and gives them a short back and sides anyway. He likes to see the look of disappointment on the children's faces at the end; it's all because he's a sick, little fuck.

Tom's salon, let's use that word in the loosest sense shall we, still looks like a house from the outside and there is no signage to allude to the fact that he's a barber. Having said that there are always at least five customers waiting for Tom's services at any one time, his business has just grown by word of mouth really; he's not in the *Yellow Pages* and I don't even know if the salon has a name.

In the summer months you'll get a bottle of lager with your haircut, whichever brand is on special offer at Macro Superstore that week. No, he doesn't have a licence to serve alcohol, but this is Tom's unique selling point and most of the regulars will occasionally bring in a six pack to ensure the tradition remains.

Inside the salon the walls are painted white, *were* painted white at some point in the distant past, and are covered in marks where customers have rubbed them with the back of their chairs whilst waiting for Tom's aforementioned short back and sides.

There is one barber's chair in dark brown leather, sat in front of a tall IKEA mirror (As I said earlier, I cannot stress enough how fucking great IKEA is.) and the six chairs for waiting customers are upholstered in a delightful, light brown leatherette, rather like those chairs you get in doctor's surgeries. They probably *are* from a doctor's surgery; I've never asked him where he got them from.

A ritual of sorts has evolved in Tom's Barbers, initiated by Colin of all people. Tom used to ask the regular customers if their haircut was satisfactory and the answer would generally be, 'Yes, it's fine thanks,' until Colin started saying 'No, it's shit, I don't know why I bother coming here,' and from then on, by word of mouth, everyone started saying the same as Colin.

Tom has since given up asking for feedback and when the occasional patron does offer a compliment or suggestion for improvement, Tom's usual response is to point to his face and say, 'Bothered?' in the style of Catherine Tate.

The 'salon' used to be Tom's gran's house and she left it to him when she died, severely pissing off the rest of the family who were left the grand sum of fuck all, but then Tom was the only one who went to visit her.

To be fair, Tom only stopped off at his gran's when he couldn't be arsed walking the extra half mile to get to his own home, so he'd stop off at his gran's instead.

Tom's gran lost a lot of her hearing as she advanced in years, not that this mattered as she would talk non-stop bollocks for hours on end and you couldn't get a word in edgeways.

She would go on and on about rationing, the psychedelic seventies and how Tom's grandad Jack had got her totally trashed on a funny cigarette once and she hadn't been right for days.

It was great in winter when Tom would take me and a couple of other friends from school because she wasn't one of these tight pensioners who never turned on the heating, she'd have it set on that Mediterranean setting that only old people can find on their thermostat. We'd all take turns falling asleep in front of the telly with one of her multi-coloured crocheted blankets, made of scraps of wool left over from Christmas jumpers and the like, wrapped around us. The TV had the volume turned down so low that you had to be able to lip read if you wanted to know what was happening on any of the programs anyway.

We were twats really as we would all be playing our personal stereos while Tom's gran was talking and occasionally cast her a sideways glance to mumble, 'Really?', or 'Yeah, you're right', or some other affirmative comment just to show our impeccable manners. She wasn't stupid though and probably called us worse than shite after we all left.

She was a great sort though: we'd all be snoozing on the sofa and she'd still be talking complete and utter bollocks but managed to keep the cups of tea and mint and orange viscount biscuits coming—she was a fucking star.

She would always be wearing a knitted twin set, she must have had hundreds of them as I don't think I ever saw her in the same colour more than twice, and a thick woollen skirt made of tweed or some similar fabric. She'd shuffle along in her pink slippers from Marks & Spencer. Tom bought her a new pair of slippers every Christmas, or should I say his mum bought them for him to give to his gran, and Tom told us how she would act all surprised and grateful every Christmas morning when she opened them.

Gran's are great at hiding their true feelings. When I look back now at some of the presents I bought my gran when I was younger they were absolutely dog shite, and she'd say, 'Ah, that's lovely,' or 'That's just what I wanted,' and then she'd put whatever I'd bought her on display.

I remember buying her some brass ornaments that I picked up from one of those 'Everything's A Pound' shops. You could chose from about six well-known global landmarks, so I picked the Eiffel Tower, the Taj Mahal and one of those Egyptian pyramids. Anyway, they weren't even a pound, they were three for a pound, so thirty three pence each; you could just feel the quality, and if you felt too hard the brass came off on your fingers—Fucking shite.

She had those shitty ornaments on one of the shelves of her bookcase for years, I don't think I'll ever love anyone enough to display that sort of junk in my house—I'd best not have any kids then.

I do think that Tom's gran was a bit of a sly, old bird though as she once picked up on the fact that Tom had said the word 'blow-job', when only a fucking dog could have heard it and, like a terrier with a bone, she wouldn't let up until Tom had explained what the term meant.

On this particular occasion, and for reasons unknown to the rest of us, Tom chose the medium of mime with which to explain to his gran what a blow-job was. As Tom grasped an imaginary cock and moved his hand up and down the shaft, his gran copied his every move. Then Tom placed the aforementioned cock into his mouth and the look on his gran's face was fucking mint. The horror of such an act was etched onto her face and her rocking hand came to an abrupt standstill.

One of my fondest memories in my later years will be of that cold, dark winter night when, safely tucked up in my crocheted blanket, I watched Tom and his gran pump air cock together.

July

Time passed quickly, before I knew it Neal had been staying with me for six weeks and I was doing less and less — *result!*

We even had a visit from the Food Safety Inspector and Neal took care of it. Apparently, he told the Inspector that there would be no problems as I was anally clean, the Inspector commented that that was good to know but he only wanted to check the kitchen.

Nikki: Any hot bedroom action with old green eyes yet then?

Me: Not a sniff.

Bev: He must be homosexual if he doesn't fancy you.

Me: Well that's exactly what I was thinking, he must be.

Tom: Sweet Jesus.

Neal was standing behind the counter, I shouted over to him.

'Neal, which side of the stamp are you licking?'

Neal: Eh?

Me: Well are you a tits and arse man, or just an arse man?

Tom: Jules wants to know if you're a cackpipe cosmonaut.

Me: A cackpipe cosmonaut?! I much prefer the term 'rusty bullet hole engineer'.

Bev: Chutney ferret.

Amanda: Big, brown bear hunter.

Nikki: Sausage jockey.

Neal: How old are you lot?

Pause …

Me: Well do you dance the chocolate Cha Cha or what?

Neal: Or what.

Me: That's a relief.

Nikki: Are you a boobs or bum man?

Neal: Definitely a boob man.

Me: If you were a woman for twenty four hours, would you stay at home and play with your tits all day?

Tom: If you were a man for a day would you have a tug?

Me: Of course.

Kam: I'd get the biggest thing possible and stick it up me.

Tom: What like a traffic cone?

Kam: Yeah.

Bev: Nice to see you boys understand what a girl really needs.

And from then on, Neal and I started to flirt. I still wasn't too sure that I wanted to shit on my own doorstep, but the flirting was definitely an ego boost. I even started getting out of bed fifteen minutes earlier in the morning just to put some makeup on and make myself look presentable. Then he asked me if I wanted to go to the flicks the following weekend, I suppose it was going to be our first real date.

Bev: What are you going to see?

Me: I don't know, some shit about a guy who finds out that one of his best friends, who happens to be a girl, is getting married and then he realises that he loves her and sets out to ruin the wedding day. There we have it, I don't really need to go now.'

Nikki: Watch out, he might try the old 'cock-porn' trick.'

Me: Cockporn trick?

Nikki: You know, where a bloke sits with a bag of popcorn on his lap and he's made a hole in the bottom and stuck his dick into the bag. Then he asks you if you want some popcorn so you touch his tail.

Me: Where did you grow up? Jersey wasn't it? Is that really all there is to do on a night in Jersey then?'

Amanda: Have you got some condoms?

Me: Steady on, I'm only going to the flicks with him. Mind you I might pay the beauty salon a visit; you could plait my bikini line at the moment.

Amanda: Waxing smarts like fuck, no man's worth waxing for.

Bev: What if he asks you for a shag afterwards?

Me: He'd better be a vampire then; It's that time of the month I'm afraid—every four weeks, seems to be some sort of cycle going on there.'

I decided to make an effort and scrub up for this date, my bush looked like a dead badger so I got the Remington Bikini Trim out. Blokes have it easy, I thought as I was sat there on the towel trimming my thatch: no waxing, plucking, exfoliating ... ooh, what the fuck was that? My bikini trim made a noise like I was trying to cut through a scouring pad with it. Bollocks! I'd just cut the string off my tampon.

I sat for a few moments pondering what I should do next, then I dressed and started to look around the flat for something with which to hygienically retrieve said tampon. I made my way into the kitchen—*voila*. After I'd removed my tampon with the barbeque tongs, I completed the trim and went to bed.

The next evening Neal and I went to the cinema as planned: the film was absolutely average and I didn't have any of Neal's popcorn. Afterwards, we walked out of the cinema, crossed the road and went for something to eat in the Purple Onion.

The Purple Onion is a French restaurant with deep red and gold décor and a romantic ambience. I might even start to look attractive to Neal after he'd downed a few pints; not too many though, it was a bit pricey and I didn't want to push him back over the edge into alcoholism again. Apparently, he couldn't have any alcohol, being a reformed alcoholic, so it was a cheap date.

Me: What are you having?

Neal: Are you having a starter?

Me: No, I'd rather have a dessert.

Neal: Me too. I'll have the salmon.

Fucking marvellous, kissing him will be like licking Whitby Fish Market's floor.

Me: I'll have the vegetarian lasagne.

Neal: Are you a veggie?

Me: Yes, I've been veggie for about twelve years now I think.

Neal: Do you not like meat or is it for other reasons?'

Me: I just don't like the way the animals are kept, you know in cages with hardly any room to move, and then electrocuted and skinned alive.

Neal: Yeah alright, stop before I feel sick.

Me: Mind you, saying that, I am wearing leather boots and a leather jacket.

The food was wonderful and I had a really nice time, I think he did too. Finding something to talk about was easy with Neal: there were no awkward silences, and when there was silence it felt comfortable.

There's always live music playing at Doc Brown's every Sunday night, so we ended the evening there. As we walked in the band were singing about a girl with big tits— class with a capital C.

When we got back home to the Funky Doughnut, there was an awkward moment just as we separated to go to our bedrooms but, all in all, it was a pretty good night; I hoped, the first of many, but next time with a bit more 'getting jiggy with it', if you know what I mean.

I'd just started to drop off to sleep when the phone started ringing. Kam was calling to tell us that Jamie had been hit by a Land Rover outside of his house and was in the trauma unit of James Cook hospital; we got back into the car.

They charge you two quid for the first hour that you park at James Cook hospital! At least Dick Turpin wore a fucking mask; nowadays it's the 'Pay & Display' machines that commit highway robbery.

'Hello dickhead,' was my affectionate greeting when we arrived at the trauma unit. 'Would you care to enlighten us with this little gem of a story?'

Kam: He hasn't got a clue; he's pissed.

Jamie: Its red hot in here, open the window before I pass out. Ooh, my pelvis hurts.

Kam: This fool pulled straight out into the road without looking to see what was coming.

Jamie: Then, when the wanker had impaled me on the front of the fucking radiator grill of his four by four, he thought, 'I'll just reverse and flip this daft bastard over'. I landed with my arm under the chair, I think I've broken that as well as my pelvis.

Me: What, the chair or your arm?'

Jamie: Both: the chair's a write-off and I've bust my wanking arm—fucking marvellous.

Me: Where are all the nurses?

Kam: Jamie's already asked them all if they want to see his tail so I think they've gone off to get a male nurse.

Jamie: They can't resist, they fucking want me, the filthy sluts, Ooh, it hurts.

A nurse walked over to us. I noticed his name badge straight way: it read 'Dave'. Jamie noticed it too.

'Did our Beverley wank you off the other week?' Jamie innocently enquired.

Dave: Your friend seems to be suffering from concussion, perhaps I should sedate him.

Me: Perhaps you should take his temperature the old fashioned way, just in case he starts fitting. And then, just to make sure, you should put the thermometer in his mouth as well to double check it was right the first time.

Pause …

'On second thoughts, perhaps you should just put him down.'

Dave: Would you sign the consent form?

Me: No problem, by the time I've finished with the form it'll look like a fucking petition.

Jamie: HELLO, I'm still here.

Neal: Is there anything we can do?

Dave: Not really, the doctor will come round a see him later. Get yourselves off home.

Kam: We'll see you in the morning then.

Jamie: Don't leave me on my own.

Me: You're in the best place.

Jamie: I might call my mum.

Me: Leave your mum alone, she'll only get worried, tell her in the morning. Kam, take his mobile off him.

Jamie hugged his mobile phone to his chest.

'Will you come back tomorrow?' he pleaded.

Me: We might do.

Bed at three thirty; start at seven am—*result!* God was I ropey that morning, luckily the shop was quiet.

Hospital visiting times are five thirty until eight o'clock in the evening so we grabbed an Indian takeaway on the way over and took some cutlery and plates from the cafe; you just know you'd rather eat your own faeces than hospital food. As we walked along the hospital corridor the smell of tikka massala, jalfrezi and peswari nans wafted behind us.

Walking into Jamie's room we were confronted by Nurse Dave taking Kam's blood pressure.

Me: What's wrong with you?

Kam: Nothing, but I thought I'd have it checked. When was the last time you had your blood pressure taken?

Me: I can't remember, years ago probably.

Dave: Do you want it checked?

'Go on then,' I said, rolling up my sleeve.

'How did you manage to get a room on your own? Are you going private?' I asked the patient, as Dave proceeded to slip the blood pressure strap around my arm.

Jamie: You're jesting aren't you? Anyway, you're treated quite well here on the trauma unit.'

Dave: One hundred and nine over sixty-nine: it's a bit low.

Pause …

Me: And?

Dave: It's just a bit low that's all. You should keep an eye on it.

Me: Why? What's gonna happen?

Dave: Nothing.

Me: There's nothing you can do or there's nothing going to happen?

Dave: Well there is nothing you can do about low blood pressure. You can take tablets if your blood pressure is high but low blood pressure is less common.

Me: And?

Dave: Just keep an eye on it.

Pause …

Me: What do you mean keep an eye on it?

Dave: Well, you should visit your doctor regularly to keep a check on it. You shouldn't let your blood sugar get too low either, eat little and often.

Neal: There's no problem there: every time I look at her she's eating a fucking doughnut.

Me: I wish I hadn't bothered, I was alright when I came in here and now I'm worried. Cheers Dave, you're a star.

Jamie: Shut up, I'm the one with the broken arm and pelvis.

Me: Are they smarting like a bastard?

Jamie: Oh yes, the doctor reckons I'll be signed off for six weeks.

Kam: You lucky, lucky bastard.

Jamie: Oh yes, let's see if I can't stretch that out a bit longer. Anyway, let's get the chicken tikka served up, I'm starving.

Me: I've got to sit down, I'm feeling a little light headed.

Jamie: Shut up. Where's everyone else?

Me: I asked if they were coming but they said they didn't even like you.

Jamie: Fair enough.

Me: Nah, they're coming later so let's get this curry eaten before we have to share it with them. Come on Kam, you must be a dab hand at serving up curry.

Kam had brought an old Playstation into the hospital for Jamie, so we took turns playing *Tomb Raider 2*.

Tom rushed in thirty minutes later looking excited.

Tom: Have you seen that nurse out there? She's fucking gorgeous.

He stood in the doorway to Jamie's room like a prairie dog, twisting his head left and right trying to find her.

Tom: She smiled at me. I know she wants it.

Jamie: Yeah, I am feeling better. Thanks for asking.

Tom: Whatever, try telling someone who's interested. How can we get her in here? Jamie, press the buzzer.

Jamie: And say what?

Tom: You need something.

Jamie: Like what?

Tom: A dump.

Jamie: But I don't need a dump.

Tom: Just pretend. We need to get her in here for a couple of minutes so that I can work my magic.

Jamie: How can I pretend I need a dump? I've broken my fucking pelvis you know, you thoughtless twat.

Tom: Please, she'll get to spend some time in here with me. What sort of a friend are you? You shithouse.

Tom already had his hand on the buzzer. At the nurses' station Dave stood up to attend to Jamie.

'SIT DOWN!' Tom whispered loudly. 'He wants the other nurse.'

Dave: You mean Ashlea?

Tom: Ashlea is it? Excellent.

Pause …

Tom: Jamie, press that buzzer again.

Jamie tutted and pressed the button again.

Ashlea walked out of a ward two doors up the corridor and back to the nurses' station; she sees that Jamie has pressed his attendance buzzer and that Dave is still sat on his arse doing nothing, smiling smugly at her.

'I'll get that, shall I?' Ashlea sarcastically asked.

'If you wouldn't mind,' Dave replied.

'Work shy, lazy bastard,' she muttered as she walked towards Jamie's room.

Tom sat down quickly and hid behind a magazine trying to look cool and uninterested; it didn't work because he picked up a copy of Woman's Weekly that Jamie's mum had left earlier in the day: the front cover advertised how to bake the perfect apple pie and the pattern to knit yourself a scarf and matching bobble hat. Ashlea noticed this and she tried to hide her smile.

Ashlea: What's wrong, Jamie?

Tom: He's needs to empty his bowels.

Ashlea: OK Jamie, you're going to have to relax, not strain, just go with the flow. You should have no problems after that chicken tikka, especially if it's from the Taj takeaway down the road.

Jamie shot Tom the look of death, Tom looked on pleadingly, Jamie relented. After much oohing and aahing, Jamie was moved to a portable toilet chair and wheeled into the bathroom, where the door was closed and he was left to do the business, so to speak.

Tom started his schmoozing.

Tom: So how long have you been a nurse, Ashlea? May I call you Ashlea?

For a moment I thought Ashlea was having a seizure but then I realised she was just rolling her eyes into the back of her head.

Ashlea: Just over eight years now.

Tom: I have the greatest respect for nurses, you do a marvellous job, especially under the current economic climate with the lack of NHS funding and staffing levels at an all time low. It must be hard for you and your colleagues to keep morale up.

Neal: If he goes on like this any longer, I'm really going to be bringing this chicken jalfrezi back up.

'I'm finished,' Jamie shouted from the bathroom.

Tom ignored them both and continued, 'So, would you have any time free for me to take you out sometime so we can continue this conversation in private, over dinner perhaps?'

Ashlea: And what would you suggest that I do with my two kids?

Tom: You have children? ... Fantastic, I love children: boys, girls or one of each?'

Me: Ooh, good recovery, Tom.

Jamie: I'm finished.

Ashlea: I should see to your friend.

Tom: He'll be alright. So what are their names, your children's names?

Ashlea: Sadie is seven years old and Oliver is five, and I really must see to your friend now.

As Ashlea disappeared into the toilet with Jamie, Tom turned to us and whispered with a fixed smile, 'Will you pack of bastards just shut the fuck up for five minutes?'

Me: But I'm enjoying this. You really have the shittest chat up lines ever, it's fucking hilarious. I can't wait to see how this pans out.

Ashlea wheeled Jamie back into the room and helped him into bed; Tom continued his harassment.

Tom: Anyway, Julie's just offered to babysit your kids so is Friday night OK?

Me: EH?!

'I'm not likely to hand my kids over to some complete stranger to go on a date with a complete stranger, am I?' And with that Ashlea left the room, with Tom following her like a lost puppy.

He returned to Jamie's room five minutes later with a cheesy grin on his face, 'Friday night. Get in there!'

Me: How did you pull that off?

Tom: I was thinking of telling her I was dying of cancer, but I decided on a more subtle approach.

Me: Thank God for that.

Tom: I just said that I found her really attractive and that I'd really like to take her out sometime.

Me: Did you beg?

Tom: Yes.

Me: We've got to go now Jamie, visiting time is over.

'Thanks for coming to see me. I really do need a shit now,' Jamie tutted. 'Nurse?'

We all left him to explain to Ashlea why he needed another shit.

The next night we decided not to visit Jamie—just to leave his mum and dad to lecture him all night on the dangers of operating electrical machinery whilst under the influence of alcohol.

If any of us had been at the hospital visiting Jamie, his parents would have gone easy on him, so we all stayed in the cafe to allow him the full brunt of the lecturing—we're all a little bit sick like that, and because he drives that chair like an idiot and needed to learn a lesson.

August

Nikki: So how did your date with Neal go?

Me: Really good. He was lovely to me.

Bev: He seems like a nice bloke, even with his suicidal tendencies.

Colin: Of course he'll be nice to you, especially if he thinks there's a chance of riding you bare back.

Me: Shut up.

Amanda: Have you, er … had any *jiggy jiggy*?

Me: Not yet. I've bought some new underwear though, but this thong feels like cheese wire.

Nikki: I hate the first few times after you've shagged someone. There's no bedroom etiquette guide for you to follow.

Me: Like how long before it's OK to fart in bed.

Amanda: It's never OK to fart in bed. But if you really do have to fart then tell him you thought you heard someone moving about outside and crack one out while he's looking for the intruder downstairs.

Kam: How many dates before you let someone shag you?

Me: Normally a couple of weeks, obviously joining the mile-high club on the way to India was an exception to the rule.

Nikki: Depends really on how attracted you are to them.

Tom: Did one of the last blokes you shagged really get up the following morning and say he had to go home and feed his dog?

Nikki: Your point being?

Tom: Did you ever see him again?

Nikki: I'm going to treat that question with the contempt that it deserves.

Tom: Did he even have a dog?

Kam: How many dates before you ask them if they take it up the arse?

Me: Everyone to their own but my poo shooter is a one way system.

Amanda: Blokes only like it because it's more degrading for the woman.

Tom: Your point being?

Kam: Anyway Jules, you've had colonic irrigation, that should have loosened you up a bit.

Me: They don't use a piece of guttering Kam, it's just a piece of hosepipe they stick up your arse.

Amanda: Have you ever taken revenge on a former partner when you've been dumped?

Nikki: Once I found out my boyfriend had gone on holiday for a week with some fat, ugly slut from where he worked, when he was supposedly on holiday with the boys. So I emptied two buckets of water over his mattress and sprinkled a packet of cress seeds on it. It was summer and I turned the central heating on full whack, opened all the curtains so it was nice and bright and then smeared dog shit over every door handle in the house.

Tom: Can we stop this now, before it goes too far?

Amanda: It hasn't already?

Right on cue, we heard the not so dulcet tones of an ice-cream van. Nikki's boyfriend, Phil, had decided to change the familiar sound of Green Sleeves on his ice-cream van to something a little trendier; Ice Ice Baby just didn't do it for me, but it obviously did for Nikki. He drove his van along the street outside of the coffee shop at the same time everyday, with military precision. We heard him coming from three streets away.

'How do I look?' Nikki asked, and without waiting for an answer, she rushed off to the toilet.

Me: Come on, while she's looking in the mirror let's give this shitpipe some grief.

Nikki started seeing Phil eight months ago and he's been promising to leave his wife for the last four months. We just know he's talking complete bollocks; We hate him.

Me, Bev and Amanda snuck across the road.

Bev: Hello, Cuntface, aren't you dead yet?

Phil: Come on ladies, there's no need to be like that. How would you like to try my new rum and raisin flavour ice-cream?

Me: No thanks, I'd rather eat my own shit.

'Look, I'd really like to get on with all of you,' Phil said, pushing his glasses up his nose and giving us all a smile that made me want to grab his ice-cream scoop off him so that we could all take turns beating the fucker to death with it. 'I know how much you all mean to Nikki. I know it's not an ideal situation but I am going to leave June, she just doesn't understand me anymore.'

Amanda: What? She doesn't understand why you fuck other women behind her back? No shit, Sherlock.

Nikki joined us.

Nikki: I'm glad to see you're all making the effort to get on.

Bev: No problem Nikki, as long as you're happy.

We all curled our lips up, and flared our nostrils at Phil as Nikki climbed into his van, Amanda rocked her hand backwards and forwards in a wanking motion and I mouthed, 'You are a wanker,' at him. Then we all smiled when Nikki turned to look at us.

Me: Take care, we'll see you later.

Later the next day, when the shop was closed, I was sat in the coffee shop with the girls. It had been just over two weeks since my date with Neal and I was about gagging for it now. I had to make that embarrassing move from just flirting to asking for penetration and I needed a bit of moral support and advice from the girls.

Bev: The trouble with you is you don't drink. There are no problems after a few drinks when you've both lost your inhibitions and you drunkenly fall into bed together.

Amanda: Ply him with a few drinks then it'll be easier.

Me: He's a recovering alcoholic. I don't want to push him over the edge again, poor bastard, don't forget where we met him. Anyway, in my experience, when drunks can manage to get it up they go like a train but never get to the station.

Nikki: Phil's abused me with the ice-cream scoop and a Walls Mini-Milk before.

Me: Please tell me he boil washes his equipment every day.

Nikki: Of course he does, he's got a certificate in food hygiene, just like the rest of us.

Bev: I can't remember the certificate covering how to clean an ice-cream scoop if you've been using it in sex play with your girlfriend?

Nikki: No, I think they must have missed that eventuality out of the final exam.

Me: Come on then girls, you've been fuck all help so far. What can I say to Neal to suggest the merest hint that, if he plays his cards right, I might possibly be interested in getting jiggy with it?

Bev: It's been a while Jules, I've always been pissed.

Amanda: Look we've established he's not gay, and you've got breasts and a pulse so it should be game on.

Me: And I'm fucking stunning with a fantastic personality.

Nikki: Yeah, whatever.

Kam and Tom joined us.

Me: Boys, what do you look for in a woman?

Tom: She's, erm ...

Nikki: Deaf?

Tom: No, she's, erm ...

Me: Paid by the hour?

Tom: NO.

Bev: *She no speak velly good Engrish.*

Tom: Fuck off.

Kam: And when you're watching the footy, she has to keep the dips and chips coming. What do girls look for in a bloke?

Nikki: Since when have you been American, Kam?'

Kam: What?

Nikki: She has to keep the dips and chips coming? That's an American thing and a bit sophisticated for you isn't it; don't you still eat a packet of Monster Munch every day?

Tom: Ooh, what flavour?

Kam: Pickled onion's my favourite.

Bev: I like Frazzles, they're tasty.

Me: Salt and vinegar Discos.

Bev: Ooh, yeah.

Nikki: You fucking heathens, I can't believe you eat that shite when there is so much good food around.

Me: Would you do Jamie Oliver then, Nik?

Nikki: I might do, I mean, I wouldn't go out looking for someone with a short tongue but, yeah, I'd probably do Jamie Oliver.

Me: I'd make him cook for me afterwards, naked, and not wearing an apron. I'd make him flambé something.'

Amanda: I'm looking for someone who can lick his own eyebrows.

Bev: Someone with a bit of girth.

Nikki: Apparently, it's singles night at Safeway in Ingleby Barwick on a Thursday night.

Me: Really! I didn't know that, I used to live in Ingleby Barwick.

Bev: When are we going then?

Me: Tomorrow by the looks of it.

Nikki: I thought you liked Neal.

Me: I do, but I'm thinking of Beverley and Amanda. I'm thoughtful like that. Anyway, Bev, I thought you liked Dave.

Bev: Not particularly, I mean he's OK but it was just a hand job.

Amanda: What time then?

Me: Straight after work. How exactly do you pull in a supermarket? Do you gently stroke a courgette while looking longingly in the direction of some guy you might find vaguely attractive?

Amanda: I was thinking of gently caressing a couple of plums then rubbing them gently against my breasts. What attire would you recommend?

Bev: Slutty: I don't want anyone thinking I'm there for the groceries.

The next evening Safeway was absolutely dead, obviously everyone in Ingleby Barwick is getting it. I bought some bleach and Dettol sanitising wet wipes; oh, we live the high life. Back to square one for the girls then.

Then Nikki announced that her grand-daughter was getting christened in two days time, and apparently we were all invited.

Me: What should we buy Ocean then?

Nikki: None of that cheap silverware if you don't mind.

Bev: What, no silver first tooth box?

Me: Ah, why not Nik?

Nikki: Because it's shit, and don't forget it's a Catholic service so you'll all have to be on your best behaviour.

Bev: Do you think random drugs test should be introduced when people register the birth of their children?

Me: What do you mean?

Bev: Well take Ocean as an example. It's a fucking ridiculous name. Perhaps the registrar should have said to Amy, 'You're obviously still off your tits after the epidural you've been given, go home and come back next week, when you're clean'.

Amanda: Is Amy putting on a spread afterwards then?

Nikki: Yep, upstairs in The Central.

Bev: Are we all buying new dresses for the do then?

Me: You're joking aren't you? In The Central? I'm wearing the oldest outfit I can get away with; it'll be going to the Red Cross shop the next day.

The service started at two o'clock on Sunday afternoon, at least we missed morning mass.

Amanda: I bet this takes ages. I hate catholic services.

Me: I'm starving already, I knew I should have had some lunch, I hope it's a decent buffet.

Bev: Which hymn are we murdering then?

The number twenty three was displayed on the hymn board, and flicking through the hymn book we were happy to find that *All Things Bright and Beautiful* had been chosen. Our mood lightened.

When it came to church services we'd all rather perform bowel surgery on ourselves with a flick knife than attend a religious ceremony, but this particular hymn always brought a smile to our faces. It has to do with the first line of the second verse, which we always sing with gusto.

'The purple headed mountain,' resonated around the church. Nikki's daughter, Amy, turned to us and curled her lip. Like us, she probably couldn't remember singing that line at school. We all chuckled.

After the service Amy commented, 'Mum, you witch, I can't believe you chose that song.'

Nikki: It's all shit anyway. When was the last time you were in a church?

Amy: When I got married.

Nikki: My point exactly.

Buffets, at the social occasions we attend, are usually similar to taking your position in a rugby scrum. Form a queue my arse; get the food piled on your plate before any fucker else, by any means possible, and today was no exception.

The christening reception was being held in the room above The Central, in Middlesboogie. Not the most salubrious of venues, I might add, but the lager's cold and the food is free. As usual, we were at the front of the queue for the buffet.

Me: Beef in gravy looks like a dangerous choice.

Nikki: Bollocks, I'm sticking to dry food in this stampede.

As we spoke a bloke filled a ladle full of beef and gravy and lifted it carefully over the head of the woman in front of him. Most of the gravy dripped down the back of the woman's cream suit, she didn't flinch, she just continued shovelling chips onto her plate.

Me: I've decided I'm going to ride Neal hard tonight.

Amanda: How are you going to bring up the subject, so to speak?

Me: Fuck knows.

Nikki: Have you got any condoms?

Me: I think I've still got that chocolate one from Amsterdam.

Nikki: Surely you're not going to use that.

Me: No, I bought some last Christmas. The expiry date on them is putting me under some pressure: 2012 I think.

We'd exchanged pleasantries, so to speak, with everyone and there was no food left so we all left at about six o'clock. Tom suggested coffees at my place but I gave him a stare that could turn anyone to stone; he quickly changed the subject and everyone went their separate ways.

Back at the Funky Doughnut, I made cups of tea for me and Neal and we sat playing 'Who Wants To Be A Millionaire?' on the Playstation.

'What is another name for a spy?' Neal asked.

A> Beaver   B> Badger
C> Squirrel   D> Mole

Me: It's squirrel, Secret Squirrel was a spy.

Neal: It's *mole* you clown.

Me: Oh, yeah.

Somehow we managed to get up to half a million quid.

Me: If I won a million pounds I don't think I'd want to know you lot.

Neal: Forget the million, I don't admit knowing you lot now.

It was after nine o'clock and I was starting to think that I couldn't really be bothered with a shag, the sexual tension had hit its peak around seven thirty with the 'What's another name for a spy?' question, when we'd briefly made eye contact and then the next question came up; now I'd be happy with a pash and to be in my cot for ten o'clock.

And then, from nowhere, he gave me the look that you can interpret as, 'I'm gonna rut you all over this apartment'. Oh, yes. He leant across the sofa and planted a soft kiss on my lips.

I remembered I'd been eating Stilton cheese at the buffet so I thought I'd just pop into the bathroom and freshen up before the grand finale. I stood in front of the sink: I'd scrubbed up OK and there was no running mascara, and I resisted the urge to squeeze the blackhead I noticed on my chin because I thought it would only start bleeding and ruin the moment. I gave my armpits the sniff test, no nasty surprises there, and smoothed my hair down one last time. OK then, rock-and-roll.

I opened the bathroom door, walked out onto the landing and straight into Neal who was standing straight outside of the door.

'What the fuck? You scared me you … erm, you're naked,' I mumbled.

Neal: Time is of the essence, My Love; we've got to get up at six o'clock.

Me: Will there be any foreplay?

Neal: Of course there will, now you go into the bedroom, I just need to take a slash.

Me: It's not like this in the movies.

Neal: We're in Saltburn, Julie.

I rushed back into the bedroom to set the scene. I managed to light a candle and had turned on the TV and started flicking through the channels to find MTV, or some other appropriate source of background music. When Neal came back into the room, he grabbed the remote control off me and proceeded to violate me for a full fourteen minutes—*result!*

I didn't think it was appropriate bedroom etiquette, when taking a woman from behind for the first time, to shout, 'Who's the Daddy?' in midstroke. I put my hands between my legs and gently squeezed his testicles to remind him of the fact.

Neal was quite a considerate lover. I wasn't really looking for fireworks; I'd set my standards quite low really and just hoped he'd get a hard on. We even talked for five minutes before we fell asleep.

I slept like the dead afterwards, that first awkward shag was over now, and even though we'd been shagging the whole time to motorbike racing on Sky Sports 3, it didn't bother either of us.

Over the next couple of weeks we were at it like rabbits, everywhere, anytime—it was fucking marvellous. It wasn't even Christmas and I was getting my Yule Log a little earlier this year.

'Do you think we can buy a new bed?' Neal asked a few nights later.

Me: Why?

Neal: Because this is a single bed. You're only meant to pull the other mattress out from under it and use it as a double bed occasionally. It's like sleeping on a wallpaper pasting table.

Me: Stop bitching, you're worse than a chick.

We decided to buy a new double bed though as Neal somehow managed to trap his testicles in between the two mattresses later that night. I'm sure he did it on purpose.

Then Kam hit us with a blinder.

Kam: I'm getting married.

Bev: Eh?!

Kam: Don't get me wrong, I had my reservations at first but I've met her and she's a fucking stunner. Her name is Shabira, she's got a Masters in Psychology and she works for Social Action for Health: it's a community development charity focusing on health equity. She works with hard to reach communities in London but she should get a job no problem up here. And she's an excellent cook, she made some fantastic daal last night when our families met up. She's got a fantastic figure on her and she seems like really good fun.

Nikki: I hate her already.

Kam: I can't wait to get jiggy with her.

'Get jiggy with who?' Tom asked, as he sat down at the table.

Bev: His soon to be wife.

Tom: Are you happy with this?

Kam: Look, I know it's hard for you lot to comprehend arranged marriages but my parents have really looked into this, they haven't chosen some nutter for me; she's well educated, beautiful and I really like her.'

Me: But wouldn't you like to chose your own partner?

Kam: What, like you did?

Me: Fair point. I want you to be happy, and if she makes you happy then fair play to you.

Kam: Anyway, why did you and your hubby split up?

Me: Because he was a knob.

Kam: Is 'because he was a knob' written on the divorce papers, or did you go for irreconcilable differences?

I didn't feel the need to answer.

Me: What are we going to buy you and your missus as a wedding present?

Amanda: Aren't we supposed to pin money on them or something?

Tom: I'm just going to flick pound coins at them.

Me: Do we do the rice throwing thing or is that just a Western tradition? Where did rice come from anyway?

Tom: What about rice pudding? Can we throw rice pudding at them?

Nikki: Shut up, fool.

'What's this then?' Tom asked, pointing to the jug I'd just brought to the table.

Me: I went into Costa Coffee the other day and they do these drinks blended with ice, and I thought I'd try making a few myself.

Tom: I don't know why you bother with this shite, the majority of your clientele are more than happy with Tetley tea and Nescafe instant coffee. Hot chocolate is considered risqué around here with the high prevalence of diabetes among your clientele. What's in it anyway?

Me: This is raspberry flavour.

Tom: How did you make it?

Me: Well, the woman at Costa told me the raspberry flavour had a vanilla base, so it's a Muller Fruit Corner in with some crushed ice, I've put some ice-cream in as well. What's it like?

Tom took a big gulp of the drink.

Tom: It tastes alright, actually. Ooh, I've drunk too much, I've got an ice-cream headache.

Me: Well you shouldn't drink it so fast you greedy bastard.

Tom: Ooh god, I think I'm having a mild stroke.

Me: Kam, are we all invited to this wedding then?

Kam: Too right. It's on the tenth of August, it's a Sunday, at the Sikh Temple on Lorne Road in Middlesbrough. Be there for midday.

Bev: Is there a Sikh Temple in Middlesboogie? How long's that been there? I can't wait, I've never been to an Indian wedding before. Can we wear Saris?

Me: What, *this* August, as in this month?

Kam: Us Sikh's don't fuck around, none of this planning for two years shite that you Christians do.

Nikki: I've never worn a Sari before though, they're supposed to be a right bastard to put on.

Kam: Don't worry, you can buy them already stitched in place.

Bev: They look gorgeous.

Me: Are you going to nail Shabira before the big day?

Kam: You're joking aren't you? Not a sniff, but some things are worth waiting for.

Tom: Don't you think you should try before you buy, so to speak?

Kam: I just think that Shabira's really nice, I'm sure it will all work out in the end.

Me: By god, you've changed your tune. You've always been a right fanny rat, what's stopping you this time?

Kam: Time to settle down and have a family of my own, I'm thirty years old next year.

Me: I'm nearer forty than thirty, I hit thirty-nine this year; I wonder when I'm going to want to settle down? Again. So what's it going to look like then, this wedding?

Kam: The formal part of the ceremony, the Anand Karaj, takes place in a *Gurdwara*, you know, the place of worship.

Bev: No actually, we haven't got a clue. Is it like a church?

Kam: No, Sikhs don't have idols or altars in the Gurdwara. The main feature of a *Gurdwara* is that it has a *Satguru* in it, the holy Sikh scripture. Then, after morning tea, at about eleven o'clock, everyone goes into *Darbar Sahib* or main prayer hall. Now you don't have to wear a Sari, but you have to dress appropriately in the Gurdwara.

Tom: Can I wear my arseless chaps?

Kam: Er ... No.

Jamie: What about my gimp mask and dog collar? Can I bring Jules to the wedding on a leash?

Kam: Er ... No.

Nikki: What about — —

Kam: I don't want to see any pink skin, money shots, or any part of your body that doesn't normally see daylight, and I mean fucking *normally* as in ninety-five percent of the population. And you'll all have to sit on the floor for forty-five minutes, cross legged, so no mini-skirts.

Tom: What the fuck am I going to wear then?

Me: I think I'll go for a sari, sounds easier.

Early on the morning of Shabira and Kam's wedding there was glorious sunshine, bright blue skies, and it felt like a great day to be going to a wedding. Obviously, that all turned to shite by nine thirty when the rain started to piss down.

I then trapped my sari in the car door, which left a dirty, great black mark right along the hem; Bev nearly caused a six car pile up on the A66 dual carriageway when her sari got caught around the gear stick and I accidentally dropped down into second gear instead of my intended fourth, rapidly reducing my speed and causing everyone behind me to brake.

By the time we got to the temple my nerves were frayed. Nikki then stepped into a deep puddle as she got out of the car and wet about four inches of the bottom of her sari, so from then on everyone was a cunt.

But, oh my lord, Shabira was the most beautiful bride I have ever seen. These Indians get it right on the old wedding front, Shab wore the traditional Hindu wedding dress, a red and gold sari, it was just beautiful.

Where the fuck did us Christians get that virginal white dress idea from? It's shite compared to what I'm seeing here.

Colin was looking, well you know what I mean, at the wall.

Me: Tom, turn the daft lad towards the procession, he looks like he's bored and ignoring everyone.

Tom: Don't worry about him, nothing can top his entrance into the temple where he tripped on the step, landed in Kam's grandmother's lap and got his hand caught down the front of her sari. He nearly pulled her tits out of her dress.

Colin: I'm in love.

We all took a deep breath and rolled our eyes—rock and roll.

September

So here I am. I finally got around to making that appointment with a counsellor; it only took me six months, so I'll give myself a little pat on the back for that one. I say six months, but really it's taken me about sixteen years to get my finger out and organise the appointment but who's counting?

I picked at my fingernails as I waited for my counsellor. The waiting room smelled of tobacco, tobacco from a cigar or a pipe, and I imagined my counsellor would be wearing a tweed jacket or thick knitted jumper and something in corduroy.

I was sitting on an uncomfortable chair, upholstered in brown velour that was wearing thin, and the foam inside had seen better days; my arse could feel the wooden frame underneath. I was paying sixty quid for this session, one hour, surely they could afford some decent chairs. I must tell them about IKEA.

Another person was waiting in the room with me. I wasn't sure if that was appropriate really; Saltburn's a small town so there's a good chance I could know this bloke and I don't know if I want anyone to know that I have a few, erm … *issues*, if you like to call them that.

Anyway, I digress. This bloke was in his mid-forties and every couple of minutes we would make eye contact; he'd give me one of those close lipped smiles and a nod that sort of acknowledged that we were both damaged goods.

It was one of those rare, bright, sunny days where the sun was blazing in through the large window in the waiting room, making me squint. I must have had a look on my face like one of those tortured souls who's been through a lifetime of torment and abuse, and been fucked by various family members.

I just wanted to know why I couldn't really see anything through to the end, but you hear about these sessions uncovering all sorts of shit, I mean, I can't remember being fucked by any family members and if I found that out today I'd be gutted. Anyway, that's the worst case scenario—let's look on the bright side, shall we? And out of all the members of my family, who would I most prefer to have been fucked by? I was pondering this question as I heard my name called in the distance.

'Julie?' a voice called from one of the doorways leading off from the waiting room.

It took a few seconds to register that someone was calling my name. When I did realise I was being summoned, I quickly stood up and massaged my arse cheeks, trying to encourage some circulation in them, as I walked into the counsellor's room.

Upon entering, I immediately noticed the large, brown sofa and I considered, momentarily, whether I should actually lay down on it like they do in all those cartoons and comedy sketches. Anyway, this was no time for frivolity, I was about to find out if I'd been fucked by a close relative.

The room was bland, bland, bland; I hate magnolia coloured paint, it's shit. Perhaps it's meant to be calming but to me it just spells boring in capital letters.

There was a tall bookshelf against the wall opposite the sofa, it's from IKEA: I recognised it from the catalogue, and had thought about buying one for my place.

So, from my seated position on the sofa I looked straight at my counsellor, whose name happens to be Gail, sat in her black, leather armchair, with the IKEA bookshelf, full of self-help books behind her. I'm not sure whether the books were there to impress the clients and make me feel overawed by Gail's knowledge, or to make me more aware of how little I knew. I was just going to shut up and do whatever she recommended anyway.

Gail smoothed down her corduroy skirt (See, I told you, corduroy.), sat down and picked up her notebook. It was quite a thick book, I suppose it would have to be, there are some crazy bastards out there and I could feel that I was about to fit into this category.

'So, Julie, what would you like to talk about?' Gail asked.

She had a voice that was calm and soothing.

'Well, I thought we could work that one out together,' I replied, scratching my head. 'I've just heard that these sessions can make you work things out in your head.'

Gail: Like what?

Me: Erm … things and stuff.

Pause …

Me: Well, I never seem to finish anything. I've just opened a coffee shop and everything's going well; it's only been open a few months though and I'm just wondering when I'm going to get bored and want to do something else.

Pause …

Me: I'm a bit bored now really.

Gail: Explain what you mean when you say, 'I never seem to finish anything'.

Me: I get bored easily. I can, erm … finish little things, like, erm … decorating. I can finish decorating a room but then I struggle to paint the whole house.

Gail: What about a really big jigsaw?

Me: I wouldn't even start a jigsaw, I think they're shit.

Gail: I like jigsaws, I like the sense of achievement you get from finishing them and revealing the picture. You can get jigsaws now where they don't actually show you any picture, you just have to put it together and let it surprise you.

See what I mean, there's crazy bastards everywhere; some are even disguised as counsellors.

Gail: Give me an example of something that you haven't finished.

Me: I started an Open University degree and only managed to finish the first year.

Gail: What subject were you studying?

Me: Social Anthropology.

Gail: That's a really interesting subject.

Me: It bored me rigid.

Gail: What was boring about it?

Me: I'm not really interested in reading about trading in the Western Pacific in the early twentieth century, I'm not sure how relevant it is today. After I'd finished reading Bronislaw Malinowski's *Argonauts of the Western Pacific*, I wanted to stab myself in the eye with my pen.

Gail: Can you switch to another course?

Me: Probably.

Gail: Are you going to?

Me: I don't know yet.

Gail: What else haven't you finished?

Me: Language courses. I'd love to learn another language. I seem to start a course and then I get bored and can't be arsed to go to the classes.

Gail: Do you learn anything?

Me: I can count to ten in about five different languages, ask for directions to the nearest railway station and order a weak latte with milk and sugar.

Gail: Are you frightened of failing?

Me: I wouldn't know I never finish anything.

Gail: How's your relationship with your family?

Me: Fantastic: I don't see them.

Gail: Oh? And why is that fantastic?

Me: Because they're not very nice people; they don't make me feel good about myself.

Gail: In what way?

Me: They're big fans of reverse psychology, you know, where they call you worse than shit in the hope that you try harder to better yourself. Personally, I think my dad got a kick out of making me cry.

He probably went off to the bathroom for a wank afterwards.

Pause …

Gail: Right. Do you ever get angry when you think about them?

Me: I used to but what's the point? They're not going to change and being angry only eats away at you.

Gail: What did they used to say to upset you?

Me: It was my dad who used to say the nasty things really, my mum just used to sit there and not say a word, and then slag him off when he left the room — the spineless bitch.

Gail: What did he used to say?

Me: There was never anything positive that I can remember. Everything from 'this cup of tea that you've made me is shite' to 'why did you only get one A grade in your 'O' Level exams. Wanker. He's only got one 'O' Level in Maths, and I'm sure he only got a C grade, at least I got fucking eight 'O' Levels and an 'A' in Maths. I only ever made him one cup of tea, he told me it was shit, so I never bothered again.

Gail: How did these comments make you feel?

Me: Hurt, always hurt. I can't remember any other feeling when I was growing up except hurt, and waiting to feel hurt. I can honestly say, though, that when I think of them now I don't feel any anger or bitterness towards them. I feel nothing. Anyway, fuck em.

Pause …

Me: Do you reckon one of them has had sex with me?

Gail: I'm sorry?

Me: Well, you just hear about these sessions opening up doors to all sorts of memories. Can we keep that one particular door closed? Tightly, very tightly?

Gail: OK.

So, over the next half an hour, we diagnosed that I was quite fucked up really, and would probably need a few more sessions to understand why I behave in certain ways, in certain situations. Why I don't finish anything big? I felt hurt when my dad used to criticise me; I don't want to feel that again.

Now no-one criticises me but myself, and I can be just as cutting as that dickhead.

October

It was Ashlea's daughter Sadie's seventh birthday and we all got invited to go as moral support … *for Tom?*

'What do you do at these sort of occasions?' Tom asked us, as we walked along the street to Ashlea's house.

Amanda: What? Kids parties? You must have been to hundreds of them when you were a kid.

Tom: They all pale into insignificance after the introduction of lager.

Amanda: Shouldn't you have been here earlier to help Ashlea set all this up?

Tom: Should I?

Bev: You've shit it now Tom, the least you could have done is help with the party. You need to think more about this Tom, she's got kids and she's a single mum, it's bloody hard work, and I suppose you'll be expecting a shag later.

Tom: Well, yeah.'

Nikki: So what's happening at this party then?

Tom: It's a painting party.

Bev: She's got all the kids painting her house for her, go girl.

Tom: No, she taking all the furniture out of the dining room, covering the floor with a plastic sheet and then giving the kids loads of paint and crayons and locking them in there I think. Sadie loves painting.

Me: What have you bought Sadie then?

Tom: No idea, I gave Ashlea thirty quid to sort something out for her.

Me: That's fucking shit Tom, you didn't even go out and get her a present? You cunt.

Tom: Right everyone, no more swearing, we're in children's party mode.

We had arrived at Ashlea's place and the noise of a houseful of screaming kids greeted us from the street. Luckily, it was a beautiful sunny day so the adults could sit outside in the garden and seek some refuge from the noise; you know, that high pitched screaming that only kids can do, the one that makes you want to take a cattle prod to them.

Personally, I would have thought that kids plus paint equals a fucking heinous error, but apparently the dining room needed decorating anyway and the kids were loving it.

We all sat on chairs of various descriptions in the back garden: deck chairs, plastic garden chairs and Ashlea's dining room chairs.

Amanda: How's it going with Ashlea?

Tom: You know what they say about these nurses: absolute filth. It's fucking great, thanks for asking.

Jamie: Has she checked your prostate yet?

Tom: That is none of your business, young man, but we have had a look at some of my sperm under a microscope; it's really interesting all those little tadpoles swimming along. Have you ever done that?

122

Pause ...

Me: Yeah, all the time. I get my microscope out from behind my Breville sandwich maker, Neal squeezes one out onto one of those little slide thingys you put under the lens and we spend all night watching the little sperm trying to find an egg. We usually do that on Monday nights when there's fuck all on the telly. *You crazy bastard!*

The kids couldn't quite grasp the idea of disability, especially the blind part. Today there was a run on fire engines and fairy princesses. In total, Colin was asked to critique around fifteen pieces of art work that were thrust into his face by random kids. He'd hold them up, sometimes the right way up, sometimes not, and sometimes completely the wrong way around. Jamie would quietly whisper in Colin's ear what was drawn on the paper. 'That's fantastic,' Colin would say about every single one, 'That's the best fire engine I've seen all day, apart from the other ten of course. So which would be faster, this fire engine or an ambulance?'

Pause ...

Boy: A police car.

Colin: Fair enough.

'This dog is almost lifelike,' Colin told one young girl.

Girl: But it's a dinosaur.

Colin: Oh, my mistake, sorry about that. What type of dinosaur is it then?

Girl: It's a Stegosaurus.

Colin: Really? Because of the row of bony plates on its back? Jamie thought it was a dog—what a complete retard.

Jamie: I thought it was a Golden Retriever.

Colin: Catching frisbees with its spine?

Jamie: I'm not going to help you anymore if you're going to be like that.

Oliver, Ashlea's son, asked Jamie if he wanted to play football. Jamie responded by saying that he'd love to but that he couldn't walk, to which the little boy recounted the story of his cousin and how it took him months to learn to walk and that Jamie should just keep trying—bless him.

Colin thought that Oliver had walked away when he started talking about some stupid bitch of a client that had come to see him that day.

Me: COLIN, there are children about. Oliver, that's a naughty word and Colin shouldn't be saying it. You can tell him off if you like.

'It's OK, Colin,' Oliver commented, 'it's not as bad as shit or fuck.'

The boredom started to kick in after being shown around twenty different pictures from twenty random kids, so we decided to critique each picture with a bit of constructive feedback to improve their drawing prowess, should they wish to choose the field of art as a future career path.

'Your spatial awareness is a little bit shot here,' Tom said to one young girl, 'someone's been on the crack pipe again, haven't they? Now, you've got a house here, standard four windows, pitched roof and front door, but then you've got your little, stick family standing next to the house. They're all actually bigger than the front door; the dad's actually bigger than the house. How do you propose that they actually get into the house? With a shoe horn perhaps?'

Girl: What's a crack pipe?

Tom: Go and ask your mum. Pretty good for a first attempt though, I'll give you an F for fantastic.

It was Jamie's turn next.

Jamie: Let's take a look at this little beauty, another fire engine, eh? VROOM. Now, in this instance the fire engine is actually smaller that the picket fence behind it, should I assume that this fire engine would be used for, say, wheelie bin fires? Also, it doesn't appear to have any water hoses on it; granted, you have had the foresight to put a ladder on it. I'll give this an E for excellent.

'What have we got here young Sophie? Is this a picture of your family?' Tom asked a pretty, young girl when she handed him her piece of art.

The little girl nodded.

Tom: Is this your dad? The figure with six, no sorry seven, hairs sticking out of his head?

Sophie nodded again.

Tom: Fantastic, and I think this is your mum, isn't it? With the long, yellow, curly hair?

Sophie smiled as Tom recognised her family in the picture.

Tom: You might want to draw a few more chins on your mum then, but overall pretty good, it's better than most of the, to be honest, dire pieces of work that have been exhibited here today. In fact, I'll give it a D for dire.

Sophie seemed more than happy with Tom's assessment of her work and went off to tell her mum what he'd said. Sophie's mum promptly shot Tom a look of pure hatred, and in response Tom raised his bottle of beer and nodded acknowledgement.

And then luckily, all the kids fucked off home and we could relax.

November

You know fuck all ever happens in November, except Bonfire Night on the fifth and that only happens in the UK.

If you're organised you can get some early Christmas shopping in but apart from that it's usually raining, cold and dark at around four thirty in the afternoon.

I think November's a bit shit.

December

Me: I'm going to have a Christmas dinner for us and the regulars, what should we have on the menu?

Nikki: Who are you inviting?

Me: Er, us and the regulars. The shop's been open for nearly nine months now and it's doing OK, so I think that I should say thank you to the customers for bringing in the dirty cash.

Nikki: Are you actually making a profit?

Me: Mmm … we're just about breaking even, I think.

Nikki: You are fucking clueless. Right then, what's on the menu so far?

Me: I don't know yet, give me some suggestions.

Nikki: What about orange and walnut salad to start with, followed by a traditional turkey dinner, with beef as an alternative.

Kam: No, not beef, what about pork or duck?

Nikki: Why not beef?

Me: More like, why are we having orange and walnut salad? Sounds a dodgy combination. Anyway, Kam, won't you be having Christmas with your folks?

Kam: We celebrate *Dihvali* instead, and as Sikhs we don't eat the sacred cow. They just wander the streets in India you know.

Me: What, Indians?

Kam: No, not Indians, cows.

Me: Eh?

Kam: The cows just wander the streets because no-one wants to kill them because they're sacred.

Me: Why?

Kam: I don't know.

Me: While we're on with this Sikh thing, what's the crack with turbans and why aren't you wearing one?

Kam: Bollocks to that, they're a right fucker to put on. It's something to do with the fact that Sikhs used to be the warriors of India and used to protect the Indian borders.

Me: And?

Kam: Well the turban was head protection for when the Sikhs were in battle.

Me: So wearing a turban on your head was supposed to stop you head being chopped off by a machete?

Kam: Something like that. Nike do a sports turban in India, there's no messing around with wrapping your head up in it, you just put it on like a headscarf and it fastens at the back with some Velcro. Anyway, only around ten percent of Sikhs wear turbans.

Me: Would you prefer pork?

Kam: Yeah, pork's alright.

Me: Who can I offend with pork? Muslims or Jewish people isn't it?

Nikki: Are you inviting any Muslims or Jews to the party?

Me: How the fuck would I know? Good Morning, how may I help you? You'd like a flapjack

129

and a cup of tea, I'll bring it over to you. The weather's been lovely hasn't it? Have you booked your holidays yet? Are your religious beliefs aligned with Judaism or Islam? It doesn't flow well does it? I've never seen a *Kiber* or a *Hijab* in Saltburn.'

Pause ...

Bev: What's a Kiber?

Me: One of those skull cap things that Jewish men wear.

Pause ...

Bev: What about duck?

Pause ...

Nikki: Orange and walnut salad to start with, followed by a traditional turkey dinner, with duck as an alternative, and Christmas pudding and trifle for dessert, then coffee and mints.

Me: Are you sure about this orange and walnut salad?

Nikki: Fucking Heathen.

Me: What about vegetables? What sort of vegetables will interfere with someone's dentures? Bearing in mind that fifty percent of the party may not be packing their own teeth. Broccoli might be a bit dangerous, I could imagine it getting right under your palate.

Nikki: Just stick to safe vegetables like carrots, parsnip and turnip. Don't be fucking around making mash either, you have to cook loads of potatoes to make mash, just give them roast potatoes, that way you can count out four or five pieces of potato per person and you're laughing.

Me: Sorted.

Bev: When's it happening then?

Me: What about the week before Christmas, get everybody in the spirit of things? What about the twentieth of December?

Everyone nodded.

Me: Right then, I'll send the invites out. Who wants to do what? Kam, can I count on you to be chief vegetable preparer?

Kam: Do we have to help?

Me: Yes, you're getting a free meal out of it.

Colin: What can I do?

Me: I was thinking that perhaps you could carve the meat, should be quite interesting.

Colin: Fuck off.

Jamie: What about me?

Bev: Perhaps you could provide a little light entertainment in between courses. A little tap dancing maybe or limbo dancing?

Jamie: As a member of the *handicapable* community, I have many skills that I can bring to this table.

Me: Like what?

Jamie: Let me think now, you've put me on the spot.

Me: Do you think that you two could handle the guest list? Obviously, I will give the final approval as to who's invited, so don't think that you can squeeze in loads of your mates for a free meal.

Colin: Yeah, why not.

Jamie: Sorted.

The new computer I'd ordered for the cafe arrived later that week.

Tom: What's this then?

Me: A computer.

Tom: I know it's a computer, fool!

Me: Look I know I'm not the most innovative of cafe owners but these Internet cafes seem to go down a storm.

Tom: Most of the customers are over sixty years old, what the fuck are they going to use this for?

Me: Senior citizens are getting quite hip, you know. They can buy stuff over the Internet and they won't have to leave the coffee shop to go into town.

Tom: Like DVDs and music?

Me: More like incontinence pants and Viagra, but I can see where you're coming from, Tom; it will appeal to all ages.

Kam walked over.

Kam: Right, let's get the porn on.

Me: Well, turn the screen away from the windows and customers then.

Tom: thehun.com is a good one, it's filthy.

Kam: There's frogsex.com as well.

Me: Frogsex? Is that a bestiality site?

Kam: No, just pure filth.

Me: Is it French porn?

Kam: What?

Me: Where does the frog thing come into it?

Tom: Who cares! All that matters is it's labia central. Come to papa.

A rather nasty picture of a woman being entered in both front and back passages flashed up on the screen.

Me: She looks like she's in pain.

Kam: Oh, yes. She's definitely well lubricated.

Tom: Will you two stop distracting me, I'm trying to look at porn.

Me: You're not going to start touching yourself are you?

Tom: No, I'm just collecting some masturbation material for later.

Me: Anyway, why do blokes always ask for anal sex, is it really that much better than vaginal sex?

Tom: No, it really *is* just more degrading for the woman.

I shot Neal the look of death.

Kam: But, more importantly, do you know that giving head is illegal in eighteen states in America. It's OK to carry a gun but you can go to jail for sucking cock, they're a bunch of crazy bastards those Yanks. Let me at that computer, Tom. Here we go, it says here, on Wikipedia, that oral sex is illegal in Alabama, Arizona, Florida, FLORIDA! —I got sucked off in Florida when I went to Disneyland and I met this girl from Sheffield, fucking hell, I could have done time for the dirty cow—Idaho, Kansas, Louisiana, Massachusetts, Minnesota, Mississippi.

Me: We don't need to know all the states, Kam.

Kam continued regardless, 'Georgia, North and South Carolina, Oklahoma, Oregon, Rhode Island, Utah, Virginia and Washington D.C. Where was Bill Clinton sucked off by Monica Lewinsky?

Me: I don't know. Wasn't it in the White House?

Kam: Washington D.C. then? It'll tell us on Wikipedia. I love the Internet, it's fucking great. Here it is, Monica Lewinsky alleged nine sexual encounters with Bill Clinton. It was all about her giving him head in the news anyway, I think he was saying that he'd never had sexual relations with her so he probably doesn't class head as sex. Apparently, she was once blowing Bill off when he was on the phone with a member of Congress, have you ever tried to hold a normal conversation while you're getting sucked off?

Me: I can't say I have.

Kam: It's fucking hard work, I can barely remember my own name let alone hold a conversation with a politician. Anyway, there was a twenty one day trial in the Senate and President Clinton was acquitted of all charges and remained in office.

Me: That'd be right.

Kam: What was I talking about? Oh yeah, blowjobs. So, it says here that there was a case featured in the November 1996 issue of *Marie Claire* magazine involving some woman from Atlanta who tried to have her soon-to-be ex-husband charged with rape. She had persuaded her then hubby to tie her up and then said that the sex had not been consensual. Her sister came forward and informed the court of the plot against the man. But, and this is the shocker, although the man was acquitted on the rape charge, he was sentenced to five years in jail for having performed oral sex on the woman. He had admitted to that during the course of the case and so he was charged and sentenced under Georgia law. Crazy bastards, all three hundred million of them. Ah well, at least they're all in the one country and you know what you're getting. And in Connorsville, Wisconsin, it is illegal for a man to shoot off a gun when his female partner is having an orgasm. Madder than a bag of cut snakes. Sex with animals is perfectly legal in Washington state, as long as the animal weighs less than forty pounds, so it's OK with a small dog, er ... like a Jack Russell, but they bite don't they the little terriers, but not something like a cow or a pig.

Amanda: Was California in that list of states?

Kam: No chance, it says here that California is quite liberal, they give blow jobs like they give handshakes out there.

Me: Have you finished?

Kam: Yeah.

Me: Thank God for that.

The day of the Christmas party came around a little too quickly for my liking. Unfortunately, everyone who had been invited accepted the invitation, so that was forty-two people, and I started to panic mildy.

Me: I don't think I've got forty two fucking plates.

Neal: Why did you invite so many people then?

Me: Because I didn't think we knew so many sad fuckers that had nothing better to do on a Saturday night, I was expecting a few not to turn up. Nikki's boyfriend Phil is coming, that just about made my day.

Tom: Stop being a twat and be nice to him for a change.

Me: I'd rather eat my own shit.

Jamie: How can I help?

Me: Don't you mean, *how can I hinder?*

Jamie: Bollocks to you then.

Colin: Can I — —

Me: Colin, fuck off.

Colin: Okey-dokey.

Nikki entered the kitchen, with a smile like she'd slept with a coat hanger in her mouth. 'Hello everybody.'

Me: You look happy.

Nikki: I am. Phil, or cuntface as I've been told you like to call him, has just left his wife for me.

She shot me a disapproving look.

Me: Really?! Fuck me, it must be the season for miracles, next thing you know Jamie will get up out of his chair and walk.

Nikki: I love him, now accept it, *biatch*.

Me: I want you to be happy; if he makes you happy then I'm happy. The ice-cream scoop thing still makes me uncomfortable though. Give me a hug.

Phil walked into the kitchen. 'Can I have a hug?'

Me: Fuck off.

Kam: Jules, someone has changed the screen saver on your PC to Rudolph fucking a turkey.

Me: That would be you then, Kam.

Pause …

Kam: Yes.

Me: Rudolph is an improvement on the woman with the world's hairiest beaver that was my screen saver last week. Also, some bastard's put a password on the internet access. You wouldn't happen to know what it is, would you?

Kam: *I love it up me.*

Me: Thanks.

Kam: All lower case, no spaces.

Bev: Looks like we're about done.

Me: Has anyone seen Marie? She said she was coming.

Bev: I haven't.

Neal: Me neither.

Then Tom turned up with Ashlea and her kids and we were finally ready. We served dinner and it went down a storm. There was only one person who wet themselves, and Mr Jackson lost one of the crowns from his teeth, which he thinks he may have swallowed along with one of the walnuts in the salad but he couldn't say for sure.

Ashlea's son, Oliver, insisted that it was only five sleeps until '*Farmer* Christmas' came to visit. Tom tried to convince him that Santa was on the CIA's most wanted list and that he shouldn't get his hopes up, as the US Marines had probably already killed him and taken Rudolph and his gang to Guantanamo Bay.

This upset Oliver and we all told him not to worry as Tom was possibly the most stupid person in the world; that once, when Tom had diarrhoea, and he was walking across a nearby field to get home after a night on the beer, he had pulled his pants down to have a poo and when he pulled them back up he realised that he had actually pooed in his pants.

Oliver thought this was very funny, but for some reason Ashlea decided that it was time for her and the children to leave.

After dinner Tom brought out Pictionary, and set up the flip-chart we'd bought specially for it.

Tom and Kam had done a booze trip, to France, the week before so everyone was well on their way to being completely wankered.

When it was Neal's turn, he drew a picture of a man ejaculating over a woman's breasts.

Bev: Is that a pearl necklace?

'Yes.' Neal said proudly.

Mrs Jackson: Is that a penis?

Me: Yes, Mrs Jackson, it's a penis.

Mrs Jackson: Oh'

On her way out of the shop, Mrs Jackson slipped over, which may end in a potential hip replacement, but as she was drunk at the time I don't think that she can pin a lawsuit on us, although, I may be wrong there.

When there was just our gang left it was time to bring out Articulate. If you haven't got this board game then I highly recommend buying it, almost as highly as I recommend befriending the disabled in order to gain rapid entry into most tourist attractions. On second thoughts, I would recommend Articulate more highly.

The rules of the game are that you have to get your team to say the word on the card in front of you. You work your way around the board by moving your game piece by the number of correct answers each team gives in a time limit of forty seconds. Where you are on the board depends on which type of words you have to describe, for example: places in the world, things to do with nature or just everyday objects. If you get the spade symbol, like the spades in a pack of cards, then you could be describing absolutely anything.

Phil: Who's in which team?

Bev: Boys versus girls.

Phil: Why?

Bev: Because we always kick your arses.

Me: We'll give you a chance and let you go first.

Tom: OK, what are we on?

Jamie: Ooh, it's the random one, we could be describing anything.

Amanda: Are you ready? I'm turning the egg-timer over now.

Jamie: Wait a minute, I haven't got any cards yet, just hold on.

Amanda: Are you ready now?

Jamie: Right, erm … he was the labour politician who resigned over the, so called, 'weapons of mass destruction' in Iraq. He was ginger.

Silence.

Jamie: OK, erm … his surname is what you do to food: if you bake it, fry it, what are you doing?

Tom: Cooking it?

Jamie: Shorter.

Tom: Cook.

Jamie: Right. And his first name is a bird associated with Christmas.

Phil: Turkey.

Jamie: Fucking turkey! Pass, pass onto the next one. It's a city in China. It's been given back to the Chinese. It used to be a British colony.'

Silence.

Jamie: Sounds like Ping Pong.

Kam: Hong Kong.

Jamie: Yes. It's a type of insect.

Tom: Grasshopper?

Jamie: Ooh, nearly.

Kam: Ladybird.

Colin: Stick insect.

Jamie: You might do this in a church.

Tom: Cricket?

Jamie: Cricket? What the fuck are you lot on?

Tom: I was still thinking of an insect.

Amanda: Right, time's out. Our turn.

Jamie: Fucking Turkey Cook! Who the fuck's Turkey Cook? It's Robin Cook, you pack of complete cocks, and this last one was a preying mantis. How many did we get?

Bev: One.

Jamie: Great. Feel free to join in at any time boys.

Phil: Fuck off.

Tom: I was still thinking of insects.

Nikki: Right ladies, it's us.

Me: Come on Bev, you can do the honours.

Jamie: You've got the people category, are you ready?

Me: Wait a moment. Bev, are you ready?

Bev: Let the games begin. That Roman guy who ordered Christ's crucifixion?

Me: Pontius Pilot.

Bev: Yep. Another word for a can, like a can of beans.

Amanda: A tin?

Bev: Yes, say it twice.

Amanda: Tin Tin.

Bev: Cock on. That fucking songwriter you were on about at the airport when we went on holiday to Amsterdam.

Me: Burt Bacharach. Get in there, I knew he would come in useful.

Bev: That suffragette woman.'

Shab: Emily Pankhurst?

Bev: Yep. Pop star who got caught being sucked off in some toilets.

Nikki: George Michael.

Bev: Yes. Actor who— —

Jamie: Stop, our turn.

Me: That'll be five for us then.

Jamie: No, no, you got four.

Amanda: Ah, Jamie, shush now, you can catch up in this round.

Phil: Can I have a go?

'This should be interesting,' Nikki whispered. 'He's dyslexic.

Phil: Right, are you ready with the egg-timer?

Nikki: Go for it, Big Boy.

Colin: What subject have we got?

Amanda: Objects.

Phil: Right, they tried to ban these a couple of years ago, they might have actually banned them, er … they involve foxes and hounds.

Colin: Hunting?

Phil: Shorter.

Colin: Hunt.

Phil: Yes. Erm … they come in bunches, it's a fruit.

Kam: Grapes.

Phil: No.

Kam: Bananas.

Phil: No

Kam: What else comes in a bunch?

Phil: They say one of these a day keeps the doctor away.

Tom: Do you mean apples?

Phil: Yes.

Tom: Whatever.

Phil: If you smash something into lots of little pieces then these pieces are what?

Tom: Fragments?

Phil: Yes.

Nikki: Are you cheating? Can you see his cards?

Amanda: Time's up.

Nikki: Can I just look at those cards and see if you're cheating.

Phil: You cheeky cow, what do you take me for?

Jamie: We got three answers fair and square.

Nikki: Right then, what answers did we have? Hunt, apples and fragments. I'll give you apples, the other answers should have been hut and fragrance.

Tom: Can't you read?

Phil: Not very well. Sometimes I get the letters a bit muddled up.

Tom: Give me those fucking cards. I can understand you getting fragrance wrong, but hut?

Jamie: I'm playing Articulate with the retarded.

Me: That's one point then.

Jamie: Why do you have to be so competitive?

Let's just say the girls tortured the boys, it was great fun.

No one had seen Marie all day; it was a shame she'd missed the party. Neal and I decided to get some fresh air and walk around to see if she was OK. I went upstairs to get my coat and heard moaning noises in the front room. I slowly opened the door and found Amanda riding Colin hard on my brand new, wool rug. Luckily, I'd had the good sense to pay the extra forty quid to have it stain guarded—tis the season to be jolly, apparently.

Outside it was a beautiful night, very cold but the sky was clear, and you could see thousands of stars. We both looked up in awe at the stars and then I lost my balance and keeled over backwards, I'm sure I've got a neurological disorder ; I grabbed onto Neal and took him down with me.

It only took us five minutes to walk around to Marie's place: she rented a flat in a large house on one of the 'jewel' streets, named after, surprisingly enough, jewels. I always get the street wrong anyway and walk down Diamond Street instead of Emerald Street or whatever; they're all parallel to each other anyway so Pearl, Ruby, Diamond, you're going to get to the right one eventually.

There are some beautiful, old Victorian terraced houses down the jewel streets, with five or six bedrooms in each, and landlords have converted these into bedsits or apartments. I use the word apartments in the loosest context; it almost makes them sound habitable, when some are rank with damp and freezing cold in winter.

Marie lived on Ruby Street and when we got there the place was in darkness except for one solitary light at the top of the building. Unfortunately, the building that she lived in was totally shit: the front bay window was boarded up and the whole place reeked of neglect. There used to be a small water feature in the middle of the front garden, it might have been a small fountain, but now it was home to three empty cans of Carling Black Label and a Tesco's carrier bag.

I went to open the gate and then realised that there wasn't one. We rang the bell for number six: Marie's place. There was no answer. The front door was wide open so we walked in anyway.

Me: I'm a bit worried about her. I think we should go up and see if she's alright.

Neal: It smells of piss in here.

Me: It's just damp that's all.

Neal: Because everyone keeps pissing in here.

Me: Shut up. You don't know you're born, living in luxury at our place. We sleep under one hundred percent Egyptian cotton sheets, I'll have you know.

Neal: I was living on the streets six months ago so stop talking complete shite.

He was right; it was an awful place: damp walls with seventies wallpaper hanging off the walls, and by the looks of it there used to be a pattern on the carpet, but it was long gone under all the muddy footprints—I hoped it was mud. Marie's flat was up three flights of stairs; I was breathing out of my arse by the time we got up there.

Me: God, how unfit am I?

I knocked on the door; it was slightly ajar. There was no answer so I pushed the door slowly open. Marie was laying on her back in the middle of the floor, eyes closed and deathly white.

'Marie?' I called out softly, there was no answer.

I walked over to her, knelt down and touched her arm. There was no response. And then I saw the three empty pill bottles next to her.

'Fuck me, she's tried to do herself in!' I looked at the labels in the bottles. 'I think they're sleeping tablets. Fucking hell, how many has she taken? Marie, Marie, wake up, darling. I gently tapped her face but she didn't move. 'She's still warm so I don't think she's dead yet.'

Neal: Let's lift her up onto the bed. You take her feet.

We lifted Marie up and her head shot back; I thought she was starting to convulse.

Neal: Fuck! She's having a fit.

Me: You're stood on her hair.

Neal: Oh yeah.

I called the emergency services and the ambulance arrived within ten minutes. I went with Marie to the hospital, holding her hand and telling her everything was going to be OK. She awoke briefly in the ambulance, saw me and started to cry.

'I'm sorry, so sorry,' she sobbed.

Me: Don't be soft, you're going to be alright.

They pumped her stomach at the hospital. Apparently, she'd tried this before. I couldn't believe it—I thought I knew her but I didn't have a clue. I blamed myself because I'd been so busy lately that I hadn't really sat down with her and got to know her better, but it looked like she was going to be OK, so I'd get a second chance to be a better friend.

The nurse told me that Marie was sleeping and that I should come back in the morning with some clean clothes and toiletries for her.

I got a taxi home to find Neal waiting up for me.

Neal: How's she doing?

Me: She's going to be OK. I need to take some clothes and stuff in for her tomorrow Is her flat locked up now?'

Neal: Yes, but I've got the key.

Me: I'm going to go around now and pick up some stuff for her.

Neal: I'll come with you.

We walked back to Marie's flat and filled one of my holdalls with some of her stuff, turned off the lights and went to walk out of the door.

Neal: What was that?

Me: What?

Neal: That noise.

Me: What noise?

Neal: If you shut up we might be able to hear it.

We could hear a faint, pathetic meowing sound coming from the far end of the room.

Me: Turn the light on.

Neal: Let's just go.

Me: We can't, there might be an animal trapped in here. It sounds like it's coming from over there. Turn the light on.

Neal: It might be a rat.

Me: A rat that meows like a cat; that would be fucking novel. We won't know until we turn the light on though will we?

There was a little squeak coming from behind the sofa, I knelt down on the floor to look under it. I found two big, green eyes reflecting the light from the room.

Me: It's a cat. Hello there.

I stretched out my hand and stroked its head.

Neal: It might bite you. Watch what you're doing.

Me: This one's not going to bite me, it's purring away to itself.

Neal: OK, I'll say, 'I told you so,' when I have to peel it off your face.

The grey and white cat walked out from its hiding place and rubbed itself against my legs.

Me: The tag says he's called Beano. He's beautiful.

I picked him up.

Neal: What are we going to do with him?

Me: Take him home.

Neal: And do what with him?

Me: Look after him.

Neal: I hate cats.

Me: Shut up.

A fat man with a big, red nose and a crusty, bald head stormed into the room; no really, his head was crusty like the top of an apple pie.

'Where is she?' Crusty demanded.

Me: Who are you?

'The Landlord,' he growled.

'I knew it!' he said pointing at Beano, who was by now curled up in my arms. 'I told her she wasn't allowed any pets, and she's behind on the rent. Tell her not to bother coming back; I was going to throw her out anyway, she's been nothing but trouble. All that shouting and carrying on.'

Me: She's in hospital.

Landlord: What's she done this time? Taken some more tablets? The stupid bitch!

It was four o'clock in the morning and I really couldn't be arsed with this complete knob head giving me grief. Beano hissed, so against my better judgement I threw the cat at him.

Beano did Marie proud, locking himself like an alien onto the Landlord's balding, crusty head; he scratched and chewed at his face. The Landlord swung his arms wildly trying to remove the cat from his head, and managed to fall backwards down the stairs onto his arse. Beano released his grip.

'Tell her not to come back!' the Landlord screamed and ran into one of the rooms at the bottom of the stairway.

Me: Get in there Beano, you little minx.

We took Beano and his cat-litter tray home.

Neal: He's not coming into the bedroom.

Me: Oh, yes, he fucking is. Animals are dead sensitive, you know; I bet he's frightened.

Beano jumped softly onto the bottom of the bed. He sat down and looked at us, unsure of what to do next, as if he didn't really know if he should be there.

Neal: Don't be leaving chocolate kisses all over this duvet cover, puddy twat.

'Come here Beano,' I patted the bed next to me and he trotted over to me purring.

Neal: I fucking hate cats.

Neal woke me in the middle of the night with a scream. I looked over at him and saw Beano sat on Neal's chest, looking down at him.

Neal: Fucking cats. I hate 'em, I really do. Take him over on your side, he's ruining your one hundred percent fucking Egyptian cotton sheets, you know.

Me: I'm trying to sleep, will you be quiet. Come over here Beano, you don't want to be near him, he's a complete cock anyway.'

We opened the coffee shop a little later than usual that day. Neal stayed to look after it while I visited Marie in hospital. I bought some grapes and bananas and a few magazines for her. I was a bit nervous really; I had no idea what I was going to say to her.

Marie was in a room on her own. When I walked in she was looking out of the window. She turned her head towards me, and then turned back towards the window, she'd been crying.

Me: Hello there. How are you feeling?

Marie: OK.

Me: I've brought you some clothes and shampoo and stuff. Beano is staying at our place. We've locked your flat up. I've brought you a newspaper, a couple of magazines, and I've got you one of those word-search puzzle books. Shit, I've forgotten to get you a pen.

Marie: Thanks.

I sat down next to the bed and an uncomfortable silence filled the room. I had no idea what to say, and Marie must have felt really embarrassed, so I just went into automatic bullshit mode and talked absolute bollocks about the weather, about how the doughnuts had gone up in price at Tesco's, and that Mr Jackson had lost one of his crowns at the Christmas dinner; then I remembered that she hadn't come to the Christmas dinner.

Me: What happened yesterday?

Marie: I'd have been no fun at your party.

Me: Do you really want to die?

Marie: I don't know.

Me: The nurse told me you've done this before.

Marie: I have my dark times, when I feel really down.

Me: What makes you feel so sad that you'd want to take your own life?

Marie: I have my reasons.

I got the feeling that Marie didn't want to talk about this anymore, so I asked one of the nurses if she had a spare pen and I started one of the word-searches. I caught Marie looking at me a couple of times and then she picked up the newspaper. I looked at her and smiled, she forced a smile out between tightly closed lips, and then we just sat in silence for the next hour; me with the word-search and her with *The Daily Mail*.

Later that day, everyone came to the shop at closing time for tea.

Amanda: How's Marie?

Me: She's OK, I'm going to see her tonight.

Nikki: Why did she take all those tablets?

Me: No idea. She doesn't want to talk about it at the moment. Anyway, let's talk about Marie later, she's in safe hands. Amanda, were you riding Colin hard in my front room last night, and may I add, on my brand new wool rug?

Amanda: Yes.

Me: Oh, alright then.

Nikki: What?! When did this happen?

Me: Last night after the Christmas party.

Amanda: Colin was feeling a little bit dizzy.

Me: I bet he was, all that blood rushing to his cock.

Amanda: So, I took him upstairs for a lie down. One thing just led to another, you know how it happens.

Me: No, I don't really know at all.

Amanda: He's moving in with me.

Nikki: Bloody hell girl, you don't waste any time.

Amanda: I've liked Colin for a while now, I don't see any point in taking my time, I've been on my own for ages now, he makes me happy.

Me: Bev, are you seeing Dave then or was it just a wank?

Bev: I might as well, he's a nice bloke so why not? Having said that though, I sent him a text the other day, telling him I was feeling rough as fuck after I'd got hammered sometime last week, well one of the times, I can't remember which, and have a listen to this.

Bev reached into her handbag, brought out her mobile phone and started flicking through the menu, trying to find something.

Bev: Ah, here we go. It says, *'so sorry to hear u r not feeling well. I pray u start to feel heaps better soon.'*

Me: Eh?! I pray?!

Bev: It doesn't stop there. *'I'm sending you love and healing thoughts, may the sun start shining and brighten you back up.'*

Me: Fuck off. Let me see that.

'Please take care, kiss kiss kiss,' she finished, passing the phone to me for confirmation.

Me: I feel sick; the hairs on the back of my neck are standing on end. Have you replied?

Bev: Of course, I told him if he ever sent me shite like that again I'd stab him in the eye with a syringe.

Me: Is he one of the 'God Squad?'

Bev: No, he just said it was a turn of phrase. Fucking weirdo.

Me: I'm going to see Marie, is anyone else coming?

Bev: Yeah, come on, I'll drive.

All the girls piled into Bev's car. Bev drives like a maniac and is inclined to a touch of the old road rage. We got about half way to the hospital when some boy racer, in a crappy, old Orion Ghia, cut us up at the roundabout near Asda supermarket.

Bev: Ooh, you fucker! Come to Mama.

We all gripped the edge of our seats; Bev chased after him. Luckily, he was turning right at the next roundabout and we were headed straight on, so the chase was almost over before it started. We did stop at the roundabout long enough to give Bev the opportunity to hurl some verbal abuse at him.

'Are you going to McDonalds?' Bev screamed out of her window.' Are you working in McDonalds? You daft cunt! I'll have fries with that! Wanker!'

The poor lad just looked totally confused and then stuck his middle finger up as he drove off.

Bev: He's a fucking idiot. Why have you all gone quiet?

Me: You're a fucking nutter when you get behind the wheel of a car. We nearly mounted the kerb coming up to that roundabout.

Bev: I think I'm a good driver; I've never had a crash. My motto is that you should always approach roundabouts with speed and confidence. Ah, fuck, there's a copper behind us; he's flashing his lights I'm going to have to pull over.

Amanda: Everything's all right though isn't it, Bev? You don't have anything to worry about.

Bev: I think I'm still over the limit.

Me: Eh?! What did you have for breakfast? Have you been putting Bacardi on your cornflakes again?

Bev: I was fucking hammered last night.

Me: Why didn't you ask me to drive?

Bev: It's a bit late to think about that now.

We came to an abrupt stop in a parking lay-by on the A66. We just looked at her and shook our heads. Bev's eyes never moved from her wing mirror as she watched one of the Policemen get out of his car and make his way towards us. Bev's face broke into a wide smile.

Bev: Thank fuck for that, it's my cousin Stuart, we should be laughing here.

'Good Evening, Madam,' the Policemen said. 'Oh, hiya Bev. You got yourself a new car?'

Bev: I got it last month; it sticks to the road like shit to a blanket.

'We noticed. You must learn to curb that fucking temper of yours, you fiery bastard,' Stuart commented and then looking at us he added. 'She never fucking changes. We saw you chasing that young lad in the Orion Ghia.'

Bev: Did you see him cut me up at the Asda roundabout? The twat.

Stuart: Whatever. Look, my Supervisor's in the car with me so I'm going to have to give you a right royal bollocking and breathalyse you.

Bev: You can't, Stu, I'm over the limit.

Stuart: You're fucking joking aren't you? You soulless witch.

Bev: We had a party last night, I was hammered. I woke up in bed this morning naked and couldn't find my clothes, I looked out of the bedroom window and they were all over the front garden: I found my knickers and bra hanging from the front door handle. What the fuck was that all about?

'How the fuck are we going to get away with this?' Stuart asked, slowly setting up his breathalyser.

Bev: You're going to have to take the breath test for me, Stu.

'It's not really regulation this, you know, Bev? Do you know what she did when I was five?' Stuart continued. 'My mum and her mum went out shopping together and left her to babysit me; she must have been about twelve years old. She only locked me in her mum's garden shed with her psycho cat that used to attach itself to my face, any opportunity it got. I was in there for over an hour; I nearly lost a fucking eye. The cat was fucking ginger too; they should have called it Beverley.'

Bev: I hated baby sitting for you, Stu: you were a little bastard.'

Stuart leaned against the side of Bev's car, blocking his Supervisor's view from behind, and quickly exhaled into the breathalyser.

Me: What did you do to Bev to make her lock you in the shed?

Stuart: Fuck all! You didn't have to do anything, she's just the spawn of Satan.

At that point the breathalyser gave a beep and Stuart looked at the reading.

Stuart: Fuck! I'm over the limit.

Bev: Right then, I'll just drive calmly away.

Stuart: Just give me a moment to clear this thing and then you can fuck off out of my life … there we go.'

Bev: See you on Sunday at Aunty Audrey's then?

Stuart: Yeah, see you later, Bev.

Marie seemed a little embarrassed when we all walked in to see her.

'What did you think you were doing, you daft cow?' Bev said as she gave her a hug. For working in a hospital all these years her bedside manner is appalling. I just smiled at Marie and rolled my eyes, she smiled back.

Marie: They've said I can go if I want to.

Me: You can come back and stay with us; we've got a spare room.

Marie: It's OK, I'll go back to my flat.

Me: Er, I wouldn't recommend that.

Marie: Why?

Me: I don't think that the landlord wants you back there, something about cats not being allowed, mind you, I did almost have to peel Beano off his face.

Marie: Really?

Me: Well, I did throw the cat at him. So, I think you should stay with us.

Marie: OK. Thanks.

Me: You don't want to be in here over Christmas.

Bev: Come on then, get your stuff together and I'll drive us back.

We had an incident-free return trip.

'We've got no mince pies left,' was how Neal greeted me when I returned to the shop.

Me: I'll get some tomorrow.

Neal: Connie from across the road wants to know if we're opening on Christmas Day. I think she's going to be on her own.

Me: Really?

Neal: I get the impression that there's going to be a few like that at 'Heartbreak Hotel' over there.' He pointed across the road to the retirement housing.

I know I'm quite selfish at times but I can't stand the thought of anyone being on their own at Christmas. When it gets cold in winter I always think of homeless people and wonder how anyone can last a single night without a thirteen and a half tog quilt, a hot-water bottle and copious amounts of hot chocolate.

Neal raised his eyebrows and I could feel myself turning into a complete sucker.

Me: Should we have like a social outcasts' dinner?

Neal: Why not?

There were more social outcasts than we anticipated: fourteen accepted our invitation. So that was seventeen including Marie, Neal and me, and then eighteen when Phil decided to dump Nikki two days before Christmas to go back to his wife.

'Can you do the menu for our 'Norman No Mates' themed Christmas special then?' I asked my now single again, miserable mate Nikki.

Nikki: Go on then. Mmm … cheese soufflé to start with, I think, then, erm … I don't know if I fancy the traditional turkey dinner, we had one two weeks ago at your party and every other Christmas party I've been to.

Neal: What about chicken nuggets?

Me: Chicken nuggets for Christmas dinner?

Neal: I like chicken nuggets.

Nikki: Beef Wellington, followed by …

Me: Chocolate.

Nikki: Chocolate what?

Pause …

Me: Chocolate something.

Pause …

Nikki: Chocolate and raspberry meringue, and coffee and mints. Oh, and a cheese-board.

Me: Do you know anyone who orders the cheese board in a restaurant? I don't.

Nikki: I have it sometimes.

Me: Nah, you've got to have a dessert for afters. It's got to be sweet, served with ice cream, and you've got to feel sick as fuck when you've finished. Are you going to help me with all this cooking then, Nik?

Nikki: I might be busy on Christmas Day; I might be washing my hair.

Me: And opening all your presents?

Nikki: Yeah.

Me: So you'll be here for breakfast then.

Nikki: Yeah.

Me: Fabulous. I'll get some croissants in then, let's go Continental. I think I've got some Nutella in the cupboard.

If there's one thing that gets me in the mood for Christmas it's the carol service at the local church on Christmas Eve. All of the gang make it a habit to go and usually bring mums and grans and aunties along; so, it's a great time to catch up and savour that Christmas feeling when you all add up how much you've spent on food and presents, and anticipate a frugal January when your credit card bills come in and bite you on the arse.

The choir was fabulous, which is more than can be said for the congregation who usually belt out the first two lines of every carol and then mumble the rest because, let's face it, who knows even one Christmas carol all the way through. No, Jingle Bells doesn't count.

'O Little Town of Bethlehem' goes something like, 'O Little Town of Bethlehem, how still we see thee lie, above the sheep and dreamless sleep, the silent stars go by, yet mmm mmmmm mmmmm' (I don't even know if the sheep part's right, it might be sweet not sheep, or deep.)..

Anyway, I love the Christmas carol service, and then it was back to the shop for coffee and mince pies.

I'd made a real effort this year on the decoration front. I'd managed to squeeze a real tree into the shop and I'd found these lights in B&Q that looked like snowballs but had lights in them, which I'd draped across the front windows and counter. Every table had a cream candle in the middle, surrounded by holly and mistletoe berries—I love candlelight at Christmas. I tried to make the place look classy.

I remember when I was a kid, we used to have shit Christmas decorations at our house. We used to have these four multi-coloured, paper streamers where my mum would pin one end to the light fitting in the middle of the living room and the other end to each of the corners of the room, they looked tacky as fuck! We used to hang so many baubles and so much tinsel on the tree that not one branch was visible; the tree was practically at breaking point.

We kept hanging decorations that we'd had for years—stuff we'd bought as kids had to go onto the tree. I remember this little dog I'd once bought, I think it was a bit like a beagle only without the cigarette, and it was plastic with a velvet feel to it; we hung it on the tree for years. What is the point of hanging a dog onto a Christmas tree? It looked ridiculous.

When me and my sisters no longer believed in Santa, we used to have two piles of Christmas presents: one for 'thanks this is lovely' and one for 'what the fuck were you thinking, can I have the receipt?' We got some shit presents over the years. I remember my mum holding back a present for each of us until New Year once, and I got really excited thinking it was just like Christmas all over again. I ripped the paper off my present to reveal this rattan, waste-paper bin and the look on my face must have said everything that needed to be said.

My mum said, 'You're so ungrateful, I won't bother next year.' No nine-year-old in their right minds is going to jump through fucking hoops over a fucking rattan, waste-paper bin. What was she thinking?! Fucking clueless! Anyway, I digress.

I'd spent a fortune on presents. Thankfully, Boots had a 'three for the price of two offer' on their gifts, so I'd bought shitloads of bubble bath sets and chocolates and games. I just think that everyone should get at least one present at Christmas— preferably fifty but at least one.

George, one of the blokes from the retirement home, talks non-stop about World War Two, as he was joining us for Christmas dinner I decided to buy him a book on the subject. Whilst I was in WH Smith, buying a book on the Battle of Britain, I noticed that there was an appeal, sponsored by the local radio station, for presents for underprivileged children in the area. There was a shortage of presents, for boys aged ten to fourteen years and newborns, in the area.

Well, let's face it, the newborns aren't going to thank me for a Christmas present, but to think the older kids might not get anything really upset me, so I bought a 'Learn How To Juggle' and a 'Make Your Own Kite' kit and donated them.

Now on the present side I had a bit of a dilemma: what should I buy Neal? I'd been knocking him off for a few months now—should I go the whole hog and spoil him rotten, would I look desperate and frighten him off, or should I buy him a couple of token gifts and look tight as a gnat's chuff?

I decided bollocks to it, and I bought him a new outfit, a bottle of aftershave, a couple of CDs, a DVD, some chocolates and Bill Bryson's *Down Under* travel book. That was our aim: we'd go to Australia on holiday together.

I bought Nikki the new Nigella Lawson cookbook, some chocolates and a scarf. Bev got an AA road atlas: she's always getting herself lost and I thought if she at least had directions then she was less likely to be prone to an attack of the old road rage—she'll fucking stab some poor bastard to death one of these days. I also bought her a wine carrier from Tesco's, filled with six bottles of various wines, under the three bottles for a tenner offer.

Now, Amanda is a bit of a posh bird, so I needed something that looked expensive but wasn't.

So, I bought her some Beverley Cobella shampoo, conditioner and styling spritz from Boots, that had yet another three for two offer on them, and a chocolate fondue set from Marks and Spencer.

Marie stumped me. I was tempted to buy her a self help book, but would I then find her swinging from the rafters by her neck anytime soon? I was also conscious of the fact that we now had the Internet and you could look up various ways to kill yourself on Google, so I decided to play it safe. Judging by the amount of personal belongings we'd brought back from her place she had very little—she was in need of a serious treat. I bought her a pamper package from a local beauty parlour, a new top to wear on Christmas day and some smellies.

Beano got a mouse filled with cat nip, and I bought the boys the usual: fuck all.

I woke up with a warm feeling inside me on Christmas morning, I was really looking forward to this one. Nikki arrived early and made breakfast for us, and we sat and opened our presents.

Neal had bought me a road map of Sydney, Australia, and some chocolates (Always a winner.). He looked embarrassed because he didn't have a lot of spare cash, and wanted to buy me more, but I didn't care; I loved what I got.

We had a really relaxing day actually: we took our time serving dinner and we took about three hours to eat it all. The look on the pensioners' faces was one of sheer gratitude that they got to spend the day with someone, and not on their own. They didn't care about the food or the presents; it was the company that mattered most to them. They had all gone home by eight thirty.

I sat up talking to Marie until around two o'clock in the morning. Apparently, she had been fucked by her grandad from the age of eleven; there's no polite way of saying it really, and I'm not even going to try putting into words how evil that act is. I didn't know how to respond to that piece of information so I just put my arm around her and listened to what she had to say.

'The worse thing for me,' Marie said, 'is that my parents didn't believe a word I was saying. I couldn't handle that. They should have believed me shouldn't they? I never lied to them; I was a child.'

'I can't understand how they would think that you'd made that up, you were fucking eleven, you don't come out with shit like that off your own back.'

'He had dementia, my grandad,' Marie continued.

Me: He hadn't forgotten how to fuck though had he, the shithouse.

Pause …

Marie: My mum and dad just let him stay in the house, in the room next to mine. He used to visit me at night, it felt like every night, but I kept quiet as a mouse. I couldn't scream; I was terrified of him. Then one night, when it had been going on for three years, I heard him open his bedroom door and I just knew he was coming for me. When he was stood at the side of my bed I picked up the bedside lamp and hit him over the head with it.

Me: About fucking time too, you had no other choice, Marie.

Marie: And then he fell over and cracked his head on the floor and ended up in a coma. And then he got pneumonia and died.

Me: That's the best result all round if you ask me, and it's Christmas today, who knows Santa might have brought your mum and dad a fucking spine each.

Marie: I got some sleeping tablets from the doctor; I used to have nightmares about him and I couldn't sleep. The doctor gave me a couple of prescriptions at a time, so that I didn't have to keep going back to him and I made a stockpile of them.

Me: When did you leave home?

Marie: About six months ago. A teacher helped me, Mrs Brown. I didn't tell her everything, she just knew I needed to get out of there. I don't ever want to see my mum and dad again but I don't think I've ever felt as alone as I have these last few months. I haven't had anyone to really talk to. You know that time you came back into the coffee shop and Colin was pretending to work the cash register?

'Yeah,' I replied, I could vaguely remember it.

Marie: Well, my dad had just come into the shop to tell me that my mum wasn't very well, and that I should go home and look after her. I just told him to fuck off and die and then went out the back into the kitchen.

Me: Nice turn of phrase, very concise.

Marie: I hear you lot say it all the time.

Me: It works for us: says everything you need to say really and in only four words. Look, I can't really give you any advice, I can only say that you now have a great opportunity to choose your own family, like I have. There is a closeness that you get with blood though that I'm not sure you can recreate with friends; we can't expect the same support from friends but it's better than being in a damaging environment that's going to continue to fuck you up further the longer you stay there. Do you feel that leaving your mum and dad was the best thing to do?'

Marie: Yes.

Me: Then you're on the right track. You should get some counselling, you know. I went to see someone a couple of months ago.

Marie: Really? How did it go?

Me: I'm all sorted now.

Marie: Really.

Me: No. It'll take a few more sessions just to crack the surface I suspect, but eventually I'll get my finger out and book another appointment. Are you OK?

Marie: I'll be alright.

Me: Right then, let's get to bed.

'The twenty-ninth of December is a shitty day to have as your birthday,' Jamie informed us. 'You either get a decent Christmas present and get told that this is for Christmas and birthday combined—I fucking love that word 'combined'—or you get a shit Christmas present, followed by a shit birthday present because everyone realises that they have to buy you two presents within four fucking days. Even my mum and dad have tried that old chestnut. My birthday is on the twenty-ninth of December every year, they should be able to budget and buy me a fucking decent birthday present.'

Me: Have you finished?

Jamie: I wish I had my birthday in June, the twenty-fifth of June. Bang on half way through the year, when you consider Christmas, and it would be warm so that I wasn't always going home in the pissy, wet weather after my birthday night out.

Me: Now have you finished?

Jamie: Yes.

Me: Thank fuck for that.

Tom: Are you having a party?

Jamie: Yes.

Nikki: When?

Jamie: What about this Friday? Friday is the twenty-ninth?

Nikki: Can't we just combine it with New Year's Eve?

Jamie: No we fucking can't! Did you listen to a word I just said?

Nikki: No, not really.

Me: Sounds good to me. Do you want us to bring anything?

Jamie: Just the food and drink. Oh, and don't forget my present. I'm expecting something blinding after my soap-box speech from two minutes ago. The sales will be on now, so no excuses. Get yourselves down to the shops and get me something nice.

Jamie left and we all huddled around thinking of the shittiest presents we could possibly buy him.

Kam: I'd forgotten about it to be honest. Anyway, blokes don't bother about presents.

'Let's all buy him something decent, and also something really shit,' Amanda offered. 'But really cheap, and then give him the shit stuff first and hold out on the decent gear until he gets really upset, possibly until he starts crying. What do you reckon?'

Bev: I reckon you're a right bitch.

Amanda: I don't usually let flattery go to my head but thanks.

Me: There's a pizza shop just round the corner from Jamie's isn't there?

Kam: Yeah, Speedy Pepper's.

Me: Excellent, that's the food sorted. You can bring your own drinks.

So, all the girls went shopping for Jamie's present on Friday afternoon en-route to the party.

Amanda managed to find *The Best of Burt Bacharach* on CD.

'Look it's got, *Raindrops Keep Falling on My Head*, *The Look of Love*, (Wasn't that a Dusty Springfield number?) *I Say a Litte Prayer*: was that Diana Ross?' Amanda was quite excited by her little find.

Me: No, wasn't it Aretha Franklin?

Nikki: Yeah, Aretha sang it.

Amanda: Whatever. *They want to be, close to you.* Now I know that one, it's The Carpenters. This is great.

Nikki: Buy one for yourself as well.

Amanda: I'm might just do that.

Nikki: Freak.

Bev managed to find some nipple clamps in the Ann Summers shop, and Nikki, thinking Jamie had been piling the beef on lately, bought him a can of strawberry flavoured SlimFast.

I was browsing through British Home Stores and found a fantastic fridge magnet in the shape of that old, Russian leader, Lenin. Lenin was standing naked, except for a pair of white Y-fronts, with the Soviet symbol of a star and sickle imprinted in red on the front. You could dress him up in a variety of outfits: an American Cheer Leader, a nun or a football player—*result!* I also bought him some aftershave as he was currently wearing some piss based fragrance, High Karate, Old Spice, or something like that.

Ten large pizzas later and we were on our way to Jamie's. We arrived to find Jamie comparing his 'easy reach' (Those long metal rods that people use to pick up cigarette ends and crisp packets in town centres when they're doing community service.), with his next door neighbour, Errol.

'I,' declared Jamie proudly, 'have an easy reach that enables me a twenty-one inch reach compared to Errol's pathetic nineteen inches.'

Nikki: Oh, you live the high life, baby.

Jamie: Where's my presents?

'Here they are birthday boy.' Amanda smiled as she waved the ALDI carrier bag in front of him.

Jamie bade his neighbour a fond farewell: 'You're boring me now, Errol. I'm going inside to open my birthday presents.' And then he drove himself into his bungalow.

'They better not be shit,' Jamie said as he positioned himself in front of his living room table and waited to receive his presents. 'I know you've only put them in an ALDI carrier bag to wind me up. Come to daddy.'

Jamie's mum came in from the kitchen and greeted us all with a hug; Mrs Dennis is one of the warmest people I know, and a fucking saint to have not had Jamie adopted.

Mrs D: Come on then Jamie, let's get them opened.

Jamie: Don't get too excited Mum, they'll be shit.

Mrs D: Don't be so ungrateful.

My present first.

Jamie: It's a fridge magnet.

Me: I know.

Jamie: It's shit.

Mrs D: Jamie, you are so ungrateful.

Me: I know, I blame the parents. Look, you can dress him up as a cheerleader or a nun, the possibilities are endless.

Jamie: It's shit.

Kam: And it looks nothing like John Lennon.

Jamie: *Lenin*, not Lennon, you tit. You shouldn't be allowed to breed, Kam.

Kam: Cheers mate.

Jamie: Is this it? Is this all you've bought me?

Nikki: I've got you something decent.

Jamie: Come on then, let's see it.

We managed to hold back the giggles as Jamie unravelled the wrapping paper to reveal two cans of strawberry flavoured SlimFast, with a whole

'Twenty-five percent extra free' emblazoned across the label. I'm not too sure how that's supposed to help you lose weight, by giving you more to drink, I didn't think that diet products worked the same way when it came to jumbo sizes. Anyway, hey ho.

Jamie: You pack of bastards!

Amanda handed Jamie his Burt Bacharach CD, which he unwrapped in silence and then proceeded to throw it immediately into the plastics recycling bin. Bev's nipple clamps he shoved straight into the drawer next to his computer table, muttering something about 'at least I've got something useful', then he turned to face us all with a full sulk on.

Me: Only joking, baby, here's your real pressie.

Jamie's face lit up as he realised that we'd got him something decent.

Jamie: Ooh. Some Boss aftershave. I think I've got some of this.

Me: I think you have, but it's two years old and smells of piss.

Pause …

Me: Sorry, was I thinking out loud again. Let's get into those pizzas.

Mrs D: Have you said, 'Thank you,' Jamie?

Jamie: Oh, are you still here, mum? You'd better get a move on, the strippers will be here in ten minutes.

Mrs D: Yeah, right. I'll see you all later then.

All: Bye Mrs D, take care.

As it was Jamie's birthday he didn't have to provide any alcohol, but he gladly partook of everyone else's, and before long we were left with one bottle of Finlandia vodka and nothing to go with it. We always forget the soft-drinks at these occasions; everyone brings a bottle and forgets the mixers.

Bev: So what star sign are you, birthday boy?

Jamie: Capricorn.

Bev: So what traits are common with Capricorns then?

Jamie: Fucked if I know.

Me: I'm a Taurean, a lover of fine things, with a tendency to be overweight because I stuff my fat face with rich food, I'm loyal and good with money.

Bev: I'm a Cancerian. Apparently, there's a high percentage of Cancerians with red hair.

Tom: June must be a slack month for birthdays in China then.

Bev: Shut up fool.

Jamie: I can't be doing with neat vodka, especially not this cheap shite, it takes the lining off my stomach.

Tom: What have we got to mix with it?

Bev: Fuck all, birthday boy asked us to provide alcohol and food and then hasn't even provided any mixers.

Our eyes scanned the room for something to add to the remaining bottle of alcohol. I mean, we had to finish it, it would be rude not to. All eyes came to rest on Jamie's birthday presents, we all looked at one another and nodded our silent agreement: the Vodka Slimfast was born.

Kam: This tastes alright. Can you smell it on my breath? You could get away with drinking this at work.

Jamie: I feel sick.

Me: Don't be starting with that line, birthday boy. Last time I had to clear up your vomit I thought the fucking *Exorcist* had been in your bed.

'I'm not kidding, I think I'm going to be sick.' Jamie wheeled himself into the kitchen.

We were only kept waiting momentarily before the background noise of retching joined our conversation. A minute later the noises ceased and we continued chatting amongst ourselves, dreading the moment that Jamie would call for one of us to clean the chunks off him.

'Help.'

We could almost get away with pretending that we hadn't heard Jamie's feeble cry for help. We knew that inevitably the cries for help would get louder, and eventually we would have to go to his aid, but we could delay our response for just a few seconds longer. It was going to be messy.

'Help.'

'You know, I'd go if I could help,' Colin whispered.

Bev: You lying git. It's always the girls that go to help him.

Tom: Bollocks! We pull our weight.

Nikki: Remind us of the last time that you lot helped if there were any bodily fluids involved.

Tom: Let me think. You've put me on the spot.

'Help. **Help! Help!**'

The girls slowly rose from their seats and went to Jamie's aid. He was sitting in a pool of his own sick.

Jamie: I couldn't quite reach the sink.

Me: No shit, Sherlock.

Jamie: I need a shower.

Me: That's OK, we'll wait in the living room for you.

Jamie: Will you help me?

'Why me?' I ask, looking around me for the other girls only to find that they'd already fucked off into the other room.

'Because you like seeing my tail,' Jamie said with a cheeky little grin that made me feel a little uneasy.

I wheeled him into the shower room and started to help him strip off.

The smell of vomit made me baulk: I have the greatest respect for nurses managing to stop themselves puking all over their patients, it's fucking rancid.

I hauled Jamie onto his shower chair and then wheeled him under the running water.

'Can you help soap me down?' Jamie begged, slowly circling his nipples with his index fingers and wagging his tongue at me like a pervert.

Me: No.

Jamie: Ah, come on, help me.

Me: No.

Jamie: I'm going to tell everyone that you've touched my tail anyway.

I grabbed hold of a face cloth with Jamie's easy reach and edged towards him.

'Don't bother,' he said before shouting, 'That's it Julie, just there, ooh that feels so good, now suck on my right testicle, where are you putting that finger? Ooh, cheeky.'

At this point I was actually six feet away from Jamie, sitting on the toilet reading an old copy of *Zoo Magazine* that was lying around, with a couple of the pages stuck together.

By the time he'd finished in the shower everyone from our crowd had gone home. Neal and I left a clean Jamie still partying with his neighbours well after midnight and claiming that I had given his testicles a damn good lathering in the shower.

January

I mean, really, who in their right mind would want to fight over Phil the ice-cream man? He's about six feet tall, probably nine stones wringing wet. He's the type you wouldn't want to shag too hard in case you cut yourself, and wouldn't want to leave your kids with.

He's going bald, wears glasses (You get the picture.), and unless he's stinking, filthy rich, is absolutely hilarious or can lick his own eyebrows, you wouldn't give him a second glance.

Nikki says that he makes her laugh; isn't love blind. I've never even cracked a smile when I've been around the smarmy, lecherous little cunt.

So imagine mine and Amanda's surprise when, one crisp Saturday morning in January, June barged through the coffee shop doors and demanded that Nikki step outside with her for a chat. Even Nikki's daughter, Amy, was there to witness the spectacle, along with her own daughter, Ocean.

I'd never met June before but she looked like a right hard case: short, dark hair, a petite build, but you could just tell that she was going to kick Nikki's arse all over street.

June could have easily passed for the butch half of a lesbian couple: I'd have assumed that Phil was short for Phillipa if I'd had to take a guess at June's sexual orientation.

Nikki straightened up in her seat, took a deep breath and slowly got up from the table.

Nikki: Are you girls coming outside to offer a bit of moral support?

Amy: I am not letting my daughter watch her grandma fight in the middle of the street.

Me: It's a bit chilly, Nik, you'll be alright; you'll soon work up a sweat.

Nikki: Where's Bev?

Me: She should be here by now, just keep June talking until the cavalry arrives.

Nikki: You pack of cock-sucking whores.

Amanda: Good luck, Nikki.

I'm glad the girls decided to go outside for their 'chat' as there were five customers in the shop at the time. Now Amy, Amanda, the five customers and I settled ourselves into the bay windows at the front of the cafe and tried to lip-read Nikki and June's conversation from where they stood, across the street at the bus stop.

One of the customer's commented that this was better than an episode of East Enders, and, on this occasion, I had to agree with her.

Nikki was wearing her big, black winter coat, more to soften the body blows that June was about to inflict on her than to protect her from the cold weather. At least June wasn't wearing her Scholl sandals this time, or any high heels; she was dressed in hiking boots of some kind—she was definitely dressed for business.

I can honestly say that I have never seen a more gracefully choreographed start to a fight scene as the one that Nikki and June now performed.

June slapped Nikki across the face with her left hand, catching Nikki by surprise, as I think she was talking and may have been mid-sentence at the time. June then cupped the back of Nik's head with her right hand and brought it downwards to meet her upward-travelling, right knee. Nikki's head and June's knee made perfect contact, momentarily stunning Nikki.

June then made the heinous error of standing back to admire her handiwork, giving Nikki the vital moments she needed to compose herself and push June hard into the number 262 bus stop to crack her head on the metal time-table.

From inside the cafe we all took a sharp intake of breath as June crumpled to the pavement. It was then Nikki's turn to stand back with that all encompassing smirk on her face.

Amanda: It's like this in the movies, isn't it? They all wait for their opponent to compose themselves before hitting them again. I suppose it's for dramatic effect, but I would just get in there and kick fuck out of them until they couldn't get up and hit me back.

Me: I must remember to get the first punch in next time we're having a fist fight, Mand.

Amy: Dear God, let me be adopted.

Nikki and June's fight had now reduced to random bitch-slaps and hair pulling as they swung one another around the bus stop. The number 262 bus was actually due any minute and a small crowd had started to gather in the vicinity, mindful of the ensuing battle they all kept at a safe distance just in case they were accidentally caught in the fray.

Approximately one minute after the fight started we all heard a screech of brakes as Beverley pulled abruptly to a halt outside the café. She swung out of the driver's seat of her red, Hyundai Coupe, leapt across the road and, with the precision of a martial arts Grand Master, smacked both girls' heads together and dragged them across the street, by their hair, into the coffee shop.

'I've lost an earring,' Nikki sulked, rubbing her ear lobe between her thumb and index finger. 'It must be in the street somewhere.'

Bev: Along with your fucking dignity? That cock-sucker isn't worth it, you can both do much better than him. He drives an ice-cream van for fuck's sake, aim higher girls, *higher*, much fucking higher. I'm going to lock my car up, don't fucking start anything in here, you pair of twats.

No-one said a word until Bev came back, not even the customers, who sat quietly drinking their Earl Grey and English Breakfast teas—they'd probably need to take some blood-pressure medication by the time this saga was finished.

'Right then,' Bev announced as she waltzed back into the shop. 'Tea all round, Jules.'

I was a bit hesitant at having to leave the table as I thought I might miss some of the conversation; I've never in my life made three cups of tea so fast in my life, and never will again.

Amanda: I could do with a top-up Jules.

Me: No problems, help yourself, Mand.

Amanda mumbled something under her breath and I smiled a sickly sweet little smile at her; this was too much fun, she could get her own fucking tea.

Bev: Right then, you pair of crazy bastards, what's the story with this dickhead, Phil?

June: He's my husband, has been for nearly five years now.

June glared at Nikki and Nikki shuffled uneasily in her seat.

Nikki: He told me that he was separated from you when we met.

June: He was on a night out with the lads. Didn't you wonder why he wouldn't go home with you?

Nikki: He said that I meant more to him than a one night stand and that he wanted to get to know me better before we got jiggy.

Bev: There you go, Nik, you should have realised he was a liar as soon as he fed you that line of shite. Any single man with a pulse is going to get jiggy on the first night if you offer it to him on a plate.

Nikki: I did suck him off in the car park.

Now it was June's turn to shuffle uneasily in her seat.

Me: Eh? In my car? The Corsa? Oh, I feel sick just thinking about his DNA being all over my passenger seat. How much is valeting?

Bev looked at me with a raised eyebrow, which I wisely translated to mean, 'Shut up, Jules,' and continued, 'So, ladies, what's it going to be?'

Nikki: You can have him, he's really already yours, I don't want him back. I'm sorry if I hurt you, I did love him.'

June: I came here to give you a slap and tell you that you can have him: I threw him out three days ago. I was expecting to find him here with you until one of his mates told me that he was shagging some slag that supplies him with the ice-cream wafers. She's only seventeen, and she wears one of those eye patches because she's got a lazy eye.

Following about three seconds of shocked silence we all cracked up laughing, even June the poor cow. See, I told you Phil was a complete cock.

I brought some caramel slices to the table, topped up everyone's tea, and sat back down with the girls to talk crap shags, shitty chat up lines, and generally to bitch about men folk. Nikki even told us the full story about the guy she took home, who could barely get it up, and when he did he kept trying for a trip up *Bourneville Boulevard* ,saying, 'Oops, wrong hole again'. When he woke up the following morning he made some excuse about having a dog and needing to feed it, before rushing off home.

Nikki asked him what breed the dog was and he said it was a *damnation*, which she thought meant a Dalmatian, as he followed this answer up and said its name was Spot.

Bev: So, we can all agree that Phil is a knob.

We all nodded in agreement.

Bev: Fabulous.

February

Me: What are we going to do for Valentine's Day then?

Bev: I might check Dave's prostate.

Me: No, but really.

Bev: No really.

Me: OK then, for those of us who are not medically trained, what are we doing to do for Valentine's Day?

Nikki: I was thinking I might plot some revenge on Phil.

Me: Ooh, this sounds novel, more a festival of hate than a festival of love.

Nikki: Well, it's been a couple of months now since I've had any contact with the cock-sucking bastard so I reckon I might be able to get away with it now, he probably won't suspect that it's me.

Amanda: What are you going to do?

Nikki: I haven't decided yet; I need to give it some serious thought.

Me: What about you, Mand?'

Amanda: Everywhere is a complete fucking rip-off, I was thinking of cooking Colin a meal and having an early night.

Me: Rock and roll.

Amanda: Well, Valentine's Day falls on a school night this year.

Me: You look like you could do with a few early nights, Mand: you're looking pale.

Amanda: I'm knackered. It doesn't matter how much sleep I get, I'm just fucked all the time, and I feel a bit ropey really.

Nikki: Have you eaten something dodgy?

Amanda: Not that I know of. Here, let me out Jules, I need to go to the toilet.

I slid along one side of the booth and stood to one side at the end, to let Amanda pass. Amanda didn't manage to stand up; she just leaned forward and vomited all over my feet—it looked like that scene from *The Exorcist*. To top off the whole scene, I was wearing my Birkenstock flip-flops—fucking marvellous.

I stood there for a few seconds in horrified silence, wiggled my toes, and felt the chunks of Amanda's vomit slide in between them.

Me: *What … the fuck … happened …there?*

Amanda: I think I might be pregnant.

Bev: Really?! Are you sure? Have you taken a test?

Me: Can someone get me a damp cloth?

Bev: When did you have your last period?

Amanda: Ages ago, I can't remember when; I've never been that regular though.

Me: Please, can someone get me a cloth.

Nikki: What's the chance of you being pregnant? Have you been riding bareback?

Amanda: We haven't been as safe as we should have been.

Me: PLEASE GET ME A FUCKING CLOTH. IF I DON'T GET RID OF THESE FUCKING CHUNKS FROM BETWEEN MY TOES I'M GOING TO HEAVE!

Bev: If I get you a cloth will you shut up?

Me: YES!

Bev passed me a dish cloth and I slipped my feet gingerly out of my flip-flops, wiped the puke off them and carried my newly decorated Birkenstocks into the kitchen at the back of the shop. I quickly changed into some fresh shoes, slipped out of the back door of the cafe, and rushed over to the chemist to purchase a pregnancy testing kit.

The assistant behind the counter in the chemist looked at me suspiciously, I vaguely remembered her from school.

Assistant: Congratulations may be the order of the day then?

Me: It's not for me, thank god. I like children but your parents ruin the first half of your life and then your kids ruin the rest—you're fucked either way. Have you got any kids?

Assistant: Three of the little bastards. If the test is negative start using some contraception.

At last, a parent who is honest. I mean, I always say 'Congratulations' to anyone that tells me they're pregnant, what's the point of reminding them that their life is over?

I walked back into the Funky Doughnut and placed the ClearBlue pregnancy test in the middle of the table; we all stared at it for a few moments.

Bev: Would you like to be pregnant?

Amanda: I suppose so, why not?

'Right then, let's get this confirmed,' I said, opening the pack and unfolding the instructions. 'What do we do with this?'

Amanda: What are we looking for? Is it a blue cross or a blue strip?'

Me: No. I've gone for the digital version, it's even easier than that, it says 'pregnant or not pregnant'. You've got two options: you can piss on this stick for five seconds, don't forget to take the blue cap at the end off; or stand the stick in a pot of piss for twenty seconds. There's no pot provided.

Amanda: Have you got an egg cup I can use?

Me: No.

Amanda: What, you haven't got an egg cup?

Me: I haven't got one that I'm prepared to let you piss into. You'll have to go with the first option.

Amanda: I haven't got a full bladder and I'll probably piss all over my hand.

Pause ...

Amanda: Give me the fucking stick.

Bev: Hurry back, Mand, don't keep us all in suspense. Oh, have you been drinking any Dandelion and Burdock?

Amanda: Not since I was twelve.

Bev: OK then.

Amanda: Why, might it harm the baby?

Bev: What, Dandelion and Burdock? Don't be so fucking daft, but apparently it can give you a false reading on your pregnancy test.

Me: I can't find that on the instructions. I used to like Dandelion and Burdock.

Bev: And cream soda.

Me: No, cream soda was shit.

Bev: Fuck off, it was magic cream soda.

Me: We're going to have to agree to disagree on that one Bev, because cream soda is shit with a capital S.

Bev: Just go and take the test, Mand.

We watched Amanda disappear into the toilet.

Bev: Who do you reckon she'll have as godparents?

Nikki: If she's got any fucking sense, none of us.

Bev: Why not any of us?

Me: We don't even believe in God, why would she choose us?

Bev: It's got fuck all to do with believing in god, it's about being part of the kid's life.

Nikki: Don't be surprised but I think you'll find that a Christening ceremony, where godparents are sworn in if you like, is held in a church, which is, funnily enough, the house of God.

Bev: Whatever.

Me: Does it also mean baby-sitting duties? I wouldn't know what to do with it, you could help out in that department, Nik.

Nikki: Fuck off, I've done my bit. I do my best to get out of baby-sitting my own grandkids, I'm not looking after anyone else's.

Bev: I work shifts at the hospital so it could be difficult to arrange.

Me: And you want to be godmother? You'd be a shit godmother.

Bev: So, you think you'd be a better choice?

Me: Do I fuck, I'm just saying that we'd all be shit godparents. I'll buy it a Christmas and birthday present but that's about it. Here she comes. And?

Amanda: I don't know yet, I've only just pissed on it.

Me: Did you use the new hand-wash I've bought? Milk and honey, it's lovely isn't it?

'Funnily enough, I didn't pay much attention to the hand-wash, I'm more interested in finding out if I'm going to have a baby,' Amanda confessed as she stared intently at the ClearBlue pregnancy stick.

We all stared at Amanda for what seemed like an eternity.

Me: Bloody hell, how long's this going to take? It says three minutes on the box.

'Er … it says I'm pregnant,' Amanda announced.

Bev: We don't want to be godparents.

Amanda: What?

Me: Congratulations, Mand, I don't know what to say.

Bev: How do you feel?

'Er … shocked I suppose,' Amanda replied, a smile slowly appearing on her face.

Me: Say something, Nik.

Nikki: You've ruined your life.

Me: Something *nice*, Nik.

Nikki: I'm really happy for you.

Me: Do you feel different?

Amanda: No wonder I've been feeling knackered lately, I'm knocked up.

With that Tom and Colin arrived at the coffee shop.

'What fantastic timing, we can all watch Amanda ruin Colin's life,' Nikki mumbled.

Tom: We've just been called homosexuals.

Bev: Who by?

Tom: Some blokes driving past us in a Renault Clio. I mean, how can they call us homosexuals when *they're* driving a Renault Clio?

Nikki: Why? What were you doing?

Tom: Helping Colin across the road.

Bev: What were you holding? His cock?

Tom: No, Beverley, I had hold of his arm because you know he can't walk straight across a pedestrian crossing, he walks into the cars waiting for the lights to change. It's like watching a fucking bad episode of Starsky and Hutch. And these two blokes, let me again emphasise that they were driving a Renault Clio, it wasn't even the sports model, rolled down their window and shouted 'Homosexuals!' at us.

Colin: And then I asked where the homosexuals were and Tom said that it was us!

Nikki: It appears that we're getting a better class of scumbag in the neighbourhood. They'd normally just shout 'Puff!' and be done with it, but *homosexual?* That's almost middle class.

Me: Yeah, but I bet they couldn't spell it.

Nikki: So Colin, how's it going with Amanda?

Colin: Are you trying to catch me out, you conniving bitch? I know she's here, I can smell her perfume.

Amanda: Really, is it that strong?

Colin: Not as strong as Tom's BO, but you know I've got a sensitive nose. Anyway, what's happening?

Bev: Mand was just telling us how good you weren't in bed.

Colin: Ah, now fuck off Bev, you're only jealous because I'm not digging you. I'm pretty good with these hands of mine, you know, and I must say that your friend gives fabulous head.

Amanda: Colin?!

Colin: Well you do. Last week I thought I was going to pop a bollock.

Amanda: Er ... thanks, I suppose.

Me: Do you want a drink Colin?

Colin: A tea please, Jules.

Nikki took Tom by the arm and we all moved to another booth.

Colin: Where's everyone gone? Why are we alone? Are you doing to dump me?

'No, it's marginally better than that,' we heard Amanda say before she started speaking in hushed tones to tell Colin the news.

She must have been beating around the bush, talking about the events of the day or something because there was no reaction from Colin, unless of course he's the coolest person in the world, which he isn't.

Colin is like me in that we wave our hands around when we speak, our body language is very expressive of how we're feeling, and when he stopped moving and his body went deathly still, I knew she'd told him.

He sat like a statue, for what seemed like an eternity, before lurching toward Amanda and kissing her passionately on the left eye (It must be a blind thing.), jumping up and shouting, 'I'm gonna be a dad, I'm gonna be a dad. Fucking hell!'

Bev: Happy then?

Colin: Hell yes!

'Well done mate,' Tom said, shaking Colin's hand vigorously. 'You always said it was big enough to fill a pram.'

Me: So when are you going to tell your mum and dad, Mand?'

Amanda: At the weekend, we're going around for Sunday dinner. My mum will be over the moon, she thought she'd never be a grandma.

Colin: What about your dad?

Amanda: Well he thinks no one is good enough for me anyway but he'll be fine.

Colin: What? He doesn't think I'm good enough for you?

Amanda: Not really.

Colin: Why?

Amanda: The fact that you're a masseur put him off a bit: he just thinks that you're a bit of a pervert really, you know, feeling the clients up.

Colin: A pervert?! Your dad thinks I'm a pervert?!

Amanda: Just a bit, not completely, but he'll be fine once he's come around to the idea.

Tom: Have you slipped any of your clients a finger Colin?

Colin: Only you, Tom. Let's get back onto the subject of how your dad came around to thinking I'm a pervert, Mand.

Amanda: To be honest, I probably had a small part to play in this story.

Colin: Pray tell.

Amanda: I told my dad that you more or less molested me after you'd given me a massage one time, I was only joking but he didn't think it was funny, my mum laughed, so he just assumed that you would provide the same after sales service to some other clients. You know, like a happy ending.

Colin: Fucking great.

Amanda: I didn't tell him about you shagging that hooker in Amsterdam.

Colin: Well there's some good news, I suppose. Let's look at the positives. It does explain why you've been an emotional wreck over the last couple of weeks: I caught her crying at some advertisement for life insurance on the telly the other day. I asked her what the matter was and she tried to tell me in-between sobs. You know what women are like when they cry, they talk in a pitch only a fucking dog can hear. Roll on Sunday dinner.

When I look at Bev, Nik, Mand and me, I'd probably only get jiggy with Mand because the rest of us can be hard work sometimes. We never lose an argument with blokes either, we may change our minds but we never lose, and around *that time of the month* events can be interesting.

I don't get PMT; however, for about three days before my period my bullshit tolerance level is fucking zero. And I can never remember when I'm due on, it happens roughly every four weeks but it's not like I mark it on the calendar with a red dot or anything—it doesn't bother me when it happens, it just happens.

On the bullshit tolerance issue, just before my period I get the impression that blokes usually spend fifty percent of their time talking about footy or rugby, reminiscing about being drunk and pissing in inappropriate places, and pussy or their cocks. The other fifty percent of the time they talk complete and utter shite. They're just fucking weird.

When they do talk shite, I usually just ignore what they say, roll my eyes and occasionally rock my hand back and forth in a wanking motion. But, just before *rag week*, I am possessed by Satan and I have to have the last word in any argument / discussion / you're making it into an argument / you're a complete bastard / look, you've made me cry.

Nikki's even worse, sometimes she gets so angry she spits when she talks: she loses it big time. I've known Bev to knock blokes out; she must get her period every two weeks. *Nightmare.*

This brings me nicely onto my three PMT stories for the month of February: the first of which involves me giving Neal a first degree burn on his left testicle, with my GHD hair straighteners.

Like I said before, I don't keep track of when I'm due on but Neal has the timing worked out to the exact day and revels in winding me right up.

Neal doesn't tend to argue with me, he just does things to annoy me. For example, he'll never replace the toilet roll when he's used the last sheet, he'll just leave an empty tube on the holder, especially when I go to take a dump. He could possibly leave empty toilet roll tubes on the holder all month round, but there's only three days when I feel the need to stab him in the head with a fork over this particular issue.

Neal will say something ridiculous, I will lose the plot and argue back furiously, and then he'll give me a cheeky little wink and I'll tell him to go fuck himself. He's not even funny—he's actually starting to get on my tits.

Take the other evening for instance. Neal can never just blow out a candle, he has to play with the melted wax by tipping the lighted candle back and forth, seeing how close to the edge he can get the wax without it spilling over the edge. And when he finally does blow the candle out he doesn't just gently blow it, *oh no*, after he's got wax all over the top of the candle he then blows out the flame like a three-year-old blows out the candles on their birthday cake: I find wax and his spit halfway up the wall and all over the bedside table. Wanker!

So, this particular evening, after he'd dropped the red candle that sits on my bedside cabinet on my cream eighty percent wool axminster, I fucking lost it.

I was sitting at the dressing table, straightening my hair in front of the mirror, when he came up behind me, and apologised profusely for dropping the candle instead of actually cleaning the mess up.

I saw his reflection in the mirror and must have misjudged how close he was stood near me, like in the overtaking mirrors on your car when it says, 'Objects in the mirror may be closer than they appear'. Anyway, I turned around to bitch at him and, as I was holding my straighteners in my right hand, I used them to point at him and accidentally on purpose caught his left bollock with one of the one hundred and eighty degree, pre-heated, ceramic plates. Needless to say, he dropped to the floor nursing his nuts.

I said, 'Sorry,' and finished straightening my hair; well, I only had one section left to do, and then we went to the bathroom and I made Neal hold his nuts under the cold tap in the basin for a couple of minutes. You should have heard him whinge, mind you the water is pretty cold in February.

He ended up with a massive blister on his ball though, and I know when I get a blister on my foot from wearing new shoes I always pop it with a needle and it always feels better, but Neal was having none of it.

He whinged and moaned for so long that I finally ended up calling Bev and asking her if she'd come over and have a look at it. She said that she was busy but if I could give her three and a half minutes she'd be there—something about she'd have to see this. While we were waiting for Bev I decided to call

Nik and Mand and update them on the medical emergency—we did giggle.

'Come on then stud, let's have a look,' were Bev's first words to Neal when she walked through the door into the bedroom.

Neal: Are you sure you know what you're doing?

Bev: I'm a nurse, dickhead, of course I know what I'm doing. We did an entire module on burns when I was training.

Neal gingerly pulled down his undies.

'You shave your balls, eh?' was Bev first observation, as she gave Neal a cheeky wink. 'Porn stars shave their balls you know, apparently it makes their cocks look bigger. Anyway, you've only got a first degree burn, it didn't even go through to the second layer of skin.'

Me: Should we pop the blister?

Neal: Will you fuck off?

Bev: No just leave it; it'll heal over the next few days.

Neal had to sleep on his back with his legs apart: I asked him how much of the bed he needed. He grunted some profanity under his breath and I started giggling again.

The second story involves Dave and Beverley who often work the same shifts at James Cook Hospital, on the trauma unit. Dave hadn't bought Bev anything for Valentine's Day: he *had* bought her a card and a bunch of flowers from some service station on his way over to her place but, as Bev later said, that is the equivalent of buying her absolutely fuck all. There was no real effort made and she was well pissed off.

On the Saturday morning after Valentine's Day, both Bev and Dave were working the morning shift, from six o'clock until two in the afternoon. Dave was supposedly going away with some friends for the weekend and had brought his overnight bag to work with him, so that he wouldn't have to go home first to change before he set off.

While Dave was away from his desk, Bev decided to write him a saucy, little note, telling him what she was going to do to him when he got back on the Sunday night. She carefully folded the note up, sprayed some perfume on it (Didn't you stop doing that when you left school?) and thought the best place to leave it would be in Dave's toiletry bag, as he was sure to find it when he brushed his teeth; as opposed to hiding it somewhere in between his undies, because it was a boy's weekend and he might not even change his underwear.

Bev lifted Dave's overnight bag onto the desk in front of her at the nurse's station, opened it up and quickly unzipped his toiletry bag to find a three pack of Rough Rider condoms staring her in the face, complete with a picture of some leather clad slut on the front straddling a motorbike.

'You fucking cunt,' was Bev's statement on the find, at round about the same time as some lovely, white-haired, old lady approached the counter. The lovely, white-haired, old lady took a sharp intake of breath upon hearing Bev's comment and Bev quickly explained that it wasn't directed at her, but at Bev's cheating, or soon to be cheating, boyfriend.

The lovely, white-haired, old lady advised that the best thing to do would be to staple her love note to said box of Rough Rider condoms; not just the one staple mind, but to empty the entire stapler into the box, until she could no longer make out the leather clad slut on the front. Bev took the lovely, white-haired, old lady's advice and placed the massacred box of condoms back into their rightful place.

At this point it was just coming up to two o'clock and Bev and Dave's shift was coming to an end. Dave returned to the nurses' station, already having changed his clothes, and announced to Bev and the white-haired, old lady that, as Bev's Valentine's present, he was taking her away for the night to a day spa in the Lake District and he'd already packed a bag for her and it was in the back of his car.

Bev was gobsmacked and couldn't bring herself to admit her dastardly deed to Dave. Obviously, he found out what Bev had done when they got to their hotel bedroom and he went to brush his teeth; he laughed and said that he was hurt that she could think that he would do such a thing, and the least she could do was give him a blowjob.

This leads me onto the third little story linked to good old PMT, that Nikki had dreamed up during what was to be an eventful pre-period week.

Still hurt by Phil's betrayal (How dare he sleep with his wife?), Nikki planned her revenge.

On a crisp afternoon, late in the month of February, I received a call from Nikki urgently requesting our presence in one of the streets that make up Phil's ice-cream run.

Ice-cream run? He used to call it a 'run' to make it sound exciting; he sold broken wafers, Cornettos and 99s—Wanker!

'Don't bring Mand,' Nikki said.

'Why?' I asked.

'She'll be sick,' was Nikki's reply.

Bev drove: she's a fucking maniac, and we arrived at our destination to find a large crowd gathered around Phil's ice-cream van.

'What's happening, Nik?' Bev enquired.

Nikki: Let's take a closer look, shall we?

We slowly, at breakneck speed, made our way towards the crowd. We noticed the road behind the van was spattered with blood. As we reached the front of the crowd we were greeted by a gruesome sight.

Tied to the back of the ice-cream van, by a long piece of old rope, was a large, black dog. Do I need to go any further? OK then, I will.

The large, black, now three-legged dog had obviously been dragged some considerable distance by Phil's ice-cream van. The large, black, three-legged, earless pooch was not looking in the best of shape: I wasn't too sure if it still had a nose.

Phil was protesting his innocence to the Policeman at the scene, who was taking notes in his little, black book; I'd like to get hold of that notebook because we couldn't hear the conversation. Phil was actually in tears, he was sobbing and kept wiping his nose on the sleeve of his white, catering coat.

'Nik, I know that Phil is a cheating, smarmy cock-sucker but on this occasion I am going to have to ask if there are any boundaries that you wouldn't cross if someone really pissed you off?' I asked, nonchalantly.

Bev: I'm fucking speechless. Didn't you used to be a vegetarian, Nik? I saw a documentary once on serial killers, a lot of them start off killing people's pets before they move onto people. What were you thinking?

Nik: My next door neighbour found the dog dead in her allotment yesterday.

Me: Thank fuck for that.

Nik: It was really heavy carrying it into the back of my car and then driving it over to Phil's place and tying it to the back of his van. Luckily he always parks his van in his carport, ready to drive straight out on his run, he's a bit anal like that, so I knew he wouldn't actually see the dead dog when he got into the van.

Bev: So, you actually had a plan? You saw the dead dog and this little plan just popped into your head? You're going to have to remortgage your home to pay for the therapy required after this little episode; you are one sick little puppy, Nicola.

Nik: Have you noticed the finishing touch on the back of the van?

Phil's ice-cream van is cream with swirling patterns in pink, blue and green across all sides. On the back of ice-cream van there is usually signage reading, 'Mind That Child,' in big, red lettering, but today Phil's van was sending a different message.

Me: 'I fuck kids.' That's a bit harsh isn't it Nik?

Nik: He's shagging a seventeen-year-old, she's not an adult.

Bev: I am never going to fuck with you, Nik.

Nik: I wouldn't recommend it, Beverley. Do you think Phil may have experienced a drop in sales today? Mmm … do you?

Bev: How did you manage to change that? It looks really good.

Nik: I designed it on the computer at work using Microsoft Word, marvellous piece of software you know, and then the guys in the print room produced it on this clear plastic laminate, it's really sticky stuff. He'll need a complete re-spray to sort it out.

Bev: I'm still a bit uncomfortable with the dog thing.

At that moment, Phil made eye contact with me. I gave him a cheeky little wink and we disappeared into the crowd. Revenge, it's wrong but it feels so fucking right.

We walked slowly back to our cars, stealing backward glances at what would become known as 'The Ice-Cream Incident', and giggled our little heads off—well me and Nikki did, Bev was still a bit upset about the dead pooch.

All in all, I was only gone from the coffee shop for about forty-five minutes. As Bev drove me back there I pondered what to do with my life next; I was getting a bit bored after ten months of serving Earl Grey tea and custard slices to pensioners.

I thought I'd done really well in the customer service stakes but, as far as I was aware, none of the oldies had written me into their wills yet—the tight fuckers.

I needn't have worried about what to do next really because when we got back to the cafe the fucking thing was on fire.

'What the fuck is going on here?' I questioned the fireman who restrained me from approaching the coffee shop.

'There's a fire,' he responded.

Me: No shit, Sherlock.'

Flames were spewing out of both of the upstairs windows, blackening the outside walls and licking the roof tiles. Through the windows in the shop front I could see that the kitchen was also ablaze.

All we could do was watch. After five minutes I remembered that we usually had quite a few customers in the shop at this time of day and I wondered if anyone was trapped inside.

I saw Neal making his way towards us, pulling Colin through the crowd with one hand and holding a squirming, angry Beano in the other.

Me: What's going on here?

'Don't worry Jules, we're OK, thanks for asking,' he replied sarcastically. 'I was in the backyard,' he continued, 'sorting out the rubbish when I looked up at the upstairs windows and could see the living room was on fire. I tried to go up the stairs but there was too much smoke.'

Me: Where's Marie? Is she OK?

Neal: I send her to the 'cash and carry', we were running out of coffee.'

Me: Really, I only just bought some last week.

Neal: Business is booming Jules.

Me: Did you leave Colin in charge?

Neal: What?

Me: You know, the blind guy?

Colin: What's your point here like?

Me: Keep your voice down, Colin. I'm just wondering if I'm actually covered by the insurance I'm paying an absolute fortune for.

Colin: Ah, point taken.

Neal started to speak and decided against it, his eyes flicked nervously between me, Colin, Bev and Nikki. Fortunately for Neal all my sharp knives were happily burning away in the kitchen and therefore I was unable to take one in my hand and inflict multiple stab wounds on the daft cunt until he was dead. I knew it wasn't Neal's fault but there was no one else to blame; he'd have to take the brunt of it.

So, we just stood and watched the fire consume the coffee shop and all my personal belongings: my oil paintings of the Eiffel Tower and the Moulin Rouge from Paris, my silk rug from China, my war mask from some dodgy blokes on a beach in Kenya and my kangaroo testicle bottle opener from Australia.

That was all the sentimental stuff gone, and then there were more pressing matters, like the fact that I didn't have a clean pair of undies to my name or a toothbrush, or fuck all really—added to this was the fact that earlier that day I'd squirted some jam from one of the doughnuts down the front of the t-shirt I was wearing—all in all, it had been quite an eventful day.

Oh, and my car keys were smouldering away somewhere in the cafe, so I couldn't use my car to go and buy any replacement clothes, and Marks & Spencer would be closed by the time I got there anyway. Even if I did get there before closing time I didn't have any money, well that's a lie I had about £3.50 in spare change in my pocket, not enough for a new pair of undies, well not from Marks & Spencer at any rate.

That's karma for you, laugh at someone else's expense, ideally at someone who is a complete cock like Phil, and then your house burns down—I can't fucking win.

After the firemen had gone, and the police had taken a statement from Neal, there was the pressing need for a place to stay that night. Jamie had a spare room and, even though he wasn't answering his mobile, he was always in at this time of night, especially on a school night, so we started walking over to his place.

I was still feeling pretty numb: I felt sure that I would shed a tear pretty soon but then, as always, the optimist (I know, can you believe it?) kicked in and I started to remember that I was getting bored with the shop anyway. It had been a whole ten months now, so perhaps I should try something new. I might even break the magical twelve month barrier with my next venture—we can all fucking dream.

After ringing Jamie's doorbell for the sixth time I got well pissed off; I knew the awkward, little twat was in: all the lights were on and I could hear music playing in the background. So we walked around to the back of his place to knock on the patio doors leading into his bedroom.

We could hear muffled voices through the glass, someone was barking orders at someone: it sounded really aggressive. I hammered on the glass and the voices in Jamie's bedroom went quiet.

Jamie: Who is it?

Me: Me. Are you alright?

Jamie: I'm a bit busy at the moment, what do you want?

Me: A place to stay, the coffee shop's gone and burned down.

'Really?' a female voice exclaimed.

Me: Marie?

Marie: Yes?

Me: What's going on here?

Jamie: The usual sort of things that go on between consenting adults in bedrooms all over the country, Julie.

Me: I need a jumper; I'm freezing my tits off out here. If you give me a jumper and let Beano in, we'll fuck off and come back in a couple of hours. You should be finished by then.

Jamie: We might be.

Beano was getting annoyed, he'd started hissing at Neal and I had visions of having to peel kitty from Neal's face. The patio door slowly opened and an old, faded, woollen jumper was thrust towards me. Beano took the opportunity to bolt through the open door.

Me: Not this old thing, have you got something nicer?

'Don't be ungrateful,' Jamie grunted, trying his best to cover himself with the net curtain.

Me: Thanks, Jamie. Are you wearing nipple clamps?

There was no answer as the patio doors slid shut.

We wandered along the promenade, lined with old, four and five storey, Victorian terraced houses: the local council had started a 'Victorian Day' in August some years previously. I remembered seeing the Red Arrows flying down Ruby Street the first year, it looked like they only missed the top of the houses by a few feet, and loads of people wore Victorian attire. The evening finished with a firework and laser display off the end of Saltburn Pier; but like most events in small town England, 'Victorian Day' died on its arse over the next three or so years. The residents stopped wearing their Victorian outfits; the Red Arrows were definitely the highlight. Of course, just like the Victorians, some of the residents of Saltburn only bathed twice a year; for them it was Victorian Day everyday.

Neal and I grabbed some fish and chips and walked over to Tom's place. Tom was out, probably examining his sperm under a microscope over at Ashlea's place, but he always left a key in one of the plant pots at the back of his place, so we let ourselves in.

Neal suggested that we should shag in Tom's Barbers Chair and I thought, 'Why not? We were mid stroke when someone pulled into one of the car parking spaces at the front of Tom's shop and shone their high-beam straight onto my arse; then they started blowing their horn, before driving off—wankers.

Two cups of tea and five milk chocolate HobNobs later, Jamie called Tom's place to see where we were, I answered and Jamie thought we were staying at Tom's place and got all sulky; honestly, he's like a five year old sometimes.

So we left a note in place of the milk chocolate HobNobs, saying, 'Yum Yum Pig's Bum', locked up and walked back to Jamie's place.

Jamie: So it's all burned down then? How did that happen?

Neal: Were you wearing nipple clamps earlier this evening?

Jamie: Did you manage to save anything?

Me: I thought you'd be a bit restricted on the old S & M thing with your brittle bone condition going on.

Jamie: Were you insured?

Me: Does Marie stand on your testicles with her stilettos? I saw that on a movie once.

Jamie: When do you think you'll be able to re-open?

Me: Does Mummy spank Daddy?

Jamie: Right, shut the fuck up.

Me: I'm telling your mum.

Jamie: You are not.

Me: Does she know that you've shagged one of your carers before?

Jamie: No.

Me: Where's Marie? She'll have to stay here tonight too.

Jamie: She's in bed. I think she's a bit too embarrassed to come out.

Me: She'll have to eventually.

Jamie: Well how long are you planning on staying here?

Me: Just the one or two, er ...months.

Jamie: That's just great.

Neal: Thanks for letting us stay.

Jamie: You're fucking welcome.

That night, in Jamie's spare bedroom, staring up at the energy saving light bulb which gave off as much light as a candle, we talked about what we should do next.

Me: I've always wanted to travel, perhaps this is a hint that I should crack on and do something about it.

Neal: Having a home is overrated.

Me: There's no way that I'm living in a cardboard box on the side of the road somewhere, I've got too many friends with spare beds that I can sponge off. I'm not used to that sort of life.

Neal: And you think I am? You don't get used to that sort of life.

Me: I'm cold enough as it is, Jamie never turns the heating up past sixteen degrees the tight fucker.

Jamie: Will you two shut up, some of us are trying to sleep.

Neal: Take your nipple clamps off then, you'll sleep better, Jamie.

'Let's go to Paris,' I whispered.

Neal: I fucking hate the French.

Me: Since when? Which French people do you know?

Neal: The French have got this thing about the English.

Me: Probably because we go over to France and ask everyone to speak English, you've at least got to try to speak the lingo. Then when you've made a complete dick of yourself, they kind of warm to you.

Neal: Can you speak French?

Me: Can I fuck? I'm sure I'll remember some of my old school-girl French when I'm living there though. I'll probably be living on omelettes in the short term though.

Neal: What's omelette in French?

Me: The same as here but you can put a bit of a French accent on and get away with it. I think they might spell omelette *o..m..e..l..e..t*, you can spot it a mile off on the menu.

Neal: What other meals can you order in French?

Me: Erm … *un baguette.*

Neal: A bread roll?

Me: *Un pomme.*

Neal: Is that an apple?

Me: Yep, *un pomme de terre.* That's a potato.

Neal: We're hitting all the major food groups here, Jules, do you know any meats in French?

Me: Er … *un chien*, ah no, that's a dog.'

Neal: So we're off to Paris via Korea then?

Me: *Un cheval*, I think that's a horse.

Neal: I think I'll be vegetarian, god knows what I'm going to end up eating.

Me: Well, I spent a couple of weeks in the middle of France with a company I used to work with. It was just outside of Limoges, they make pottery there apparently, I think it was called *Breve de Gallard*. Anyway, I was vegetarian at the time and no fucker spoke English. I ate omelettes the whole time; I didn't shit for a week.'

'We'll think more clearly in the morning,' Neal said, as he leaned over to kiss me goodnight, 'Go to sleep.'

The next morning, bright and early at around ten thirty, Neal and I went to see the coffee shop in the light of day: it wasn't a pretty sight. The roof had fallen in and all that remained of the shop were the four outside walls. The fire brigade had done a good job of containing the blaze as both the estate agent, on the left hand side of the cafe, and the jewellers on the right were both open for business as usual.

I felt numb; I had no feelings really. I just kept thinking about Paris.

We walked to the bank to get some cash. I'd had my business account with the local branch Barclays for over ten months now and I even knew the girl on the counter, I used to go to school with the witch. And today, of all days, Andrea Connor, Bank Clerk extraordinaire, decided to ask me that old chestnut: 'Do you have any identification?'

Me: Are you fucking joking Andrea?

Andrea glared at me uncaringly.

Andrea: It's standard procedure now to ask for identification for all over the counter withdrawals, when you don't present an ATM card.

Me: The coffee shop burned down yesterday, I have lost all my worldly possessions and have been wearing the same underwear for two days in a row, do you really want to piss me off today?

'If you don't play nice, I won't give you any cash,' Andrea replied, smiling through her gritted teeth.

Me: What do you want me to do?

Andrea: We'll just go through some security questions. What's your date of birth?

Me: The twenty second of the ninth, nineteen sixty-nine.

Andrea: What's the approximate balance you have in the account?

Me: Eighty-six thousand, six hundred and fifty-nine pounds and about twelve pence.

Neal: Approximately then?

Andrea: Err … yeah, that's right.

Me: I'm a bit anal about checking my bank balance.'

Neal: You don't say.'

Andrea: You were always a bit weird at school.

Me: It comes from when I used to work for a bank, and if you went overdrawn you could get sacked. Now I can check it on the internet.

Andrea: And you recently made a purchase at Next, can you remember how much that was for?

Me: Actually, I even surprised myself on this one, I spent a fortune, I think it was around three hundred and fifty-nine pounds and ninety-eight pence. I bought myself a new coat, some boots and a couple of jumpers, oh, and a pair of jeans. Fucking hell, I didn't even get to wear them, they were still in a bag at the bottom of the wardrobe.

'Right, I'll just check that this withdrawal is OK with my manager,' Andrea said, as she climbed down from her chair and disappeared into one of the rooms behind the counter.

Neal: What if they won't give you any money?

Me: That's not going to happen.

Neal: Why not?

'Because Andrea knows I'll cause carnage in this branch if I don't get some cash today, she knows who I am and she's just being an awkward twat.' I was saying, as I turned my head back towards the counter to see Andrea had already returned to her seat and was listening intently to my conversation, with her arms folded and one eyebrow raised.

Me: I'll have five hundred for now please, actually, on second thoughts, make that a thousand.

Andrea: The Manager's said that I can only give you two hundred pounds without any identification.

Me: Can you please tell your manager that I'm going to rip all the pens from the counter, then I'm going to drop my pants and wipe my arse on a Barclays deposit slip if I don't get a thousand pounds from this bank today. I've banked here for over ten months now and you went to school with me, so tell him he can stick his identification up his fucking arse.

Andrea: Only joking, he said that's fine. Would you like fifties or twenties?

Me: I'll have twenties please, and thank you for your assistance today, you've been most helpful.

Andrea: You're welcome.

Andrea passed me one thousand pounds over the counter in an envelope. I passed the money to Neal and then ran from one end of the counter to the other pulling all the deposit and withdrawal slips from their little plastic containers and throwing them into the air shouting, 'I'm rich, I'm rich.'

As I skipped out of the branch I could vaguely hear Andrea calling me a complete cock, and I couldn't have cared less.

My accountant managed to squeeze us into his diary at short notice, and then kept us waiting forty-five minutes for the privilege—wanker. He didn't even have any good magazines in his waiting room, who reads the *Financial Times*?

My accountant was an old school friend too, Mike Lesbirel, and had been a complete knob all the way through school. He was one of those nerds that ends up successful and loaded, he still a knob but now he's a knob who drives a Porsche.

He also had a stutter, which he used to great effect to ensure that you always went over your thirty minute time-slot, and then he'd charge you for an hour of his time.

'I knew you'd fuck it up, Jules,' was Mike's opening statement as he showed us into his office.

'Really?' I replied sarcastically. 'Firstly, I'd like to ask how you managed to come to that conclusion and secondly, only the two questions mind as I know you charge by the fucking question, where's your stutter gone? Surely you should have said, 'I knew you'd f-f-f-fuck it up, Jules.'

Mike: I've been having speech therapy.

Me: Anyway, enough of the pleasantries, time is money, what happens next?

Mike: Luckily the insurance company doesn't know that you regularly left the blind guy in charge.

Me: Do you mean C-C-Colin?

Pause ... death stare. I'd have this smart, little fucker back to square one in the stutter stakes in no time—fifty pounds for half an hour, the greedy bastard.

Mike: Luckily, I took you for a complete amateur and knew you'd go into a venture like this with only half a plan at best. So, I insured you to the max and you're going to come out of this little incident fucking loaded.

Me: Really?

Mike: Yes, really.

Me: Thanks for that Mike.

Mike: You're welcome. That'll be one hundred and fifty pounds, if you could pay at the reception that would be greatly appreciated.

Me: We've only been in here five minutes.

Mike: You're welcome, now fuck off.

'Get in there!' Neal shouted as we left Mike's office. 'What are we going to do now?'

Me: Right now I'm going to get something to eat.

Neal: You've just had your breakfast.

Me: You call that out-of-date muesli and a morning tea biscuit breakfast? I'm going to have to visit one of my previous competitors, as much as it pains me to do so.

Neal: I think I'll have eggs Benedict then, seeing as we're celebrating. Then we'll go shopping. Obviously, we'll be buying the essentials, like some new undies, and possibly some suntan lotion and a swimming costume.

Me: It's February.

Neal: We'll need a holiday to get over the trauma of losing all our personal effects, don't forget you're loaded now with all that insurance money.

Me: My passport's gone up in smoke, I'll need to get that replaced first. You don't even have a passport, you've never been further than Leeds.

Neal: I went to Scotland once, it's another country you know.

Me: I know Mike said I'm going to be loaded, but he doesn't mean *Richard Branson loaded*, you know. I might not have to work for a year but then I'm going to start eating into my savings: I'll have to find another job.

Neal: What are you going to do?

Me: Fuck knows, not another coffee shop though, it was boring. Anyway, let's get some breakfast.

We were treated to burnt toast and burnt coffee; I think it was instant coffee and I didn't know that you could burn instant coffee.

'Please tell me our stuff was better than this shite,' I said, curling my lip up at the offering in front of us.

Neal: You and Tesco's had a good thing going back at the Funky Doughnut. Do you reckon that the customer's knew our food wasn't home made?

Me: The majority of them see it as an achievement to make it through the day without pissing themselves or suffering a stroke, I don't think they give a shit about homemade cakes.

Neal: There was no healthy living going on there mind, I don't think I served one skinny latte or skinny cappuccino the whole time I was there. Mrs Jackson once asked Marie which herbal teas we offered, Marie mumbled something about Tetley's and Mrs Jackson ordered a hot chocolate instead. I don't think hot chocolate is a good choice when you've got Type 2 diabetes.

Me: I don't think I'll give a shit by the time I'm seventy either.

Neal: You don't give a shit now, have you weighed yourself lately?

Me: What the fuck is that supposed to mean? Don't sugar coat it for me, baby.

Neal: You're just getting a bit chunky, that's all.

Me: Chunky?

Neal: Yeah, just a bit though.

Me: Chunky?

Neal: Can we have the bill please? So you fancy Paris, eh? What about Italy? I've always fancied Rome.

Me: Well I can be chunky in Paris and you can be a cock in Rome.

Neal: Yeah, I'd love to go and visit the Coliseum.

Me: On your fucking own.

Funnily enough that was the end of that particular conversation, so we went shopping. We had so much to buy: have you ever thought about losing everything in a fire and then having to replace it all?

I like shopping but we had to go by public transport and then cart about twenty carrier bags back to Jamie's, it was torture. I got the locks changed on the car a few days later so at least I got some independence back.

When we received our insurance claim forms later that week we found out what a painful task it was to complete them—I'd rather take a disc grinder to my nipples. We didn't have any toothbrushes and toothpaste, or a hairbrush; we had to buy everything all over again.

March

We'd all lost our central meeting place. We'd grown accustomed to our end of day get togethers, so we had to flit between everyone's homes to catch up.

I decided to get into shape, as Neal said I was looking a little 'chunky', and I enrolled to go to a yoga class. It was Bikram yoga and the class was held in Redcar by the sea.

For those of you who don't know anything about yoga (I know I don't.), Bikram yoga is done in a heated room. The only way you can keep rooms that warm in Redcar is to close all the doors and windows and keep the heating on high. As a result, the room just smells of arse—inhaling other people's poo particles does not make for a pleasant Yoga experience.

I enrolled into yoga because it seemed like the easy choice; *my arse*, it's rock hard. I was sweating like a rapist; I didn't know my head could hold that much blood, I nearly passed out in the first five minutes and we hadn't even finished the warm up.

Anyway, I lasted two of those classes before I made the miraculous discovery that if you limited your food intake the weight just dropped off. I now only ate two chocolate biscuits per day and one slice of cake rather than numerous biscuits and lots of cake and doughnuts.

Mand's bump was starting to show. She'd finished with the puking but was now at the 'fuck all fits me' stage and the 'Surely, I'm not fat enough to fit into those fucking, heinous maternity clothes yet?' stage— joggy bottoms it is then, Mand; honestly, they're the height of fashion, especially when the elastic starts to show through the waistband— sexy as.

Bev was still getting jiggy with Dave, he seems alright actually. Bev must have liked him because she didn't treat him like a dog, but she still lost it regularly and Dave reckoned she's a great shag when she's angry.

Nikki was still single and finally seemed to be over Phil. Whichever way you look at it Phil was definitely over Nikki; I haven't seen his van lately either. I hope he's dead.

Tom was joined at the hip with Ashlea and had even started to give unwanted parenting advice to Amanda and Colin. Colin was expecting his parenting skills to be limited to giving the baby some sort of pat every time it come near him; Amanda reminded him that she was going to give birth to a child and not a Golden Retriever.

All in all, my accountant reckoned it would take a couple of months to get the money from the insurance company, as the roof had collapsed the Fire Brigade were struggling to give a root cause for the fire; which was probably a good thing. God knows how it got started.

I found out three weeks later.

We were invited to a party at Neal's mate's house in Loftus. I'd never met this guy Adam before, but Neal reckoned that he was a good bloke and he knew him from his time on the streets.

Adam had managed to get a council house in Loftus and was having a bit of a house warming party. I invited Nikki to join us. When we turned up there were around fifteen people already there.

To be honest, everyone was really nice. The house had two bedrooms and Adam was sharing it with another bloke, Tony, who Nikki was practically salivating over after only five minutes at the party. I think the feeling was mutual.

Towards the end of the evening I had to pay a visit to the toilet. As I walked along the landing to the bathroom my eyes were drawn to a picture frame on the wall. It was an arrangement of oil paintings, side by side, showing three Parisian scenes: the Eiffel Tower, the Arc de Triomphe and the Moulin Rouge.

'Where have I seen that before?' I pondered to myself, and a split second later I realised that it was my painting from Paris, the one I thought I'd lost in the fire.

'What the fuck is that doing here?' I asked, to nobody in particular as I was alone and still on my way to the toilet.

I stood there closely looking at my painting, checking the artist's signature and the frame, which had ended up costing more than the paintings.

'It's nice isn't it?' someone behind me asked.

Startled, I turned around to find that Tony and Nikki had followed me up the stairs; Nikki looked at the paintings and her jaw dropped as if she were about to speak. A quizzical look crossed her face and then she raised her eyebrows and looked at me.

Me: Yeah, it's really nice. Something I would have chosen myself. Where did you get it?

Tony: Oh, it's not mine, it's Adam's. He got it off a mate who was throwing some old stuff out. I think he only paid about twenty quid for it, it's from Paris you know.

Nikki: No shit, Sherlock, I bet that frame cost more than twenty quid.

Me: Probably about sixty-five quid.

Tony looked a little confused.

Nikki: What other stuff did this mate of Adam's throw out?

Tony: I seem to remember him getting a rug and some wooden mask thing: they're on my bedroom wall. Do you want to have a look?

Me: I'd fucking love to.

My blood boiled as Tony pushed open one of the doors leading from the landing and switched on the light to reveal my Kenyan war mask hanging from one of the walls.

'The fucking cunt,' I mumbled under my breath. Well, I thought I was mumbling but Tony looked at me in shock. I turned to him, smiled and announced that I really must go for a piss.

In the bathroom I stood in front of the mirror trying to come up with some rational explanation as to why my belongings were in this house, and more to the point why Neal had burned my coffee shop to the ground. I heard a knock at the door.

'It's me, can I come in?' Nikki whispered.

'I'm having a shit,' I replied.

Nikki: Let me in.

Me: There's no lock on the door, let yourself in.

Nikki: Are you alright?

Me: It's nothing a cattle-prod and a blowtorch can't put right.

Nikki: So, he didn't mention anything to you about all this then?

Me: Funnily enough, no.

Nikki: So, did he just sell some of your stuff and then burn down the coffee shop to cover his tracks?

Me: I think he just picked the best things I had and got them out before setting the place on fire.

Nikki: What are we going to do?

Me: I don't know. I want that stuff back. I'm not too bothered about my kangaroo testicle bottle opener.

Nikki: I wouldn't be either, it's shit. Let's devise a plan, not here mind, keep your mouth shut and we'll talk about it tomorrow. At the moment if the insurance company gets wind that some of your stuff was removed from the cafe before the fire you'll be fucked. And I don't trust Neal if he did all this behind your back. Neal is pissed as a skunk downstairs, looks like he's well and truly off the wagon. Let's go back to my place and plan some revenge.

Me: Nikki, can it be bigger and better than the ice-cream incident?

Nikki: Oh, yes.

I sneaked out of the party and sat in my car waiting for Nikki to say her goodbye to Tony, wondering how on earth I'd ended up in this situation. Did he think I wouldn't find out and *what the fuck was he thinking?* Burning down my cafe without consulting me? I mean, it was probably for the best, and I wouldn't have had the balls to go through with it but he'd actually burned my home down.

Five minutes passed and Nikki returned to the car.

'Let's strike while the iron's hot,' she said as she slipped into the seat beside me. 'Everyone's either off their tits or hammered in there so I think we should go and get Bev, 'cause she'll fucking love this, and then come back in a few hours and get your stuff back. Tony reckons the back door's always open. Right then, let's motor.'

I drove slowly away from the party; I wasn't in the mood for talking.

Nikki: Eh, fucking hell, who'd have thought it? Your Neal, an arsonist? What a complete cock, I told you you should have let that fucker jump into the River Tees and drown; honestly, being nice does you no favours nowadays. Did he know that you were insured up to the hilt or did he just decide to fuck you over anyway? The shithouse.

It didn't get any better when we got over the Bev's. It was just after midnight so she wasn't best pleased to start with, and after we told her that we'd found my stuff at the party she went off her box.

'The fucking cock-sucker!' was Bev's first comment on the matter. 'Right, we're going to dress the part, I've got loads of black jumpers and trousers and I think I've got three baseball bats.' Bev paced her living room as she thought her plan through.

'Why?' I asked.

'Just in case anyone tries anything.' she replied.

'I suppose I should have split that into two questions really. Why have you got three baseball bats, and are we really going to use them? Can't we just negotiate the return of my things?' I suggested.

Bev: Julie, you are possibly the most boring person I have ever met. Live a little, let's cause some havoc and cave a few heads in. He's stolen your stuff and burned your home down, are you going to just bend over and take it?

Me: Yeah, probably.

Bev: Well I'm not, I haven't hit anyone for, oh, let's see, about six months, I'm due a scrap.

We decided, or should I say Nikki decided, to drive back to the party at around two o'clock in the morning. Bev wanted to set off straight away and take them all on but Nikki managed to persuade her to wait a while; apparently, good things come to those who wait.

We drove slowly up the street towards Adam's place and I brought the car to a halt outside his house.

'That's it Julie, just stop the car outside of the house we're planning to burgle,' Nikki tutted.

'What am I supposed to do?' I asked.

Nikki: Do a bit of a drive past and park the car up the street somewhere, don't you watch the telly?'

Me: Not really. Bev this jumper you've given me smells lovely, what fabric conditioner do you use?

Bev: Some shit from ALDI, it's alright isn't it?

Me: Although, I'm a little concerned that you had three balaclavas hanging about at the back of your wardrobe. Why the fuck would you have a balaclava? I think you'd have been good in the IRA.

Bev: So, what are we waiting for? You still haven't moved the car.

Me: It's raining, we're going to get wet if I park down the street.

Bev: Sweet Jesus, I'm working with amateurs.

We watched the house, it was in darkness and there was no longer the pounding of 'Now That's What I Call Music 87'.

'So, you had no idea that Neal burned your place down?' Bev continued.

Me: Not a fucking clue, do you think you guys wouldn't have known about it? You know I can't keep secrets. He was just normal really, well apart from the bridge incident, obviously, but the perfect boyfriend really. He was good to talk to, he made me laugh and he could cook: what more could a girl want? Neal made me a quiche last night.

Bev: Dave made me cum last night and then we got a take away; you can stick your quiche up your arse. Here, let me out of this car.

Bev didn't even wait for me to get out of the driver's seat, she just lifted the catch at the side of my seat, pushed it forward and I found my face being crushed between the steering wheel and my headrest as she climbed out of the car. She walked purposefully up to the gate at the front of the house and kicked it open. It swung violently on its hinges and made enough noise to wake the dead.

Nikki and I pulled on our balaclavas and followed Bev up the garden path towards the front of the house. Up ahead, Bev cut across the grass and up the right hand side of the house; we were going to go into the kitchen through the back door and then straight up the stairs to reclaim my belongings.

Bev didn't even try to be quiet, she opened the back door, walked straight into the kitchen and promptly kicked the cat's water bowl about six feet across the tiled floor. I heard her mumble 'Bollocks!' under her breath and continue across the room towards the hallway.

The light from the street filtered in through the front door, which had a large glass panel in the middle of it, making navigation into the hallway quick and easy. Well, I thought so until I accidentally kicked the cat about six feet across the kitchen floor: poor, little bastard was only trying to find its bowl of water. It made a noise that would have put the RSPCA on high alert.

'This is going well Jules, keep up the good work. We could do this for a living,' Nikki snarled sarcastically.

I hung my head, placed my hands on my hips, took a deep breath and thought, *'What the fuck am I doing here?'*

There was the sound of snoring emanating from the living room and someone turned over in a bed upstairs, I could hear the springs groaning under their weight.

Nikki and I walked slowly up the stairs. We'd planned, I'm not sure you could actually call it a plan, to each take one of my possessions back to the car; we'd just pick up the first thing we found and leave the house with it.

As we got to the top of the stairs I could see Bev's silhouette from the light coming in through the landing window. Bev had no idea what her next move would be and turned to face Nikki and I for some direction, I pointed to the bedroom door where I had seen my war mask hanging on the wall but Nikki pressed her hand on my arm to lower it and mouthed that she would take the war mask and that Bev should take the Paris paintings from the wall to her right.

I then mouthed that I needed to take a piss and Bev and Nikki raised their eyebrows and hands to the heavens—well, it was raining and when I hear rain I need to take a piss. Neither of the girls were particularly pleased that I then proceeded to switch on the bathroom light and when I exited the bathroom Bev mouth gaped open as I realised that I had also flushed the toilet.

Nikki had disappeared into Tony's bedroom to retrieve my war mask and Chinese silk carpet; I wasn't too sure how she was going to handle the carpet as Adam had stuck it to the wall with double sided Velcro. We had briefly discussed this minor detail and decided that we should treat it much like you would a sticking plaster and rip it off in one swift movement, and then run like fuck.

We waited for what seemed like an eternity for Nikki. After, realistically, about three minutes we could hear whispering from the bedroom and strained our ears to hear what was being said. Bev and I inched slowly towards the bedroom until we practically had our ears up against the door. We heard a couple of what sounded like threatening demands and then silence. We both looked at each other and Bev pushed the door open.

The room was dimly lit by a candle burning on one of the bedside cabinets, but there was enough light to make out Nikki on her knees sucking some bloke off.

'What the fuck is going on here?' was Bev's opening comment.

'Just a bit of role play,' was Nikki's reply, 'Your stuff's by the door Jules.'

Me: Thanks.

I strained to make out Nikki's 'companion'; he had his back to me and I could just about make out the crack of his arse.

Bev: Did you plan all this then? You fucking weirdo. You're into this sort of shit aren't you? Is that why you like the *Sopranos*? They do this sort of freaky shit on that show.

Nikki: Fuck off.

Bev: Do we get an introduction?

Me: I think his name might be Tony.

Arse Crack: Hiya.

Bev: We'll see you later, Nik.

And with that, Bev closed the bedroom door and we retraced our steps back through the house and out to the car.

Although it had been quite an eventful evening, I sat in silence as I drove Bev back to her place and she didn't seem to tire of telling me how much of a complete cock Neal was. I was glad when she got out of the car and I could continue onto Jamie's in peace. I hadn't even tried to look for Neal after I discovered he'd fucked me right over and burned my home to the ground; I just wanted to ponder exactly what I was going to do to him.

I got to bed at silly o'clock and then tossed and turned for a good hour before falling into a light sleep. Jamie's carer then decided to aim for a personal best by turning up on time at eight o'clock on a Sunday morning, and began wheeling Jamie around his bungalow in his shower chair whistling a merry, fucking tune. I wanted to set the bastard on fire but it wasn't his fault I was a miserable.

Luckily, Jamie isn't a morning person either and I heard him ask his carer if he was still off his tits from the night before and would he kindly refrain from any frivolity at this hour on a Sunday morning: something along those lines anyway. I went back to sleep.

I finally got up at around eleven o'clock. I would have slept for longer but Jamie doesn't think anyone should be allowed to sleep if he's out of bed and proceeded to run his wheelchair over the squeaky dog-toy shaped like a rubber chicken, that his mum's dog played with, at least twenty times.

When I finally opened my bedroom door, Jamie asked if I was awake and then giggled to himself, like a five-year-old child. He then continued to run over the rubber chicken to wake Marie up as well, but in between laps I managed to grab the toy from the floor and put it on top of wall clock in the hallway.

Jamie went into mischievous mode and then started to open and close the front door with his automatic door key; there's no winning when he gets like that, so I just went into the kitchen to make myself a cup of tea, accompanied by a soft, morning tea biscuit and some possibly out of date muesli.

Jamie feels that the supermarket chains are too conservative with their sell-by dates, and that these dates pressure the consumers into buying replacement products when, in his words, they are still perfectly edible. Hence, soft, morning tea biscuits, out of date muesli and dairy products that require a sniff-test before use.

That morning the milk was only two days out of date—*result!*

'I've got a cracking story to tell you,' I called to Jamie from the kitchen.

Jamie: She'd sleep through anything that girl.

Me: Like I said, I've got a cracking story to tell you.

Jamie: I heard you the first time, but you appear to have mistaken me for someone who cares.

Me: No, but really, you'll like this little chestnut. I have managed to secure the return of my Paris paintings, Kenyan war mask and Chinese silk rug.

Jamie: Really?

I walked out into the hallway and bent forward towards Jamie to give the story full effect.

Me: Neal only burned down my fucking home and then sold my stuff to one of his mates.

Jamie: You are fucking jesting.

Me: We found them last night at the party his mate was having.

Jamie: Where is he now?

Me: Still at the party I assume, I left the twat there.

Jamie: What are you going to do now?

Me: Plan my revenge, oh and it will be *so* sweet.

Jamie: What are you going to do?

Me: I haven't decided yet, I'll leave the planning to Bev and Nikki as they're the sickest pair of fucks I know. Do you have any suggestions?

Jamie: Something to do with his testicles, that's always a winner. I can't help but try to cross my legs when I hear of any testicle tales.

Me: I don't want anything too violent. Extreme humiliation is what I'm looking for, like Nikki did with Phil.

Jamie: She's a right sick bitch that one, don't be taking any tips from her—poor, fucking pooch. I wonder when Marie's going to get up?

Me: Leave her alone, what's your problem?

Jamie: I've got no-one to play with.

Me: What about me?

Jamie: Are you going to suck me off?

Me: Er, no.

Jamie: There we go then. I'm going to wake her up.

And with that, he wheeled out of the kitchen, across the hallway and straight into the bedroom door, forcibly pushing it open he loudly whispered, 'Wakey, Wakey.' Marie stirred as Jamie wheeled himself to her side of the bed and began stroking her hair.

Then he gave her a quick slap on the forehead before demanding that she get up as he had no-one to play with, except me and I was shit to play with, apparently, because I took his toys off him.

Marie lifted her head off the pillow and gave me the death stare.

Me: Don't look at me like that, I was trying to quieten the little twat down to let you sleep in. Now that you're awake, though, I need a formula for revenge. Do you have any good stories?

The response was a short, sharp 'NO' and Marie then attempted to roll over and return to her slumber, while Jamie drove his chair repeatedly into the side of the bed frame.

I was on my own; I couldn't depend on these clowns for any help so I decided to take a trip into Middlesboogie.

'Right, I'm off,' I shouted to Jamie and Marie.

'Wait,' Jamie replied. 'What are we going to do if he comes back here?'

Me: Nothing, just treat him like everything is normal and that I'm not bothered about him burning my fucking home down, and tell him I've gone shopping.

Jamie: What am I supposed to defend us with? My fucking easy-reach?

Me: He only burned the coffee shop down, what do you think he's going to do? *You've got a pretty mouth Jamie.*

'Fuck off,' Jamie squirmed in his seat.

Me: You'll be fine. He'll be more worried about my reaction, let's keep him guessing.

I gave Jamie a cheeky little wink and left him searching for his easy-reach in the airing cupboard.

I'd decided that Boots the Chemist would be my first point of call for this shopping trip. Armed with Fiery Jack warming ointment and a large tube of superglue, I then headed off to Asda at Southbank and bought the ingredients to make some chocolate cookies, via Beverley's where I picked up some hospital strength laxative—I'd make this bastard pass a kidney before I was finished with him.

I returned to Jamie's and made a cookie dough mixture with a passion for baking the likes of which I had never known before. I cut up the chocolate into sizeable chocolate chips, mixed them with the dough and added oodles of laxative before placing generous dollops of the mixture onto a baking tray and placing the tray in the oven.

Now was the time to summon him home I thought; and what better way than with the medium of text message; come to mama, you little fucker.

'Where are you? Are you OK?' the message read.

'I've just left Adam's. Is it OK to come home?' was the reply.

'What fucking home? You've burnt it down, you fucking clown,' was going to be my initial response but my thoughts quickly turned to revenge and how

I wanted him to eat at least eight of my bowel-movement-inducing baked goods.

So instead, I changed it to, *'Of course it's OK. We're loaded remember?'*

A cheeky, little smile spread across my face as I sent the text, I was looking forward to carrying out this plan of revenge. I did ask myself if this made me as sick as Bev and Nik and then I came to the conclusion that being 'sick' is underrated.

A somewhat reticent Neal walked into Jamie's bungalow one hour later. I'd had to refuse Jamie, on numerous occasions during the last thirty minutes, any of my freshly baked, delicious smelling, shit-chip cookies, which did nothing to improve the foul mood that he'd woken up with that morning.

I couldn't possibly feed Jamie any; his carer wasn't due to arrive until six o'clock in the evening, the poor bastard couldn't hang on till then could he? Perhaps just the one, no, stop being wicked, Julie—I know it's wrong but it feels so right.

'I'm sorry,' Neal started to say, 'I thought it was a good idea at the time and you were getting bored with the coffee shop and I thought we could spend some more time together.'

'Let's not worry about it now,' I interrupted. 'I was angry to start with but I'm OK now, and we're going to get to do some travelling together.'

I intentionally missed off the rest of the speech I was initially planning on delivering, which would have gone something like: 'And then one night you're going to wake and find yourself naked and all tied up in the wilderness, with your cock in a precooked Asda chicken. You'll hear the sound of baying wolves in the distance, getting closer with each passing second. I'll climb into the 4-wheel drive I managed to rent under a false name, and bid you a fond farewell along the lines of 'Fuck off and die', you treacherous, little twat.'

Neal seemed to relax when I said everything was OK and I asked him if he wanted a cup of tea, he said yes and I went into the kitchen to make it.

Just as I suspected, Neal grabbed one of my shit-chip cookies as soon as he saw them and ate it with gusto. You know what they say about how a watched kettle never boils? It could have taken the rest of the afternoon for all I cared, I was feeling happier with each cookie he devoured, and by the time I passed him his cup of tea he'd devoured five of them.

As we left the kitchen and walked across the hallway into the lounge, Jamie asked if he could have a biscuit, I proceeded to hand him an out of date morning tea biscuit from his 'not so airtight' Tupperware container.

Jamie refused my offer and wheeled away furiously in his wheelchair. I didn't tell him of my plan for revenge; it wasn't fair to involve him, and he couldn't keep his fat mouth shut anyway. Nothing was going to fuck this up.

'I was thinking that we could go and stay in a hotel tonight,' I suggested. 'I'm fed up biting the pillow when we're having shag, let's go and make some noise.'

I gave Neal a cheeky wink and he smiled back at me. I passed the plate of shit-chip cookies to him and he took two—*feed away you scheming, little shit, I think that brings your total cookie intake to seven or eight.*

Me: I've already packed an overnight bag.

Neal: You're keen.

Me: I was thinking about The Grinkle Park, what do you reckon?

Neal: It's a bit pricey but nice, let's do it.

'Come on then, let's check in early,' I said, rising to my feet.

Jamie was still hanging around to see if there were any cookies left, he was still holding his easy-reach just in case there was any trouble. Personally, I would have liked to start a fight just to see what Jamie would actually do; unless you were unconscious on the floor or laid down and you told Jamie that he was free to run back and forth over your head, his choices were pretty limited.

I collected the overnight bag from the spare room, grabbed my car keys from the kitchen and before I could make it back to the lounge, a full ten metres might I add, Jamie had demolished one cookie and was gleefully holding onto a second. All I could do was roll my eyes and suggest that Neal and I should set off to make the most of our hotel stay.

Neal got into the car and I made an excuse that I'd forgotten the massage oil in the bedroom and rushed back into the house to deliver the good news to Jamie.

Me: Are you enjoying those cookies, Jamie?

Jamie: They're lovely, you should make them more often.

Me: Well, perhaps not those ones, as they're laced with enough laxative to make you pass an internal organ.

Jamie's jaw dropped and a few delicious looking crumbs fell from his mouth into his lap.

Me: That'll teach you, you greedy bastard.

Jamie: How long have I got?

Me: How many have you eaten?

Jamie: I think this is my fourth.

Me: Forty-five minutes, an hour tops.

Jamie: My carer's not here for another two hours. What the fuck am I going to do?

Jamie dropped his head into his hand and slowly closed his eyes.

Me: Where's Marie?

Jamie: She's just popped out to see a friend.

Me: I suggest you make a few phone calls. I'll see you later, after the clean-up, Tiger.

I strolled back out to the car and we set off to the hotel.

I had my reasons for choosing The Grinkle Park hotel as the venue: it's in the middle of fucking nowhere. The Grinkle Park sits in between the coast and moor roads as you head towards Whitby from Saltburn. You have to drive along a beautiful, leafy lane to get to the hotel and it's around a twenty minute drive from Saltburn, or thirty minutes if you drive slowly because you are waiting for the effects of eight laxative-laden cookies to really kick in. I was thinking that by the time I'd finished with him, Neal could walk the five or so miles to his mate Adam's, but wouldn't need to pass my door ever again.

By the time we'd reached the hotel, Neal was ashen faced and starting to perspire profusely.

'Are you OK?' I asked, in the sincerest voice I could possibly muster.

'Not really,' Neal replied, 'I think I'm going to have the shits.'

'Really? I thought we were up for a marathon session.' I teased.

'You know me, I'm still going to be good for that baby,' Neal said, giving me a sexy smile, which he quickly followed with raised eyebrows as he tried to sneak a sly fart out and realised that it was not perhaps a wise move.

Time to get him out of the car.

I had parked as far away as possible from the door to the hotel reception area and I now took the opportunity to meander slowly towards the reception, taking in the manicured gardens and casting my eyes over the exterior of the building. My overnight bag swung by my side, hiding my stash of medical accessories.

Neal, meanwhile, had walked as quickly as is humanly possible, whilst clenching his butt cheeks like a vice, towards the hotel. I wandered in a full minute later to find Neal sat on one of the sofas opposite the reception desk, biting down on his fist.

'I'll check in,' I suggested.

As there was no response from Neal, I asked if it was OK for me to check in.

'Yes, yes, make it quick,' he pleaded.

I walked up to the reception desk.

Me: Good afternoon.

Receptionist: Hello, how may I help you?

Me: I was wondering if we could book a room for the night.

Receptionist: Certainly. What type of room would you like?

Me: A double please. On second thoughts, do you have any with four poster beds?

Receptionist: Yes, we do, and they have wonderful garden views

Me: How much are they for the night?

Receptionist: Two hundred pounds.

Me: That's a bit expensive, how much is it just for a double?

Receptionist: One hundred and fifty pounds.

Me: We'll just take the double please.

I wanted to extend the check-in process but not so that it was too suspicious, and ended up sounding like a scene from a Carry On movie. I didn't want him suspecting a thing.

Three minutes later I held the room key in my hand. I walked back over to Neal and he launched himself from his seat, snatched the key out of my hand and practically ran, butt cheeks still clenched, down the corridor towards our room for the evening.

As I sauntered along the corridor towards our room I focussed intently on not laughing; I was still angry at Neal for what he'd done, but there is something about someone shitting themselves that makes me giggle.

Neal hadn't even managed to close the room or toilet door behind him in his haste to empty his bowels, and he was clearly visible from the corridor as he sat on the pot with his head buried in his hands. It took monumental effort to stifle a laugh as I entered the room and closed the door behind me. I then proceeded to close the bathroom door to give Neal the privacy he deserved and then buried my head in one of the pillows and laughed my fucking head off as he continued with the evacuation of his arse.

I switched the TV on and started to watch some documentary on BBC2 about the Roman Empire. Ten minutes later, Neal emerged from the bathroom and silently lay down on the bed next to me.

'Feeling better honey?' I enquired.

'A little bit,' Neal responded. 'I must have eaten something. Do you reckon it was those cookies?'

Me: Don't be cheeky, I made those fresh today. It was probably the breakfast at your mate Adam's, what did you have?

Neal: Just toast.

Me: That's probably it then.

Neal: What? Toast?

Me: You know you blokes, the bread was probably well out of date.

And with that Neal, jumped back off the bed and headed straight back to the bathroom, leaving me to learn more about the Battle of Carthage, which was the major act of the Third Punic War apparently between the Phoenician city of Carthage, a suburb of Tunis in Africa, and the Roman Republic. It was a siege operation, starting sometime between 149 and 148 BC, and ending in the spring of 146 BC with the complete destruction of the city of Carthage by the Romans. Those Italians were twats. Why did they have to demand the complete destruction of Carthage? You only have to watch them play football to recognise that, they blatantly dive to get free kicks—fuckers.

Neal looked whiter than before when he laid back down on the bed; I didn't think it was possible, but hey ho.

'Sweet Jesus,' Neal mumbled, weakly.

'Right then, let's get naked,' I proposed, rubbing my hands together.

Neal didn't say a word as I seductively peeled off my clothes. I knew I'd have to pull something special out of the bag for the occasion, I didn't want him using explosive diarrhoea as an excuse for not wanting to get jiggy, and I could see his eyes light up as I whipped my knickers off.

'You've shaved everything off,' Neal gasped.

'Just for you, Tiger,' I whispered as I leant forward towards him. 'Now let's get these clothes off.'

With a renewed vigour Neal stood up and started to undress, he even pulled his t-shirt between his legs like real strippers do and then must have thought it not one of his best ideas and dropped the t-shirt on the floor and kicked it under the bed.

I didn't care; I wouldn't be washing it, I just laid back on the bed and watched the performance.

A naked Neal then crawled across the bed towards me and I stopped him with my foot in his chest.

Me: Not so fast, I think I'll warm you up with a little massage first. Just lay back, close your eyes and relax.

Neal lay back on the bed, folded his arms behind his head and closed his eyes, as I went about rubbing Ylang Ylang massage oil into his chest. I'd even taken the time to sniff test the massage oils in Boots, can you believe it? I should have just mixed my own piss with some olive oil and been done with it.

Anyway, I digress, the fun was only just beginning.

I worked my way down from his chest to his stomach, Neal relaxed more with each stroke, then I massaged both his legs. When I finished with his legs I switched massage oils and filled the palm of my hand with Fiery Jack warming ointment, which I rubbed liberally into both testicles and the shaft of his penis.

Neal moaned in pleasure which rapidly changed into groans of discomfort.

'What the fuck have you rubbed in there?' he asked.

'Erm ... Ylang Ylang massage oil,' I replied, reading the label of the bottle, whilst stuffing the Fiery Jack warming ointment back under the mattress.

'It's burning my fucking nuts off,' Neal yelped as he jumped off the bed and charged into the bathroom.

I have never seen anything as funny as Neal trying to rest his nuts on the side of a basin, running the cold tap on full blast and trying to wash the warming ointment from his private parts. The whole incident must have been too much for him to bear and he farted whilst washing himself. A look of despair crept across his face as he slowly closed the bathroom door.

Me: Are you alright, Honey?

Neal: Not really, I've had a little accident.

'Ah, baby, can I do anything for you?' I asked — like I was going to help him wipe his own arse, I don't fucking think so.

Neal: No, I'll be fine.

Thank fuck for that. I shouldn't have even offered to help if I had no intention of following through with it.

My thoughts returned to the Roman Empire documentary on BBC2. Did you know that originally the Colosseum in Rome was capable of seating around eighty thousand spectators and was used for gladiatorial contests and public spectacles? As well as the gladiatorial games, other public spectacles were held there, such as mock sea battles, animal hunts, executions, re-enactments of famous battles, and dramas based on classical mythology. And today they make pizzas and wine, what a come down.

Anyway, I saw up to the part about construction of the Colosseum beginning under the rule of the Emperor Vespasian in around 70–72AD, before Neal staggered back into the bedroom and flopped down onto the bed.

Neal: I'm fucked.

Me: That's more than can be said for me. Roll over and I'll massage your back for you, let's just relax.

Neal rolled over onto his front and buried his head into the pillow. I started rubbing Neal's shoulder blades and the back of his neck, trying to release some of the tension that had built up in them. I slowly worked my way down his back towards the buttock area, where I gently massaged his cheeks.

'I need a bit more oil here.' I commented as I leant forward to grab the massage oil from the bedside cabinet, whilst retrieving the tube of superglue from beside the Fiery Jack warming ointment under the mattress.

I squeezed a generous line of superglue along the inside of one buttock and then massaged both buttocks together, holding them briefly to allow the adhesive to produce a firm bond.

As I moved down to Neal's thighs, I made the comment that the oil seemed rather sticky but continued with the massage.

Within seconds I heard a rumbling in Neal's stomach and he heaved himself off the bed in the direction of the en-suite. This movement was quickly followed by a shriek of pain as Neal stepped forward with his right leg and his butt cheeks tried to separate; good old superglue, it held fast.

It is hard to find the words that best describe the sound of tearing flesh, but easier to recount the thud as Neal hit the floor in a crumpled heap, clutching his arse.

I bit down on my lip hard to stop myself laughing, took a moment to compose myself, and then jumped off the bed and squatted down beside Neal.

Me: What's the matter?

Neal: There's something wrong with my arse.

Me: Go and have a nice, hot shower, that should loosen things up.

Neal arose gingerly from the floor and, taking little, short steps, made his way into the bathroom. He looked back at me, as he turned to close the door to the en-suite, with a look of remorse on his face. He should have known he would be sorry for fucking with me—he'd seen Bev and Nikki in action; what did he think I was going to do: sit back and take one for the team? Like shite I was.

As soon as I heard Neal turn the shower on I was retrieving my clothes from around the room and getting dressed. I couldn't find my knickers, it didn't matter, I could just go commando, he could keep them as a souvenir.

I grabbed my overnight bag and quickly stuffed Neal's clothes in it, just a little more humiliation, oh go on, I know it's wrong but it feels so right to leave him with no clothes in the middle of nowhere. Anyway, I hadn't taken everything, I left him the t-shirt that he'd wiped his arse on and if he could find my knickers he was welcome to wear them.

I left the room and closed the door behind me as quietly as I could, before racing down the corridor towards the car park to make my escape.

I climbed into my car, reversed out of the parking spot and sped down the hotel driveway with all the speed a three cylinder, one litre Vauxhall Corsa could possibly muster.

Right about then Neal would have been returning from the bathroom, hopefully having lost copious amounts of arse-crack blood, to find the letter that I had left for him on the bed. Written on the back of an old Tesco petrol receipt, he would be reading these most poignant of words:

> Dear Neal,
> I remember the first time I met you, leaning over a bridge that spans the River Tees, thinking of taking your own life. Well, I wish I'd fucking pushed you off, you complete shithouse.
> Lots of love and superglue,
> Jules xxxxx

I arrived back at Jamie's just as his clean-up operation was well under way.

'Cheers Jules, you fucking, soulless cunt, I couldn't get anyone to come and see to me earlier, so I had to sit in my own faeces for forty-five minutes.' Jamie shouted from the shower.

Me: You're welcome, Honey.

I popped my head through the bathroom door, whistled at seeing Jamie naked in the shower and winked at his carer Sue.

Jamie: Don't talk to me.

Me: Oh come on, Tiger, it's only poo. Anyway, you'll feel better after a good clean out.

Jamie: Those cookies went through me like a fucking Porsche.

Me: Sorry about this Sue, but they were special shit-chip cookies for a friend of mine and this greedy bastard had scoffed four of them before I could move them out of his way.

Sue: It's not a problem. I don't mind shit, it's puke I can't handle.

Me: I hope you've learned a valuable lesson here, Jamie.

Jamie: Fuck off.

And with that the phone rang.

'How did it go?' Bev inquired from the other end of the telephone.

Me: I think I heard the skin in the crack of his arse tear apart, it was magical.

Bev: So what's next? What else have you got planned for the fucker?

Me: Steady on Bev, I think that's enough for me, I'm quite satisfied.

Bev: I'd destroy him.

Me: I know, Honey, I know. Anyway, I think I'm going to go travelling.

Bev: Where to? I fancy Edinburgh, it's supposed to be great for a weekend.

Me: I was thinking further afield.

Bev: Like Jersey?

Me: Even further than that, Beverley. I was thinking Europe.

Bev: Jersey is in Europe. I've never been to Jersey.

Me: I was thinking I might do mainland Europe, and I might start in Paris and then see where I end up.

Bev: You're loaded, you could go anywhere.

Me: It's only a fucking insurance claim, I haven't robbed a bank or anything, I've got to go back to work eventually. I might take a year off. I think I could see that through to the end, doing fuck all for twelve months. Anyway, I'm going to go for a walk to clear my head, I'll speak to you later.

It was supposed to be spring, but all the seasons seem to merge into one shitty, wanky, grey, pissy season nowadays. I walked along the esplanade, it was pitch black as it was well after eight o'clock; I just needed some fresh air, to think things through and clear my head.

I wanted to find myself. I had no idea what the fuck that meant but everyone seemed to be doing it so why shouldn't I give it a go to see what happens?

I asked myself why it had been so easy to torture Neal, and why wasn't I bothered that he'd fucked me over. I realised then that our relationship had been absolutely average and I didn't really give a toss about him. Why had I just let the affair drag on? It's not like we were passionate or anything, we didn't always click in the sex department; sometimes I had to finish the job myself.

I thought about my parents for a split second; I must be a complete bastard, even my own mum and dad don't like me, and then I reminded myself that they don't have any friends and I do. And everything was fine again.

I considered going for more counselling. Why did I feel the need to look after people, to save their tortured souls? I met Neal when he was about to jump off a bridge into the River Tees, you don't get a more obvious fucking warning that your partner is barking mad than that. Perhaps next time I'll ask Bev or Nikki to staple a fucking warning notice to my forehead before I jump into the sack with the next total loser I meet up with.

The phone was ringing as I got back to Jamie's place; it was Nikki. I sat down on the sofa in Jamie's living room, kicked off my shoes and put my feet up as I imagined this was going to be one interesting, little gem of a story.

Me: So how did your evening go, you dirty, cock-sucking whore?

Nikki: It was a fucking nightmare. The sex was fantastic, it was like Cirque du Soleil, he threw me all over that bedroom. I felt like a gymnast, but when I woke up this morning I realised that I'd got my period during the night; the place looked like a war zone. I stripped the bed and flung all the sheets in the bath but there was no lock on the bathroom door and Neal's mate Adam walked in; I was horrified. Adam asked me where I'd hidden the fucking corpse! Anyway, how was your day?

I started to giggle as I recounted the highlights of the day and heard more about Nikki's sordid bedroom adventures. Then I decided to call Amanda and tell her what had happened—we laughed like fuck.

When I eventually put the phone down, I stayed on the sofa, closed my eyes and thought about my friends: they were fan-fucking-tastic.

I couldn't sleep that night so I switched the light on, picked up what I thought was the Dorling Kindersley guide to Europe and started to plan my trip. Only then did I realise I'd bought the European phrase book instead; I really must learn to read one of these days. It didn't have even have a fucking map in it, what was all that about?

Then I remembered that Jamie's shower curtain had a map of the world on it; someone had brought it back from a trip to Australia—yeah, that's right, a shower curtain. Madder than a bag of cut snakes.

So, I got out of bed and went into the bathroom, where I sat down on the floor and spread the shower curtain along the rail.

Ok then, forget distance, scales and shit like that; I'm sure the countries would still be in the right place even on a shower curtain, but in England the only cities highlighted were London, obviously, and Sunderland.

'What are you doing?' Jamie shouted from his bedroom.

Me: I'm planning a trip around Europe.

Jamie: While you're sat on the shitter?

Me: No, I'm looking at the map of the world on your shower curtain. Did you know that the two major cities in England are London and Sunderland?

Jamie: Which crazy bastard picked Sunderland?

Me: I suppose they do have a football team.

Jamie: Only just. And have you noticed that there are no major cities in Scotland, The Netherlands, Belgium, Switzerland and Austria?

Me: Australia's pretty well represented like. What the fuck's in Geraldton? And what's this? Tennant Creek? Never heard of it. Don't tell me that the Aussies haven't heard of Amsterdam, Geneva and fucking Vienna. Haven't they seen *The Sound of Music*?

'If they're really lucky they won't have because it's shit,' Jamie commented, as he wheeled himself into the bathroom.

Me: Bollocks! It's fucking great *The Sound of Music*.

Jamie wheeled into the bathroom, narrowly missing my feet as usual, followed closely by a sleepy Marie, rubbing her eyes to wake up.

Jamie: Your taste in movies is shit anyway, do you remember bringing *Terms of Endearment* around here one night, honestly cancer's a fucking laugh a minute. I'm never going to get that hour and a half of my life back. It's not like being in a wheelchair's a barrel of laughs and you go and bring that shit for me to watch.

Me: I liked *Pulp Fiction*.

Jamie: Liking one Quentin Tarantino movie does not make you have great taste in movies.

Me: And I liked *Kill Bill*.

Jamie: You liked *Miss Pettigrew Lives for a Day* so you should really stop talking right about now.

Me: I've never seen a *Godfather* movie.

Jamie: Enough said, that's a fucking heinous crime, you've really never seen a *Godfather* movie?

Me: No.

Jamie: There's four of them.

Me: I know.

Jamie: Shocking.

Me: So, I've done Amsterdam. I think I'll go to Paris, no … Should I go to Belgium first and then make my way over to Paris?

Jamie: My mum said there's fuck all in Belgium except the EU headquarters.

Me: Well that's settled then, Paris it is.

Jamie: Then where?

Me: Erm … Germany. Ooh, I could go to Germany via Luxembourg.

Jamie: What's in Luxembourg?

Me: Fuck knows, it's not even in the European phrase book, what do you reckon they speak?

Jamie: Probably French. There's more than one city in France you know? Are you only going to Paris?

Me: Jamie, it's two o'clock in the morning and I can't sleep. I'm hardly planning this trip with any level of precision based on this fucking shower curtain; I'm just starting to put a plan together in my head.

Jamie: Eat a big bowl of bitchy for supper did we?

Me: Go and fuck yourself.

'I've always fancied Berlin,' Marie said as she sat down on the toilet seat. 'I'd like to see the Berlin Wall.

Jamie: You're too fucking late, they pulled it down years ago.

Marie: I know, Dickhead, I want to see the remains, we studied it in history.

Me: They pulled it down in 1989, actually, the ninth of November if you want to be precise.

Jamie: How do you know that?

Me: It's a pub quiz question, you should always have information like that handy.

Jamie: You weren't even born, Marie.

Me: Fuck that makes me feel old, I remember seeing it being pulled down on the telly.

Jamie: What other information's handy for pub quizzes?

Me: Capital cities, units of currency, you should know, your dad does the pub quiz at The Acklet every Monday night. Don't you ever go?

Jamie: Do I fuck? Do you want to know what the jackpot question was last week? Name all seven Von Trapp children in the Sound of Fucking Music.

Me: Liesl, Friedrich, Louisa, Kurt, Brigitta, Marta and Gretl.

Jamie: You sad twat.

Me: Then Germany. If I go to Berlin I might as well pop into Poland; Warsaw's quite near Russia, actually. No sorry, it's Belarus and the Ukraine next, Russia's miles away. Fuck that, I'll do Berlin and then head south into the Czech Republic where I'll do Prague, then Vienna in Austria, back into Germany to Munich in the south and then Switzerland and finally Italy.

Jamie: And you'll be home by next Tuesday.

Me: Something like that.

Jamie: How long are you going to take to do this?

Me: I haven't decided yet.

Jamie: Won't you miss us.

Me: Oh yeah, like a fucking hole in the head. You're all shacked up now, Kam's got Shab, Tom's got Ashlea, we never see them anymore. The only reason I see you is because I'm living in your house, which I'll be coming back to by the way.

Jamie: Great.

Me: Yeah, I thought you'd like that. Right, my trip's planned, I'm off to bed. Aren't you at work tomorrow, Jamie?

Jamie: I am actually, will you help me get back into bed?

I tutted.

Jamie: Or you can pack your bags and fuck off, it's up to you.

Me: Well if you put it that way, of course I'll help, it will be a fucking pleasure.

Marie had fallen asleep on the toilet seat, Jamie and I just looked at each other, shrugged our shoulders and left her there.

Since Jamie had broken his pelvis I had to slide him back into bed on a banana board; so called because it's bright yellow and shaped like a banana.

Jamie positions his wheelchair as close as possible to the side of his bed, usually scraping a good, two inch long layer of paint off the side of his bed as he does so, and then I form a bridge between his wheelchair and the bed with the banana board. I then slip a plastic sheet under Jamie's arse and, sitting firmly on his bed, pull the sheet so that he makes the smooth transition from his wheelchair onto his bed.

Sometimes I pull the sheet too quickly and perform the old tablecloth and crockery routine where Jamie just stays in his wheelchair, tuts and says something patently, fucking ridiculous like, 'I'm still in my chair, Dickhead.'

That evening, in my rush to complete the task, the plastic sheet stuck to Jamie's arse like shit to a blanket; I pulled a little too severely and catapulted Jamie on top of me and nearly off the other side of the bed.

I did giggle; Jamie's language was particularly scathing, I would have been hurt if I cared.

Jamie: Luckily I don't need my pelvis to fucking walk.

'Goodnight, Tiger, sweet dreams,' I said, closing the bedroom door behind me.

As I lay in my bed I couldn't help but re-live the highlights of the day: Neal farting and shitting himself as he washed his nuts under the cold tap and then hearing the distinctive tearing of butt crack flesh, the memories brought a smile to my face and I fell into a blissfully, deep sleep.

April

Where the fuck did April go? No really, who's hidden it?

They say that time flies when you're having fun, well I did nothing in April and it still flew by. I remember Amanda's mum saying to me, on my twenty-fifth birthday, that once you hit twenty-five the years seemed to slow down.

Then on my twenty-sixth birthday I practically called her a liar for making such a steaming turd of a statement—cheers, Yvonne, another year wasted.

I was going to have to do something with my life; I suppose I'd better start looking.

May

I woke one morning in May, after Jamie had gone to work and Marie was still in her bed, fast asleep.

I practically leapt out of bed, enjoyed a leisurely, hot shower and ate my final bowl of out of date, no longer crunchie muesli, drenched in, would you believe it, milk that still had one day left until it was out of date — *result!*

I was going to start my European trip today, be spontaneous, pack my bags and, passport in hand, head off on a tour that had been planned from a shower curtain bought in some homeware store in Australia.

I'd only ever packed for a two week package holiday to Turkey before and had no idea what to pack for a long term trip. It was May now, there was still a pretty good chance of unpredictable weather in Europe, so I packed three light jumpers, fourteen t-shirts, three pairs of jeans, one pair of sandals and I'd wear my trainers.

I then packed all my undies and, as my bag was starting to get a bit heavy, I cast my mind back to a magazine article that recommended taking undies and socks in a six-to-one ratio: six pairs of undies to one pair of socks. I couldn't wear socks for six days straight! When I finally took them off someone would be serving my feet with fucking crackers.

Then I reduced the number of t-shirts to seven and added two pairs of pyjamas, and then I threw another couple of t-shirts back in and shoved my shampoo, conditioner, facial wash and body lotion down the side of my bag, and then I took the two additional t-shirts back out.

At this rate Jamie would be back from work before I'd even finished packing; Marie was still asleep.

It's not like I was going into deepest, darkest Africa: they sell shampoo and the like in France, so I emptied half of the shampoo and conditioner down the sink to make the bag lighter. Sorted.

Then I fired up the internet on Jamie's computer, booked a flight to Paris leaving Newcastle airport at quarter to four that afternoon and then booked four weeks in a shared apartment in Bastille; how much more fucking cosmopolitan could I possibly get?

Then I wrote Jamie a quick note:

> I'm off to Paris for croissants, the Eiffel Tower and hopefully a few of those eight inch French baguettes.
> I'll miss you, honest.
> Jules xxxx

I walked to the train station and then walked back to Jamie's because I forgotten my toothbrush and then walked back to the train station again.

I reached Newcastle airport after a fairly uneventful two hour train journey; by fairly uneventful I mean there that only one fight broke out and it was between two, teenage brothers, but they were at the other end of the carriage to me so I was unaffected. I knew they were related because an old woman with them tried to split the fight up and one of the boys ran to my end of the carriage.

'Come here you little bastard,' she hissed, and whistled at the same time because she appeared to have a couple of teeth missing.

'Fuck off, Grandma,' came the response.

Oh happy days; I was going to miss Middlesboogie.

This time I didn't whinge about having to pay for the sandwiches on the plane; I was going to live for one whole month in Paris—it doesn't get much better than that.

The flight from Newcastle Upon Tyne airport to Charles De Gaulle in Paris took a grand total of one hour and forty minutes. Why hadn't I got my finger out and done this before? *Shit the bed!* You can get to Paris in less than two hours; it takes eight hours to get to from Middlesbrough to Cornwall, and you're still in England.

Twenty three Euros and fifty cents later I was standing outside of my shared home for the next four weeks, on *Rue Jacques Coeur*, in Bastille.

The apartment was located in Paris's eleventh *arrondissement*, yeah I know, whatever, it means neighbourhood apparently, and had one foot in Bastille and the other in the Marais.

Then I remembered why The Bastille sounded familiar to me, it only had a fucking prison, no wonder I'd managed to rent a room so easily. I wondered if The Bastille housed really dangerous prisoners or just those charged with traffic offences, tax evasion and the like; they'd be alright.

Saint Louis Island and Notre Dame are accessible by foot and the streets are supposed to be safe by day and night. The nearby Rue Saint Antoine is filled with bakeries, cafes and shitloads of fresh fruit and vegetable shops, as well as the obligatory take away restaurants.

The closest subway stop is Bastille, a leisurely three minutes stroll from the front door of the apartment block.

The building itself is *Haussmannian?!* Exactly. I had to look it up on Wikipedia and, apparently, Baron Georges-Eugène Haussmann's boulevards 'established the foundation of what is today the popular representation of the French capital around the world, by cutting through the old Paris of dense and irregular medieval alleyways into a rational city with wide avenues and open spaces which extended outwards far beyond the old city limits'. Every day's a school day; that's definitely a pub quiz question.

The apartment was on the first floor of the building, and entry to the foyer was by security code, which had been emailed to me; probably on account of the prison nearby— God, I hoped it wasn't a maximum security prison.

I knocked on the door of what was to be my home for the next four weeks, which was answered by one of my new flatmates, Ilona. Ilona was from Hungary, and lived in the apartment with her husband Viktor. They had lived in Paris for two years but couldn't have known the area very well, as they looked puzzled when I asked them where the prison was.

The apartment was large and bright, with French doors leading out onto the balcony from the large living room and my bedroom, in which there was a double bed, a wardrobe and a TV.

I was to share the first bathroom with Ilona and Viktor. It had a bath tub, two hand basins and a small, walk-in shower cubicle; and I mean small, because when I closed the shower doors later that evening, I nearly tore my right nipple off.

Ilona commented that everyone shared the cooking duties and I asked if I could be solely responsible for the washing up as I was a shit cook and she said that was OK — *result!*

Dinner was already being cooked by another housemate who I hadn't been introduced to yet. I followed Ilona into the kitchen to find some bloke tossing the contents of a wok with a cigarette hanging from his mouth; he wouldn't pass his food hygiene certificate, that's for sure.

He nodded his head at me and dropped ash from his cigarette onto the floor.

'This is Armand,' Ilona said. 'He's a great cook.'

'I'm a chef, not a cook!' Armand replied in disgust.

'Easy, Tiger,' I muttered, under my breath.

Armand mumbled something in French and practically threw the contents of the wok into four, white bowls. I think the bowls were from IKEA, I fucking love IKEA.

'Help yourself,' Armand snapped, then walked into the living area, sat down on one of the sofas and turned on the TV.

Ilona looked at me, gave a tight, lipped smile and handed me one of the bowls. Ilona, Viktor and I sat at the glass table in the living area and ate dinner together, while Armand flicked through the TV channels and shouted out like he was a Tourette's sufferer.

I thought he was a cock, but he was a cracking cook; it was the best stir-fry I'd ever eaten.

'It's Armand's apartment,' Ilona told me. 'He works most nights but he's off on a Monday and Tuesday night, and he won't let anyone else cook on those nights.'

'Suits me,' I said, 'He can cook every night as far as I'm concerned, this stir-fry is great.'

'It needs more garlic,' Armand commented from the sofa.

'I think it's great,' I repeated.

Armand: What would you know, *Rost Beef*?

Me: What?

Armand: I said what would you know, *Rost Beef*?

Me: It's chicken isn't it?

Armand: Zat is what we French call you English, *Rost Beef*.

Me: Ah, do you mean *roast beef*? Sorry, I couldn't understand what you were saying. We call the French *Le Bell-endz*.

Armand: I've never heard zat before. What does it mean?

'I think it comes from that story about Quasimodo, you know, the bell ringer from Notre Dame.' I commented, winking at Ilona. I'd tell her later that I'd just made that little fact up and a bell-end was the end of a bloke's cock.

'I know who Quasimodo is,' Armand hissed. 'Do you know why he was called Quasimodo?'

'It's probably some French slang word for an ugly bloke with a fucking, big hump,' I guessed.

Armand: Because 'e was found abandoned as a baby in Notre Dame on a Quasimodo Sunday, ze first Sunday after Easter by Archdeacon Claude Frollo. Ze Archdeacon adopted ze baby and named him after ze day 'e was found. 'e was brought up to be ze bell-ringer of ze cathedral, but because of ze bells Quasimodo became deaf.'

Me: He was a lucky bastard then. Oh well, at least he couldn't hear everyone calling him pug fugly.

Armand: Eh? Anyway, Victor Hugo's book was originally called *Notre Dame de Paris* but through English translations it became known as *Ze Hunchback of Notre Dame*.

Me: Ah, so Quasimodo is the character from a book?

Armand: He's not a real, fucking person.

Me: I thought he was.

Armand: 'e was hideously deformed.

Me: Well, you Frenchmen don't all look like Thierry Henry.

Armand: Name one ugly Frenchmen.

Me: I wouldn't touch Gerard Depardieu with a shitty stick.

Armand: 'E's sixty-years-old.

Me: So, anyway, where's the prison?

Armand: Which prison?

Me: The Bastille.

Armand: *Ze Place de la Bastille*, just down ze road. Zey built an opera house where ze Bastille used to be and ze big ditch behind ze fort is now a marina.

Me: Oh, so it's not still used as a prison then?

Armand: Are you fucking joking?

Me: Er, no.

Armand: Ze Bastille was demolished after it was stormed on ze fourteenz of July 1789, zere were only about seven prisoners in ze place. It was a prison for common criminals, like thieves and a few religious prisoners I zink too, but some of ze prisoners were of a high rank and there was gunpowder and guns kept in ze Bastille and zat is what ze Revolutionaries wanted.

Me: How many people stormed the Bastille then?

Armand: About eight zousand.

Me: Eight thousand, don't you think that's a little bit over zealous for seven prisoners? How many guards were there?

Armand: About eighty.

Me: A hundred to one then? Mind you, the French were never very good at fighting.

Armand: What?

Me: I mean, you did win the French Revolution but only because you were fighting the French. If you put French military victories into Google and then click on 'I'm feeling lucky' you get a result of 'Do you mean French military defeats?', that always cracks me up.

Armand: *Quelle merde.*

Me: I'm sorry, my French isn't very good. I'm hoping to improve it while I'm over here. What did you say?

Armand: I said you are talking shit.

Me: Really? Can you tell me which battle you have won?

Armand: William ze Conqueror kicked ze English's arse at Hastings.

Me: Fair enough, so we're going back almost one thousand years to 1066, well before Google. Is that the best you can do Armand?

Pause ...

Me: I thought as much. So, tell me about you, Ilona. What are you doing in Paris?

Ilona: I'm an artist: I paint and draw. Sometimes I take photographs and then I sell my stuff at *Montmartre.*

Me: Montmartre's the artist's district isn't it?

'Yes, it's to the north of Paris,' Ilona managed to say before Armand interrupted.

Armand: It's on a hill, which is one hundred and zirty metres high, on ze Right Bank and in ze mid-1800s artists such as Pissarro and Jongkind came to live zere. Montmartre and Montparnasse on ze Left Bank became the main artistic centres of Paris by ze end of ze 1800s. Many famous artists have lived and worked in Montmartre, Salvador Dali, Claude

Monet, Vincent Van Gogh. Pablo Picasso and Amedeo Modigliani lived in a commune at ze beginning of ze 1900s, in a building called Le Bateau-Lavoir.

Pause ...

Me: So, what do you draw? People, places?

Ilona: Both. I like to draw beautiful things, that's why I'm here in Paris; I'm surrounded by beautiful things and people here.

Armand: See, zere are no ugly Frenchmen around here. You should see her work, it's amazing.

Me: I'd like to see it.

Ilona: I'm going to sit on the hill at Montmartre, next to the *Sacre Coeur* and draw tomorrow morning. Would you like to join me?

Me: I'd love to. Right, I think I'll do the washing up.

I was enjoying this; by the looks of it, every day's a school day at Armand's place. I wonder if his head's as full of as many useless facts as mine is? I feel a challenge coming on.

As I stood there, washing up, I could sense an impending fear of doom wash over me and I contemplated actually sitting next to an artist and drawing something. I think I must have been fourteen-years-old the last time I picked up a pencil to draw something; I dropped art in third year because it was wank. Well, really, it was because I was particularly *wank* at art.

I was picturing the scene already: Ilona and I sitting on a blanket next to the Sacre Coeur;, Ilona opens her artist's portfolio and pulls out a sketch pad and one of those tins with about fifty coloured pencils inside, some charcoal, oil paints, brushes and the full works; I pull out a packet of felt, tipped pens and a colouring book. Even one of those books where you had to join the dots first before you can colour it in wasn't going to cut the mustard with this chick. Fuck it, I'd just watch her do her thing. And I might take some cheese and a baguette. How fucking cosmopolitan?

At least I could take comfort that I wasn't living near a prison.

I took a shower in the smallest shower cubicle in the world, slipped into bed and slept like the dead.

I was woken by a knock on the bedroom door; I nearly shit the bed. It was dark, *what time was it?* I glanced at the clock on my bedside table: five forty-five. *Five forty five!* If I'm being woken at five forty-five in the morning someone better be dead.

'Where the fuck am I?' was my second thought for the day, and then I remembered, Paris. Even though I was in Paris, as far as I'm concerned, there is only one five forty-five and it's in the afternoon.

There was another knock at the door.

'Come in!' I shouted.

I wasn't so lazy that I couldn't be bothered to get out of bed, I couldn't remember where the fucking door was. The door burst open and someone flicked on the two thousand watt light bulb, positioned directly above my bed.

France was ranked, by the World Health Organisation, at the top of the world's health care systems in the year 2000, and I was going to experience this fantastic system as I now had to ask for some new retinas from the local hospital in order to see again.

Me: Turn that fucking light off!

Armand: We're leaving at six zirty, you might want to get up if you want to come wiz us.

Me: Turn the light off.

Armand: We want to get zere before all ze crowds, Paris is beautiful at zis time in ze morning.

Me: Please turn the light off.

Armand: *Non.*

Me: OK. I'm getting up then. Are you always this annoying in the morning?

Armand: Yes, are you always a miserable bitch?

Me: Yep, I don't do mornings.

Armand then proceeded to turn the dimmer switch from high to low, then low to high, so that I felt like I was in a fucking nightclub. I just stared at him, he started to giggle.

Me: The French aren't renowned for their sense of humour, are they Armand?

Armand: Get up.

And with that he disappeared from the room, leaving the light on full beam. Wanker.

I sat in silence, drinking coffee at the dining room table with Viktor and Ilona.

'You'll have to excuse me,' I muttered, 'I don't do mornings very well.'

Ilona smiled and Armand continued his annoying whistle from the kitchen.

'So, are you awake now, Rost Beef?' Armand enquired, standing over me, smiling like a clown.

Me: Is there something wrong with you?

Armand: Not at all my little bundle of joy.

Me: Actually your English is quite good.

Armand: I was fucking a Brit for a while.

Me: Was she deaf?

Armand: No, she was from somewhere in London, she spoke really good English.

Me: Is that because she was from England?

Armand: Shut up. And my grandmozer, she was from York.

Me: Ah, just down the road from me

Armand: Yes, from a place just outside of York called Thorn Abbey.

Me: Thorn Abbey? Do you mean Thornaby?

Armand: Yes, somezing like zat.

Me: Thornaby is fucking shithouse, and it's nowhere near York. In the grand scheme of things, yes, compared with earth's proximity to the nearest star in our solar system then *Thorn Abbey*, as you like to call it, is near to York. You, my little croissant, are from Middlesbrough.

Armand: Non.

Me: No really, Armand, that's funny as.

Armand: We'd better go, before all ze crowds arrive.

Me: Absolutely, whatever you say, Boro. I need to get some bread, some cheese and some croissants for breakfast. I can buy it on the way.

Armand: I don't eat breakfast.

Me: All the more for me then.

The streets of Bastille were starting to wake when we hit the pavement at ten past six. Oh well, I was on holiday so I could have a Nanna nap this afternoon if I felt like it.

We caught the Orange Line(?) on the Metro to *Gare du Nord* and then changed to the bright Pink Line(?) through *to Barbes Rochechouart*—thank fuck I wasn't alone, God knows where I would have ended up if I hadn't been with Armand and Ilona.

Then we walked towards the Sacre Coeur. The bakeries had just started to open and I slipped into one following a recommendation from Armand. I emerged with a baguette and three *pain au chocolate*, chocolate croissants to the uncultured masses; next stop, a delicatessen to pick up some cheese.

Armand: Do you know zat zere are over four 'undred French cheeses?

Me: Yes.

Armand: You knew zat?

Me: Yes.

Armand: Really?

Me: France is known as the cheese capital of the world, but you didn't invent cheese.

Armand: Who did zen?

Me: Cheese has been popular for over five thousand years, and the oldest traditions of crafting cheese come from Mesopotamia.

Armand: Where?

Me: Modern-day Iraq.

Armand: Oh.

Me: There is a drawing in the temple of the life goddess *Ninchursag*, which shows that cheese was being produced about three thousand years before Jesus was born.

Armand: You're going to buy a Camembert or a Brie aren't you?

Me: Yes.

Armand: You fucking English are so predictable.

Me: What should I buy then?

Armand: Mont d'Or is my favourite.

Me: I've never heard of it.

Armand: Zat is because you are a philistine.

Me: Do you even know what a *Philistine* is?

Pause ...

Me: They were a race of people who lived in the coastal area of the SE Mediterranean in ancient times and were often at war with the Israelites.

Armand: Mont d'Or is my favourite cheese. We might be a bit late for it as it's only usually available from October to March, but I know a little deli around the corner zat might still 'ave some. It's ze most amazing soft cheese ever: it's in the top ten cheeses in ze world.

Me: Who says?

Armand: Some English food magazine who put some shitty, English cheddar in first place. Unbelievable.

Me: Those English, eh?

Armand: I know, it's fucking ridiculous.

Ilona: There is a nice Hungarian cheese called Trappista.

Armand: ZAT'S A FRENCH CHEESE. Invented by monks in ze eighteenth century, it's called Saint Paulin over 'ere. It's pale yellow in colour and has little 'oles all over it.

Ilona: It hasn't got a strong flavour but it's really good to eat with fruit or melted on top of hot vegetables or meat.

Armand: But it's French.

Me: Let him win Ilona. He's obviously passionate about his cheese. If they'd spent less time arguing about cheese production they may have won a few more fights.

Armand led Ilona and myself through a maze of side streets and into a cheese shop that had a smell so pungent I thought someone had slipped the insole from a football boot inside my mouth; I nearly heaved.

Two hundred and fifty grammes of Mont d'Or cheese later we left the cheese shop and walked the remaining five minutes to Montmartre.

'It's only zree 'undred steps to ze top,' Armand said, grinning at me and giving me a cheeky, little wink.

'My arse!' I retorted. 'I'm catching the *Funiculaire* up to the Sacre Coeur, from the bottom of the hill. They make worship far too easy these days if you ask me.'

Armand: It doesn't open until eight or nine o'clock.

I looked down at my watch: it was just after twenty past seven, bollocks! It's only three hundred steps, Julie; the faster you climb the quicker it will all be over. I raced to the top—I detest long periods of exercise, and was helped along by my bowel which acted as a third lung. I couldn't breathe once I reached the top of the steps, sweet Jesus, I was unfit!

I practically collapsed on the grassy slope in front of the Sacre Coeur, Armand laid a blanket down for us to sit on but I couldn't move; I just needed to catch my breath.

Ilona was five minutes into her drawing by the time I sat down next to her. There was no chance of me attempting to draw in front of her, she was fantastic. She sketched the outline of two old women sitting on a nearby bench crocheting. It reminded me of Tom's grandma and the time we all watched her pump air cock – fond memories.

Armand pulled my baguette apart and smeared a large chunk of it with the Mont d'Or cheese.

'Help yourself,' I offered, sarcastically.

Armand: Are you going to do some drawing?

Me: No.

Armand: Why?

Me: Because I'm total dog shit compared to *Renoir* here.

Armand: You just need to practise.

Armand grabbed one of Ilona's charcoals, a drawing pad and turned around to face me. He proceeded to sketch me for about five minutes: I was leaning back on the blanket, stuffing my face with a *pain au chocolate*, and then presented me with his work; it was great, I looked fucking stunning.

'This is good,' I gasped.

Armand: It just takes practise.

I thought I would start with a pencil and draw something simple. I looked around me and considered drawing an old guy sat reading a newspaper on a nearby bench, because he had the biggest mous-

271

tache I have ever seen in my life: really big and bushy. It wouldn't have surprised me if it had turned out to be a small rodent that had somehow got stuck between the guy's front teeth—you know the French, they'll eat anything.

Anyway, I decided against drawing any people that day because I was suddenly cast back in time to an art class at school where we had to draw one of our classmates, I think her name was Catherine and she had ginger curly hair. I remember that there was some sort of competition where, if your drawing was any good, there was a chance that your work would be buried in a capsule somewhere in the UK, along with lots of other modern-day appliances like, er … fuck knows, but things that depicted how we lived our everyday life, just in case we were all wiped out in a nuclear attack or something like that; or was it going to be sent out into outer space?

I can't recall, but anyway, I remember really struggling to draw the hands, knees and feet. Any premiership football goalkeeper would have been more than happy with the hands I drew, they were fucking massive, I just couldn't get the hand-to-body-size ratio right—you'd have been fucked threading a needle if you looked anything like the person in my portrait.

Then there were the knees; they belonged to a person suffering from the worse case of arthritis the medical professional has ever seen. And I couldn't get them in the right place on the legs, and the legs were too short and the feet were too big. When I finished the portrait it was no surprise that I'd drawn a midget Ronald McDonald in drag, suffering from acute joint inflammation.

I shuddered at the memories and, turning myself around on the blanket, decided I'd have a bash at drawing the Sacre Coeur. I'd forgotten to bring a rubber as well, bollocks, and my sketch pad only had two hundred pages in it.

'Ze Sacre Coeur is built wiz Travertine stone. It is dug from a quarry in Chateau Landon, in ze *Ile de France* region.' Armand said, interrupting my thoughts, 'Travertine gives off ze mineral calcite, which is why the basilica is always white even wiz all the rain and pollution.'

He took another bite from a chocolate croissant.

'How many of them have you had?' I asked.

Armand: Just ze two.

Me: I only bought three, that was one each, you greedy, French pig. Give me the last one, I'll share it with Ilona.

Ilona: I'm OK, thank you.

Me: Well, just give it to me then.

I took a bite and the chocolate and pastry melted in my mouth; I was in heaven.

Armand: You 'aven't even started yet, 'urry up and draw somezing.

Me: Ssh, I'm preparing.

Armand: Preparing for what?

Me: Preparing to make a complete twat of myself; this is going to be messy.

I started to draw and bugger me, five minutes into it, I'd surprised myself and made a half decent attempt at the central dome. Obviously, I was fucked drawing people, buildings must be my thing.

'If you practice you will get better.' Armand said, pissing all over my fireworks.

Me: Is there any of that cheese left?

'A little, yes.' Armand replied

'Give it here,' I demanded, tutting as I realised I'd be lucky to thinly cover the two square inches of the end of my baguette he'd left me with. Chivalry is well and truly dead in Paris.

Armand: Have you finished drawing?

Me: Yes, fifteen minutes of drawing is enough to ease myself back into it.

Armand: Come on zen, I will show you around Paris.

And show me around he did. We must have walked ten miles: I thought my fucking feet were going to drop off, and I felt like I'd developed varicose veins—the back of my legs were throbbing like a bastard.

Firstly we walked to the western end of the *Champs Elysee*, to the *Arc de Triomphe*. The Arc de Triomphe was commissioned in 1806 by the Emperor Napoleon, when he was at the peak of his fortunes.

In the attic, above the richly sculptured frieze of soldiers there are thirty shields engraved with the names of major revolutionary and Napoleonic military victories; I didn't think that the French had won that many battles. The Battle of *Fuentes de Onoro* is described as a French victory; I'd look it up on Wikipedia when I got back to the apartment. The inside walls of the monument list the names of five hundred and fifty-eight French generals, the names of those who died in battle are underlined and there were lots of them because, as I think I may have hinted at before, the French fight like girls.

President John F. Kennedy and the First Lady Jackie Kennedy visited Paris in 1961, and after the President's assassination in 1963 his wife remembered the eternal flame of the tomb of the Unknown Soldier, at the Arc de Triomphe, and requested the same be placed next to her husband's grave at Arlington National Cemetery in Virginia. Everyday's a school day people.

And from the Arc de Triomphe we walked to the Eiffel Tower. The guidebook told me that it was 'a brisk fifteen to twenty five minute walk if you are walking with purpose'; what the fuck does that mean? Bloody French, they *no speak vely good Engrish*. Anyway, it took us fifty five minutes to get to the Eiffel Tower because I kept stopping to look in shop windows and Armand was getting increasing annoyed at me, so I stopped some more.

Anyway, the Eiffel Tower got closer and eventually it was looming over us. I cannot find the words to express how impressed I was by the Eiffel Tower, the best I can come up with is: 'It is fucking great'. I stood underneath it, looking up with my mouth gaping open, and Armand thrust a ticket into my hand.

'Over 'ere,' he said, and I followed him to one of the four legs of the tower; the west leg, or pillar (Whatever.), to be precise.

As we started to climb the steps I noticed there were elevators, travelling up and down the other legs.

Me: Armand, what's the story here? Why are we taking the stairs?

Armand: Because I bought tickets for us to walk to ze second floor and zen we get ze elevator to ze top. I know you like your exercise.

Me: You are fucking jesting!

Armand: Jesting? I am unfamiliar wiz zis word.

Me: You complete cock!

Armand: I know *zat* word. Now shut up and climb, ozerwise we will never get to ze top. It's only one 'undred and fifteen metres to ze second floor.

It was the second time that day, and also twice before midday, that I was breathing out of my arse: I am so unfit. By the time we arrived at the second floor I couldn't speak, I was so out of breath. I'd made a partial recovery by the time the elevator delivered us to the viewing platform on the third and final floor, and then I was just speechless.

Armand was in his element; he should have been a tourist guide. He spoke with such passion about Paris; it was his hometown. I had the misfortune of being born and raised in the surrounds of Middlesbrough—if there's any such thing as reincarnation, I must have been a cunt in a past life.

Armand pointed out the *Palais de Chaillot*, built on the foundations of the *Palais du Trocadero* for the 1937 World Exhibition of Arts and Techniques. The building curves to form a semi-circle around the

Trocadero gardens which sweep down to the River Seine.

We looked to our right, to the east, and Armand pointed out the Sacre Coeur and the Arc de Triomphe; we'd walked for miles. He knew the name of every bridge we could see that crossed the River Seine; the Debilly Bridge, the Alma Bridge, Grenelle Bridge and loads more but, I'd lost interest by then— there's only so long I can talk about bridges for, it's not the most riveting of subjects is it? Bridges? He gave me a bit of a spiel about each one but all I could think about were ham and cheese croissants.

Me: I'm hungry.

Armand: Already? Come wiz me. I'll show you where I work.

Me: What's the name of the place? And more importantly, how far away is it? My feet are throbbing.

Armand: Do you English ever stop moaning?

Me: No, it's our duty.

Armand: I work at a restaurant called Maison Blanche.

Me: Oh, the white house. What are we talking? An American influence?

Armand: Fuck off!

Me: What?

Armand: Does it 'ave an American influence? Are you fucking joking? It is listed by *Forbes* magazine as one of ze top dining spots for business leaders.

Me: Well, I've never heard of Maison Blanche, or *Forbes* magazine for that matter. Your restaurant sounds like an up market McDonalds.

Armand: You're a fucking peasant.

Me: You're welcome.

I couldn't have been more wrong in my assumption. Maison Blanche was quite possibly the most beautiful restaurant I have ever been to in my entire life. Sat on the top floor of the Art Deco Theatre *des Champs-Elysees*, at 15 avenue Montaigne, the entire rooftop restaurant is surrounded by glass, presenting stunning views of the River Seine and the Eiffel Tower.

There were silk lined booths along one wall of the lower level of the restaurant, in blue, peach, coffee and cream. There wasn't a sniff of black leatherette in sight. The rest of the restaurant was a sea of cream fabric, sparking glassware and polished marble floors.

I took a look at the menu. How does partridge with caramelized turnips and Szechuan style spicy peppers, doused in licorice-blackberry syrup sound? Thank fuck Armand had never been to the Funky Doughnut; I'd have never lived it down. They were batting in a different league here at Maison Blanche.

Me: The game option sounds tasty. I've never had partridge before.

'I'll make you a sandwich,' Armand grunted as he walked off.

I stayed behind in a blue, silk booth and looked out at the Eiffel Tower; I was in heaven.

There were a few waiters milling around, arranging seating for dinner reservations by the looks of it. Several of them looked in my direction, I smiled and they nodded. One of them made a comment which I couldn't quite understand so I attempted, in my best schoolgirl French, to advise that I was English and didn't speak much French.

What a fucking, heinous error that was! It was just like one of those comedy moments when people stop dead in their tracks and look at you in disgust. It was the look that I would expect to get if I'd dropped my pants, squatted on the table, curled a turd on the crisp, white, cotton tablecloth and then proceeded to wipe my arse across the silk lined booth.

It was a most uncomfortable fifteen or so seconds. Armand saved me by practically throwing a sandwich at me and barking something in French at the waiters, who proceeded to scurry away to continue arranging tables.

'I see you are making new friends,' Armand commented, sarcastically.

Me: What's in the sandwich?

Armand: It's a *jambon buerre*.

Me: Which is?

Armand: A very traditional French sandwich made wiz a baguette, butter and ham.

Me: A ham sandwich? I'm sat in the best restaurant I've ever been to in my life and I'm eating a ham sandwich. I fancied the partridge.

Armand: You are so ungrateful.

Me: Yeah, whatever.

'Jacques!' Armand shouted across the room.

A handsome waiter turned his head and then began to sashay across the marble floor towards us.

'Bonjour,' Jacques greeted me with.

I could just about manage a 'Bonjour', it was the rest of the French vocabulary I struggled with.

Armand: Jacques, zis is Julie, she's English.

Jacques: Ah, I ave a zing about ze English. How long 'ave you been in Paris, Julie?

Me: I arrived yesterday. What thing do you have about the English?

Jacques: I like them, they're not as bad as everyone makes out.

Me: Thanks for that Jacques. I love Paris. You live in a beautiful city.

Jacques: We like to zink so. What have you done so far?

Me: I've been to Montmartre, the Arc de Triomphe et La Tour Eiffel this morning.

Jacques: Ah, zat is good. I was at La Sacre Coeur zis morning, I took early mass.

And before I could stop myself, I asked the most obvious question I could think of.

Me: But aren't you homosexual?

Jacques: And your point is?

Me: Well, I'm divorced and you're a puff, so doesn't that mean two tickets straight to hell for table number four?

Jacques: Only if you believe zat shit.

Me: I don't, but I'm not the one going to church.

Jacques: I must admit, I did briefly zink about zat very point while I was knelt in church this morning, zinking about sodomising my boyfriend last night.

I could tell Armand felt a little uncomfortable, which made the situation even funnier. Jacques started to smile.

Jacques: I would be happy to show you around the city if you ave some time, and Armand gets bored.

Me: Thanks Jacques, I'll take you up on that offer.

Jacques walked away and I turned to Armand

Me: See, I've made a new friend already.

Armand rolled his eyes and said that he had to start work, so I would have to make my own way back to the apartment. I left the restaurant with confidence that I could navigate Paris' Metro with ease.

You know what it's like after lunch, you always fancy a bit of a snooze, especially when you were rudely awaken at the crack of dawn. Anyway, I fell asleep on the Metro and woke up at the end of the line in *Chateau de Vincennes*.

I decided to get off the train and have a look around. There is a fucking, massive castle in Chateau de Vincennes, hence the Chateau in the name I suppose, built in the fourteenth century and re-vamped in the seventeenth. The castle forms a rectangle measuring about one kilometre in length; three hundred and thirty metres long by one hundred and seventy-five wide, with six towers and three gates — *shit the bed!*

Anyway, I had a look around and left about fifteen minutes later. I'm European you know, a castle's a castle.

Back on the Metro and along line number one to the Bastille—*result!* I turned right out of the station when I should have turned left, but corrected myself about fifteen minutes later when I remembered it had only taken ten minutes to walk to the Metro station this morning, and nothing looked familiar.

I found a fabulous little convenience store where I bought some tea bags, sugar, milk and chocolate biscuits; not like HobNobs or anything, really posh, French biscuits. Got home and brewed myself a fabulous cuppa and opened the biscuits to find only ten, wafer thin, fucking biscuits, probably the equivalent of about four chocolate HobNobs, and I scoffed the lot.

Then I had a nanna-nap, I'm a big fan of the nanna-nap, for about an hour, curled up on the sofa. Apart from the rather harsh wake up call this morning, it had been a perfect day.

'You 'ave a date,' Armand announced, when he returned home from work that evening.

Me: Really? Who with?

Armand: Jacques.

Me: Fabulous, I'm guaranteed a shag then.

Armand: What?

Me: Never mind. Where's he taking me?

Armand: Out for dinner somewhere, wiz his boyfriend Michel.

Me: Are you coming?

Armand: No. Zey want to go to some gay bars; I'm not really into zat.

Me: And I am? I don't drink from the furry cup you know.

Armand: What? Anyway, 'ere's his number.

I called Jacques the following morning and we arranged to go out that night. I met him, and his equally gorgeous boyfriend, Michel, outside of the Metro station in Pigalle. I was a little late. Yes, I did get lost. Fuck off.

I walked with them, passed the legendary Moulin Rouge theatre, to a cosy, back street bistro.

Jacques was born and bred in Paris, Michel in Sydney, Australia. Both of Michel's parents are French so he's got the lingo cracked. Three years ago Jacques went to see some friends in Sydney; they went out to a party together and ended up in Palms nightclub, where he met Michel. Jacques sucked Michel off in one of the toilet cubicles and they've been together ever since. That's romance for you.

Me: Now correct me if I'm wrong, but men are generally easy anyway and gay men appear, to me anyway, err ... they appear to be ... err ... to be complete whores. Is that really the case?

Jacques: Well, yes.

Michel: Not me. I've tried to be a slut but casual sex just makes me feel cheap.

Me: How long did you know Jacques before he sucked you off in that toilet cubicle?

Michel: Ah, but that was different, it was love at first sight for me and Jacques.

Me: So, less than an hour then?

Michel: No. We were talking for ages before that happened?

Me: Less than two hours then?

Jacques: It was different before I met Michel. I played ze field. I 'ave no secrets from Michel, he knows he is my forty-zird partner … for ze calendar year.

Michel: He was a complete whore.

Me: So, how do you know if you're going to be compatible together?

Michel: What do you mean?

Me: Well, who's the postman and who's the post-box?

Michel: We're not even onto the main course and you're asking who's biting the pillow? That's a bit personal.

Me: I've never had a deep and meaningful conversation with a homosexual before, and I'm interested.

Jacques: We like a bit of both.

Me: Oh, fair enough.

Michel: You'll know loads of fags, they just haven't come out yet.

Me: Have you ever shagged a woman?

Michel: The idea of it turns my stomach.

Jacques: I 'ave, but it felt wrong, so very wrong. I remember grabbing a bottle of Coca-Cola after I 'ad oral sex wiz zis girl, to rinse my mouz out.

Me: When did you know that you were gay?

Jacques: Me and zis boy I went to school wiz used to suck each ozer off after swimming lessons. But I was convinced from about eighteen years old.

Me: So sucking your friend off after swimming wasn't convincing enough?

Jacques: Mmm.

They were fabulous conversationalists, no subject was off limits; well not for me anyway, I'm inquisitive by nature.

After dinner Jacques and Michel said they were going to take me to Barrio Latino; via the Metro, and three fucking trains. I started to complain bitterly that I'd be lucky to find my way home before daylight as I was navigationally dysfunctional, but I thought, 'Ooh, I recognise this place' and then realised that we had alighted at Bastille station and I was ten minutes from home—*result!*

From the outside the club was unimpressive but inside it was a weird and wonderful four floor restaurant, bar and nightclub. I felt like I was in Mexico, surrounded by wooden furniture and terracotta coloured walls, and there were intricately carved balustrades (Hark at me, I must have swallowed a fucking dictionary with my *pain au chocolate* for breakfast.) and sweeping staircases between each floor.

The first and third floors were dance floors, pumping out funky Latino sounds, and the restaurant on the second floor offered traditional Latin dishes apparently. I stole a glance at the menu; I'd never heard of any of it before.

Me: What's Brazilian *feijoada*?

Jacques: It's ze Brazilian national dish. It's made wiz beans and some pork and beef products.

Me: Pork and beef products? What constitutes a pork and beef product?

Jacques: Well I zink zat ze dish was originally invented, if you like, by ze poorer classes in Brazil, I zink it may have been ze slaves. So, ze ingredients were cheap and zey used zings like pork trimmings, erm … ze ears, tail and ze feet.

Me: Yum.

Jacques: And zen zey add two or zree types of smoked sausage and ze loin or tongue.

Me: Mmm, ears, tail, feet and testes. I think I've suddenly lost my appetite.

Jacques: It's really good.

Me: I'll take your word for it.

Jacques: What would you say the national dish of England is?

Me: Chicken tikka massala or chicken chow mein. Something with chicken in it.

Once we were seated in a darkened corner in the club, Jacques offered me a pill; I had flashbacks of my time in Amsterdam on space cake and thought I'd best not chance anything more potent, so I told Jacques that only losers took drugs.

As he opened his bag to find his illicit drug stash, I spotted, with my hawk like vision, a Cadbury Boost Bar.

Me: Ooh, can I have that chocolate bar instead of a pill?

Jacques: *Non.*

Me: Why not?

Jacques: Because I am a diabetic. If it looks like I am off my face tonight, I may well be slipping into a coma.

Me: Can I have half then?

Jacques: *Non.* Zis bar of chocolate could save my life.

Me: You're such a drama queen. If you slip into a coma tonight I'm going to have that bar of chocolate. So, this place can't be a gay club because there are too many women and all the men still have their shirts on.

Michel: This is a straight club, we like to dance Salsa so we have to come here. Can you dance?

Me: Can I shite? I've always wanted to but I've got no rhythm. If I ever do my family tree, I'll bet you a million Euros that there hasn't been so much as a hint of black anywhere in my family since *The Doomsday Book*. I'm white all the way through, no rhythm whatsoever.

Michel: Fantastic. Let's go and find someone else to dance with.

Me: Are you going to leave me on my own?

Michel: Yep, *ma petite sucez de bite.*

Me: Eh! I know what that means; it's little cock-sucker.

Michel smiled and winked at me.

Me: You say cock-sucker like it's a bad thing, and you know it's not.

Jacques and Michel made their way to the dance floor; there was no way that I was getting up to dance in here, everyone was fantastic, I'd need a few lessons before I worked up the courage to join someone at this venue.

I'd only been on my own for two minutes before some bloke walked over and started to talk to me.

Bloke: *Bonjour, aimez vous danser?*

Me: *Non, je suis* err, shithouse at dancing.

'Oh, you're English,' he replied, in a broad, Yorkshire accent. 'I'm Anton, it's nice to meet you.'

Me: I'm Jules, nice to meet you too.

Anton: So, you're on your own?

Me: No, I've come with a couple of blokes. They're out on the dance floor.

'A couple of blokes, eh? Aren't you being a bit greedy,' Anton asked, with a grin and a cheeky wink.

Me: Well, you know, you get talking to people and find out you've' got things in common. In this case, we all like cock.

After Anton's initial surprise he laughed and we got down to the small talk. I'd travelled all the way to Paris and ended up talking to a bloke from Leeds.

It wasn't like he was overly interesting or anything; he asked me if I followed the Boro in the English Premier League, I mean, what the fuck is that all about? You don't ask a chick if she's interested in footy; there's a ninety-nine percent chance the answer's going to be a big, fat no. It's a bit of a conversation stopper.

So, Anton asked me to dance; clumsy doesn't even begin to describe my dancing technique. It wasn't like I kept stepping on his toes, I kept stepping on my own toes—between my chair and the dance floor someone had sneakily swapped my feet with Side Show Bob's from *The Simpsons*. How did that happen? I kicked myself in the ankle twice.

Thank God the song only lasted five minutes. I was sweating like a pig and Anton had turned me around so many times I thought I was going to hurl all over the dance floor.

I excused myself and said that I needed some fresh air. It wasn't until I'd beaten the world record for the fifty metre dash, and was resting against a pillar outside the front of Bar Latino, gulping down lungfuls of fresh air, that I realised Anton had followed me outside.

Anton: Are you OK?

'I'll be fine,' I replied, taking another deep breath.

I'm not sure exactly what happened next but Anton took my face in his hands and planted a deep kiss on my lips.

He stared at me for a couple of seconds and then went in again for kiss number two. I was still trying not to hurl at this point and just about managed to keep my composure.

'Let's take a walk,' Anton suggested, placing his arm around my waist and guiding me across the road to a nearby park.

We sat down on a bench, in the dark, talking absolute rubbish: where we grew up—god I was feeling horny—family and friends, what we did for work—god I was feeling horny—where we liked to holiday—god I was horny. Anton loved Thai food and had spent six months in Thailand—sweet Jesus, I was horny!

We starting kissing and before I knew it there was a stiff breeze across my nipples; *where the fuck did my top go?*

When I have some spare time, and can be arsed, I've decided that I'm going to write a book on sexual etiquette; I'd make a small fortune. Surely, during your first sexual encounter with a lady, the man should politely ask if you would care to perform oral sex on him and not thrust my face into what appears to be a sword fight going on in front of your eyes. Ask nicely, and always give to receive.

I gazed at Anton's body in profile. The lights from the club behind him cast shadows on his toned body—*result!*

By now Anton was wearing nothing but a cheeky smile. He whipped a condom out of his wallet and ripped open the packet with his teeth.

Me: Don't you fucking dare! Get down there.

Anton complied; vive La France.

The wooden slats on the park bench were not the most comfortable ride ever but I was out in front on my very own Tour de France; currently riding uphill, I was almost at the summit.

I found it quite liberating being a skanky ho, and managed to find my top and most of my undergarments after only a brief search in the nearby shrubbery.

Anton walked me home and I kissed him goodnight. We both had no intentions of seeing each other again.

The next three months passed in a blur. Ilona and Viktor were easy to live with and Armand was only mildly annoying. Obviously, I was perfect.

Armand got fired from Maison Blanche for flicking a ladle of hot soup in another chef's face. The soup needed more seasoning apparently—sweet Jesus.

Armand had assaulted another chef before but this time the police were called by a customer who took offence at watching Armand repeatedly hit the other chef over the head, with said ladle, when the fracas spilled out into the restaurant.

Armand went to work with one of his friends in a local cafe, where he got me a job as a kitchen-hand / table-clearer / general shitkicker. Luckily, I didn't have to speak to the customers, as my school-girl French was still piss poor, but I did learn a few choice words from the other kitchen-hand, who was deaf when it fucking suited him.

September

When I reached the four month mark in Paris, I laid in bed one evening thinking about me (It's all about me, don't you know?) and asking myself if I'd learned anything over the past three months.

I felt a certain peace in Paris. I couldn't put my finger on what was different about me, but I just felt calmer.

Perhaps it was the fact that I was travelling, something that I'd always promised myself I would do, and that I was surrounded by so many different nationalities, personalities and cultures.

I'd met some great people in Paris; the demographic is a little more, shall we say, cosmopolitan than Middlesboogie, but on a whole the people are friendlier in the Boro than Paris, but that's the French for you.

I couldn't find the travel itinerary I'd put together from Jamie's shower curtain, so I jotted down a few places, in no particular order, that I fancied visiting: Berlin, Geneva, Vienna, Prague, Venice, Milan, Rome and Athens. The Italians were doing quite well in my list, with three cities, and I didn't have a map handy so I'd probably forgotten quite a few fantastic European cities, but I think planning is over rated.

Berlin next I think.

I woke early the next morning and went for a walk to a local bakery I'd been frequenting. I bought four, fresh *pain au chocolate* and an apple Danish. Yet again, the shop assistant tried to tempt me to buy other pastries. Surely, after four weeks of buying the same thing, she should have realised that I'm a creature of habit. I'd never been allowed chocolate for breakfast as a child and I was taking full advantage of my adult privileges now.

I got back to the apartment and brewed a large pot of coffee. I gently knocked on Ilona and Viktor's bedroom door and then hammered on Armand's, swung the door wide open and flicked the light on and off repeatedly, whilst shouting, 'Wakey, wakey, hands off snakey.' Revenge tastes so sweet.

Five minutes later we were all sitting around the dining room table, discussing our plans for the day; except Armand, who was rather annoyed that I'd woken him up.

I announced my intention to leave Paris for Berlin in one week.

'Why?' asked Armand. 'It is full of Germans.'

Me: Funny that, because it's in Germany.

Armand: But they are uncultured and only eat sausages.

Me: I like sausages.

Armand left the table, only to return five minutes later.

'Come on zen,' Armand beckoned to me, 'If you only 'ave one week left we'd better get moving, zere is lots to see in Paris.'

I pushed the last mouthful of chocolate croissant into my mouth and made my way to the bedroom. I pulled my jumper over my head, slipped my Birkenstocks on my feet and followed Armand out of the apartment.

Armand: *Le Musee du Louvre* is the national museum of France. It is ze most visited museum in ze world and ze most famous. Zere are over zree hundred and eighty zousand objects in ze museum, which is over sixty zousand square metres.

Me: You're not planning on doing this for one full fucking week are you?

Armand: Doing what?

Me: Giving me a running commentary on everywhere we visit. I don't do detail.

Armand: Ilona told me you only spent 'alf an hour at Chateau de Vincennes.

Me: It was about fifteen minutes.

Armand: You are a fucking peasant.

The Louvre was breathtaking; I stood in front of the Louvre's glass pyramid with the museum as the backdrop, I was speechless.

Armand: Should we go in?

Me: It would be scandalous not to.

We wandered around for hours, taking in Egyptian and Near Eastern (?) antiquities, Islamic Art and sculptures. In the Greek, Etruscan and Roman department we walked past the sculpture of the *Venus de Milo*; still *sans* arms, and sometime later came upon the *Mona Lisa*.

Me: Go on then, I'll let you tell me a little bit about the *Mona Lisa*.

Armand: *Merci.*

Me: You're welcome.

Armand: Ze *Mona Lisa* is shrouded in mystery.

Me: Do you know what shrouded means?

Armand: Of course, I know what shrouded means.

Me: Well I don't think I've ever used the word shrouded in my entire life, and I'm English.

Armand: So, zey are still unclear as to who ze lady in ze picture is, but zey zink it is Lisa Gherardini, ze wife of Francesco Giocondo who was a cloz merchant from Florence.

Me: A clock merchant, way back then? It was painted in the fifteen hundreds wasn't it? When were clocks invented?

Armand: Not clocks, cloz. Do you know zat ze word clock comes from ze French word *cloche*, which means bell? But ze 'ad water clocks in Egypt about five zousand years ago. Ze first alarm clock was invented by Levi Hutchins in 1787, he is from New Hampshire. Ze delicate dark veil zat covers Mona Lisa's 'air is sometimes considered a mourning veil.

Me: So, he sold clocks?

Armand: No, he sold cloz.

Me: You're fucking annoying me now.

Armand: Ze clozes you are wearing are made of cloz.

Me: Oh, cloth! Sweet Jesus.

Armand: Why are you always such a bitch?

Me: Don't sugar coat it, Armand. Anyway, I've had enough, is there much more to see?

Armand: We've only been in 'ere for just over an hour.

Me: I need a croissant.

Armand: Huh? You are a pig.

And so began one action packed, Armand packed Parisian week. Here's my top ten, in no particular order, things to do *en Paris*.

It is not surprising that food should feature in my top ten, in fact it would be criminal if it didn't, but you must eat a fresh, warm éclair straight from the oven in one of the hundreds of fabulous patisseries that dot the streets and avenues of Paris. Did you know that there is no building in Paris which is more than five hundred yards from a Metro stop? Every day's a school day people.

Read Gaston Leroux's *Phantom of the Opera* near the Paris Opera House; whilst eating a *jambon buerre*. Well read the first chapter anyway, I got bored after the first chapter—I wonder if I have ADD; I don't even know what it stands for, attention deficit deficiency? Disorder? Ooh, look ... something shiny.

Light a candle at Notre Dame, even if you're not Catholic. The cathedral of Notre Dame is one of the world's greatest examples of Gothic architecture, it's even got gargoyles. They started building Notre Dame in 1163 and true to form, this being the land of the long lunch, continued for nearly two hundred years.

The masonry and the enormous rose windows are spectacular. Climb the practically vertical two hundred and twenty-three feet to the top of the west façade and then let me know what you can see, because I couldn't be arsed.

Forget about the witch hunts of the Middle Ages and the hundreds of children sexually abused by Priests around the globe and gaze at this most fabulous of buildings, probably built from donations by individuals placing their offspring in the trust-worthy hands of sodomising clergy. Moving swiftly onto number four of my top ten.

At number four, but this top ten is in no particular order, is the Eiffel Tower. Clichéd perhaps, but I think it's great. And the Louvre and the *Mona Lisa* are in my top ten too; I overheard one guy in the Louvre saying he thought the *Mona Lisa* was a bit of an anticlimax, but I think she's marvellous.

I really liked visiting the Sacre Coeur and wandering around Montmartre close by; God, I wish I could draw. Ilona says that it just takes practice but what the fuck is that all about? I'm good at fucking and that hardly took any practice to attain my current level of proficiency.

Anyway, I digress.

And, obviously, standing at the Arc de Triom-phe and looking down the Champs Elysees in the evening is a pretty tough act to follow.

Right, where are we up to? I think that makes seven, and being a bit of a cheap bastard I'll let you know about a couple of free activities that are pretty good.

Place des Vosges is the oldest square in Paris. It was originally called Place Royal but after the French Revolution the region of Vosges, in the northeast of

France, was the first to pay taxes to the new French government. To honour them, the most beautiful square in Paris was named after the region.

Anyway, you can lounge on the grass at the Place des Vosges, listen to the street musicians, and browse the art galleries. It's free to get in.

Anyway, that'll do. I'm up to eight or nine suggestions here; knock yourselves out.

So, I booked my flight to Berlin for the following Tuesday, because it was cheaper than the Sunday or Monday. I looked for cheap flights on the internet and was directed to the Air Ninja website. It conjured up all sorts of fantastic images of the expert, martial arts, cabin crew in my head; I was so looking forward to the safety briefing, but was bitterly disappointed to find out that it was only a flight search engine and I ended up with EasyJet. I was devastated.

Anyway, I digress.

The night before I was due to leave for Berlin, Armand cooked me dinner. Ilona and Viktor had gone out to the opening of some art gallery so it was just the two of us. Scallops, asparagus and some fancy potato—he's a fabulous chef but he uses every pan and utensil in the fucking kitchen and I have to wash up afterwards, it takes me forever.

Armand lit the candles and dimmed the lights over the dining table—perhaps he burned some of the food and didn't want me to see; I can't stand burnt food.

Armand: You're still going to Germany zen?

Me: I'm really looking forward to it.

Armand: Zey are ...

Me: I like sausages.

Pause ...

Me: Can I leave some of my stuff here? I can't get it all back into my back pack.

Armand: What if I want to rent out your room?

Me: I'll fit it all into one box, it won't take up much space, you can stick it in the storage room downstairs if you like.

Armand: Are you coming back?

Me: I was thinking that I might. I like Paris, but I've hardly seen anywhere else.

Armand: When are you coming back?

Me: I don't know. If Berlin's shithouse then I'll be back by Thursday, if not I'll stay for a while and decide where I want to go next.

Armand: I zink I'm in love wiz you.

Me: These scallops are fucking lovely ... What did you just say?

Armand: I zink I'm in love wiz you.

Pause ... An uncomfortable pause.

Me: Since when?

Armand: Since you said you were going to Berlin. I realised when you said you were going to leave.

Pause ... Quite a long one.

Armand: How do you feel about it?

Me: I'm thinking.

Pause ...

Armand: How long are you going to zink for?

Me: I'm not sure. It's all come as a bit of a surprise for me.

Armand: Why?

Me: Because we're always bitching at each other, I don't think we've said a kind word to each other the whole time I've been here. What do you like about me?

'Your tits,' Armand replied, with a smile.

Me: You can't just fall in love with someone's tits, you have to like the person attached to those tits.

Armand: You don't put up wiz my shit and I'm not really a smooz talker.

Me: No shit, Sherlock.

Armand: And neizer are you.

Me: Point taken.

Armand: So we are a good match, yes?

Me: I like a bit of sugar coating occasionally.

Armand: OK, I can do bullshit.

'Sugar coating,' I repeated as I stood up, picked up the plates and started to clear the table.

Armand took hold of my hips and turned me around to face him. He took my face in his hands and planted the deepest, most passionate kiss I've ever had onto my lips. Then he took the plates from me and took them into the kitchen.

Me: Don't stop.

Armand: It's not going to go any furzer.

Me: What?! Why?

Armand: It will give you somezing to come back for.

We watched a French movie, sans subtitles, don't ask me what happened, let's be honest I had other things on my mind.

So, Armand reckoned he was in love with me. Pretty understandable I suppose, I am fan-fucking-tastic. But what about me? What did I want? I've always been with someone, well for as long as I can remember; I was with my ex for fourteen years and was just about finding my feet as … er … er … I was just about finding me, getting to know me. I can't remember the last time I was me. I needed to be 'me' before I could be part of an 'us'.

I ended up falling asleep on the sofa. It's an IKEA sofa, comfy as—I fucking love IKEA.

I slipped into bed in the early hours of the morning—Armand might have followed me, he might have given me a kiss goodnight and I might have let him go down on me but we didn't have sex. He wanted to leave me with something to come back for.

In the morning Armand and I ate breakfast, my final *pain au chocolate* for what was going to be about, ooh, three days if last night's activities were anything to go by.

As I was in the bedroom, finishing my packing, I caught Armand leaning against the doorway.

Armand: I don't want to go to ze airport.

Me: I hate goodbyes, I'm good to go alone.

I zipped up my backpack, slung it over my shoulder and turned to face Armand.

Me: I'd better go. I don't want to miss my flight.

Armand: Can I ask you a question?

Me: Fire away Armand.

Armand: You're planning all zis travelling and want to see all zese places. What are you looking for?

Pause ...
'Me.'

Lightning Source UK Ltd.
Milton Keynes UK
05 August 2010

157915UK00001B/10/P